Truth, Fiction and Lies

A MERRAN SCOFIELD MYSTERY

by Susan Curry

Across Ocean Books, Davis, CA
www.acrossoceanbooks.com

An earlier version of Part I of this novel was originally published in 2015 as a novella, titled *Unfinished Business*. The novella is now out of print.

ISBN: 978-0-944176-05-4
Printed in the United States of America
Library of Congress Control Number: 2019931106

CATALOGING INFORMATION:
Curry, Susan
    Truth, Fiction and Lies: A Merran Scofield Mystery
Filing categories:
FIC022060 FICTION/mystery & detective/historical
FIC050000 FICTION/Crime
FIC066000 FICTION/small town and rural

To Roy
My companion, my helpmeet, my love
and to my beloved family

Table of Contents

Prologue

From the *Wirrim Trumpet:* August 20, 1933

Wirrim Mother Kills Self and Three Children

Mrs. Dave Enright was just twenty-two years old when earlier this week she took her own life at the family farm west of Wirrim. That is tragedy enough, but she also took with her into oblivion, her three children, a boy aged two and a half, and two girls, aged eighteen months and six months.

Her husband told the police that he had gone to Wirrim to buy supplies, and on approaching the house in his buggy three hours later, he heard moaning. As he opened the gate, he received a terrible shock to see the four of them all lying scattered outside, his wife Colleen's rifle lying beside her. She was still breathing and managed to say, "I'm sorry," before dying in his arms. The police took possession of the rifle for fingerprinting.

When interviewed by the police as to motive, Mr. Enright told them that his wife had seemed withdrawn of late, neglecting her household duties and the care of him and the children. He said he had told her he wanted to give up the farm and return to Melbourne, citing the effects of hard times on their living conditions, and that his wife had not wanted to go because she was afraid of the city. But he never

1

would have expected something like this, he said, overcome with emotion.

He asked to be excused from further questions but mentioned that Douglas and Beverley Roberts from the neighbouring farm had also seen a change in Mrs. Enright of late and were as worried as he was. The police interviewed the couple, who corroborated Mr. Enright's story. They also confirmed Mr. Enright's assertion that his wife was familiar with guns and a good shot. They told this reporter that there had been several suicides in the district since the hard times began but that this was the first by a woman, and certainly the first murder of children.

Mr. Enright said that his parents were urging him to come back to Melbourne immediately after the burials. There was no sign of Mrs. Enright's diary, which her husband knew existed but had never read. He said it might provide clues as to her feelings and motivation at the time.

The burials are set for tomorrow. Please check the funeral notice at Ryan's store for details.

Part I
JANUARY 2017

Chapter 1
THE CARROT AND THE STICK

Merran Scofield is under her desk, patting the carpet and groping for a lost contact lens when her phone goes off. She stands up quickly and hits her head; then reaches across the desk, grabs her cell on the third ring, and scatters pages of her book proofs. Bloody hell!

She recognizes the high, wispy voice of the new chair of history at Clare College, J. L. Short. He's attempting to sound authoritative but failing.

"Please come to my office. I need to speak to you urgently."

Merran stalks down the hall, irritated. One eye is blurry; the other is twenty-twenty.

She knocks on the door to room 1012 and waits in the dim hallway, fuming. Five minutes go by. She gazes, one-eyed, out the rain-spattered window at her beloved San Francisco skyline, wishing she were quietly at home planning her future, with her fluffy mutt Hero stretched by her side, her hands wrapped around a mug of hot chocolate. Richard's sudden departure last July has set her adrift in a way that is new and unnerving.

Lost in thought, she jumps as the door opens, and is surprised to see Jess Wallace walk out, with J.L. behind her. Red-faced and tearful, Jess avoids Merran's gaze and walks quickly away. Has she been fired? She's tenured, isn't she? Then what's going on?

J. L. watches Jess walk away. He seems unperturbed. As usual he's dressed in a white shirt, knife-pressed pants, tie and jacket, not yet having adjusted to California's informality. After Jess disappears, he invites Merran in. His smile is directed at the richly coloured Persian carpet (knotted by small children, Merran thinks), and the seat he indicates for her is across his vast office. She's immediately wary.

He shuffles papers on his large oak desk, shooting uncomfortable glances in her direction. She realizes with a start that she presents a threat. He must be fifteen years younger than she is; this is his first post as chair. He's barely unpacked his boxes from Iowa and already he's pulling rank. She stares out the window, determined to wait him out. She pulls her skirt straight and adjusts her aching back. The rain is pelting now, rattling windows, and she imagines a draft of cold air curling around her legs.

"We have a problem," he says finally, his glance not quite meeting her eyes. The royal 'we' or the collegial 'we'? She waits.

"Jess has applied for leave next semester," he says. My God, his voice is shaking.

"Her mother's cancer has spread; she hasn't much time left. That's why it's such short notice." So that's it.

"I'm sorry to hear it."

"Someone needs to take over her Australian History class."

Snap, in the trap. Of course. But she plays the game anyway.

"Who do you have in mind?"

"I thought it would be obvious. That's why you're here."

"Not me. I'm too busy."

"Why not? Your résumé mentions some Australian studies. And you grew up there—that must count for something. Besides Jess, you're the only one in the department who knows anything about the place."

His message delivered, his body relaxes. He picks up his cup and sips. Their eyes meet. She draws a breath, her mind racing. Her face grows hot. These hot flashes are a bugger.

"Yes, but my studies are old news. Bachelor's." She omits the masters. "Several prime ministers back. You know as well as I do that I'm still working on my new book on Sino-Japanese relations." No need to tell him she's just received the proofs.

"*And* I'm teaching two classes next semester: Mao's Great Leap Forward, and the Boxer Rebellion." No need to tell him they are her special areas of interest and require little preparation; he might not know that yet.

He smiles and looks at the ceiling, then plays his trump card.

"Your promotion evaluation is due very soon."

She turns her head away, shocked. It's a statement with serious repercussions. She feels like a boxer lying in the ring with the ref counting down. Down and out. This step promotion comes with a significant salary increase. She's at Step V and has been scraping by now that Richard's freelance writing contributions—not large, and certainly intermittent, but adequate—

have disappeared. Without the promotion she might have to consider applying to a liberal arts college in a less expensive part of the country. Her publication record is extensive, and she has over thirty years of teaching under her belt.

Now she's reached the nub of her hurt and frustration. The faculty should have given her the chair job in the first place; she was next in line after Old Robertson had practically promised it to her. But instead, the faculty appoints this—this—teenager, a rising star, whose opinion on her step promotion wouldn't sink her but might carry some weight.

She looks up. J.L. is studying her intently. She feels the fight go out of her.

"And how do you think I'll manage to do it all?"

"You will, Merran; you will," he says. "Your reputation for fine work precedes you. Let's get together tomorrow, when you've thought it over." He walks towards the door. She sits tight, thinking quickly. This is blackmail. She must regain some control. As his hand reaches the door handle, she has a brainwave.

"J. L., I haven't been to Oz for donkey's years. I'll need a couple of weeks of research over there to get my mind around it. And some money to do it."

His eyebrows shoot up. He holds the door open for a moment.

"How much do you need?"

After making a cup of tea, she crouches and scans her bookshelves for *The Fatal Shore*, Robert Hughes' definitive account of the convict transportation system from the late 1700's until around 1850. She hasn't opened it in years. It's hefty and well-researched. Better get cracking.

Chapter 2

A Blunder

Owen Griffiths' weekly roll in the hay at the department secretary's flat is a disappointment.

It's summer here in Bendigo, a regional city north of Melbourne, Australia. By this time in January, there've been weeks of heat, heat, and more heat. The entire continent is sizzling. Valerie's air conditioning has given up the ghost, and they're both slipping and slithering, but his mind is elsewhere.

Valerie pulls away and murmurs, "Where are you, Owen?"

"Right here, can't you tell?"

"Only just. Willy seems a bit reluctant today?" She reaches over to the bedside table and passes him a glass of water.

He sits up and gulps the warm water. "It's nothing to do with you. Willy's a bit scared, actually." His frankness surprises him. Machismo has never been his strong suit, but this is a new low.

"Scared of me?" She frees herself and stares at him, pulling the sheet up to her chin. He tries his best to smile, but it's all teeth.

"Of course not. You're the gentlest, sweetest woman I've ever known. But I'm dreading the Wirrim school reunion this weekend. Tom, the organizer, rang me personally with an invite. He said it's important because it's the first school reunion ever held in Wirrim." He pauses. "You know how these events go. I'm worried about the comparisons."

"What do you mean?"

His thoughts are racing. "I've never told you this, but my schooling in Wirrim was not easy. There were the usual creeps, of course, some who got me into fights. I bled more than I should have. You know me, Mr. Under-the-Radar." Valerie looks at him with an expression he can't interpret, but he's on a roll now.

"It wasn't the bullies or fighters who bothered me most of the time, though, but a person called Merran Provenzano. She was very smart and super-competitive, tactless as well.

"She made my life miserable. I'm not very competitive, but she tried to turn every exam or test into a race to the top. The only area she didn't bug me about was athletics. She knew I didn't care one iota about sports, so she focused on someone else and made *her* life miserable."

"Are you worried she might come to the reunion?"

"Not really. I did ask Tom if she was on the list, and he said no. But it's a tiny bit possible she might turn up out of the blue. She disappeared after a few years at Melbourne Uni. Probably moved overseas. I hope so."

He stops suddenly, aware of being melodramatic. Here he is, fifty-six years old, and wary of someone he hasn't seen for over three decades.

Valerie looks puzzled at his outburst, and is refilling their water glasses when he adds, "And having to go back to work puts me off a bit. I have my summer class in forty-five minutes."

"I thought you could teach that one with your eyes closed. Isn't it full of engineering and medical school students getting their humanities credits? What do they care about Australian history?"

"Not much. They have to be there physically, but that's all. It's not even graded. They're checking Facebook, texting, and tweeting for the whole hour. It's insulting, really."

Valerie stands and looks at him. Her long, dark hair frames her face, unwrinkled except for laugh lines around the mouth, in spite of having hit fifty and being the widowed mother of five. He never tires of running his fingers through her hair as they talk after making love. It often occurs to him that he's like a devotee to a wise spiritual figure, who gives him needed strength to deal with his complicated and mostly unpleasant life.

But now she wears the same expression he'd noticed earlier: not exactly frustration, but more like decisiveness, as though his words have confirmed her thoughts. Grey thoughts. Should he have confessed something so personal? Does she think he's weak?

After a moment when neither of them dares speak, Valerie takes a breath and says, "I've been wondering…." She moves one step towards the bathroom.

What's she up to?

She avoids his eyes and brings her voice down to a whisper.

"Shouldn't we taper this off a bit?"

How can minor complaints lead to this? There must be more afoot.

She continues, "How many months has it been now? I've run into Pat a few times recently and feel like a traitor. We were at the Farmer's Market last Saturday, waiting to buy peaches. She smiled and said hello, but I think she must hate me. It's very awkward."

So that's it. Before he can stop himself, he tries to grab her and blurts out, "Pat doesn't care. She's doing all right for herself too. She meets with Colin —you know, Colin Blanchard from the English department—every week to have her own needs met." As soon as the words fly from his mouth, he wants them back. How could he have put it this way? Valerie doesn't deserve this.

She looks stunned but replies coolly with a sarcasm he's never heard from her before.

"So that's what you call it—having your needs met?"

He recovers, remembering that the best defence is a strong offence.

"Isn't that what you're here for as well?"

"No, I thought it was love, or at least affection." Her voice trembles. "My mistake."

She almost runs the few steps to the bathroom, and he hears a key turn in the lock. Water splashes, masking other possible sounds. She might be sobbing; she might be swearing. He crumples, falls back on the bed as though he's been punched. Looks like she won't be inviting him into her shower today.

Chapter 3

Conjunction

After dinner, Merran is up to page fifty-five of *The Fatal Shore*, which is still describing the voyages of discovery, and three-quarters of the way through a Barossa Valley red when Hero barks loudly. Then stops. In the sudden quiet, she detects the faint sound of her cell phone from another room and decides to ignore it.

Robert Hughes could certainly write, she thinks, but she didn't enjoy the book much last time she tackled it. It was published after she'd finished her master's, and by then she was thoroughly bored with convicts, as well as the gold rush, Federation, and all the wars. She'd already moved to the States for her PhD in Asian Studies, relishing the chance to try something new, somewhere new. Her dissertation on the Boxer Rebellion set her on the path of research that she's pursued ever since.

The phone rings again. Damn. She sees it's her mother from Rylands. Ruth is agitated but clear as a bell from seven thousand miles away.

"I've been trying to get you all day. Don't you ever answer your phone?"

"Sorry Mum."

"Dad's back in hospital. It's pretty serious. His cancer's come back with a vengeance."

First Jess's mother, now dad. Bummer!

Nevertheless, she needs to strategize. As Ruth sobs through the details, she thinks she could spare a couple of days and go straight to Rylands. It's a long way north of Melbourne, but doable. And she'd still have time for the State Library.

"Good timing, Mum, because I just found out this week that J. L.—you know, the new chair—wants me to do a bit of refreshing in libraries in Melbourne."

"What's that got to do with your area in—what is it? Something about China…Japan?"

"Long story, Mum. But I only have two weeks all told. I could spare you a couple of days early on. Say, from Friday? I'll book a flight for tomorrow night. Shouldn't have any problems. I've been too rushed to let you know—packing and all. How serendipitous is that?"

Mum loves this, a bit of the supernatural. Her voice brightens.

"Darling, I knew you'd come. Best to get here ASAP though…he's going down faster than we expected." Her voice catches as she hangs up.

Sure, Mum the worrywart. And going to see Dad will be a bit tricky, though it's unavoidable.

After polishing off the red, she gets back on her computer and nabs one of the last seats for the following day. The fare is astronomical at this point, but it's J. L.'s money.

She'd better throw a few clothes in. But then she starts idly surfing through Amazon (where she notes that her latest book is number 1,002,538, a fall of twenty points). Moving on...ads are scrolling through, and one catches her eye. The Australian Open tennis is about to begin. Images of the Great Ocean Road, Uluru, and the obligatory kangaroos and koalas go by, in an attempt to encour-age visitors. She's about to turn off her computer for the night when there's a flash of a beautifully-painted grain silo in a semi-outback setting. That could be Wirrim, the town where she grew up. Or Rylands, where her parents live now. Or in fact, any town in wheat and sheep country. Perhaps Wirrim has a website now. She pulls it up, and is astonished to read an announcement staring at her in bold lettering:

"The Wirrim P–12 School is having a reunion of former students who finished Year 12 between the years 1975 and 1980 on the weekend of January 10–11. Spouses, partners, and general hangers-on are welcome. The festivities begin on Saturday morning at nine, with a breakfast in the shire hall. Because we expect a large crowd, please reply with an RSVP." Merran frowns. RSVP means reply please, won't they ever learn that? She reads on.

"The ladies are promising a great feed. Tom Clements, chair of the reunion committee."

Tom, the pimply kid with the thick glasses? Chair of a committee now, is he? But the tenth is this coming Saturday. And no invitation? Then she remembers throwing out the last few newsletters, though there have been none for some time. After Mum and Dad moved to Rylands, she hadn't kept up with Wirrim.

So, they in turn had let her go as well. Ouch. But how come Helen Brown didn't write about it in her Christmas letter? Oh, crap. Neither of them has sent them for years.

She sits for a while, munching cheese and crackers and evaluating the reunion's importance. The stars do seem to be aligned, as Mum would say. Her Australian history refresher, dad's final illness, and the reunion are in conjunction. A reunion will shorten her research time, but she'll make it work.

But will anyone remember her, apart from Helen? And her husband Mike, that's if they're still married, but she never liked him and doesn't care if he remembers her or not. Her mind drifts. Who does she remember? Her brain throws up pictures from the past. Jenny, the fastest swimmer on the team until Merran eventually beat her. Lynne, whose parents stored hay bales in their shed and allowed the kids to leap all over them. William, the football player. He was quite a looker, but out of her league. Glenda, who married that wheat farmer right out of school. She probably has half a dozen kids by now. Owen—him! What was his last name? Griffiths, that's it. What a pain in the neck he was, always competing with her. But she was the top student; she left Owen in the dust. She smiles at the thought. Maybe it's time to let everyone know how successful she's been. And if Owen's there, it'll be icing on the cake.

The scenario looks very attractive. But there's Ruth to placate. She calls her back. Ruth has a mouthful. Eating dinner "tomorrow"—a strange thought.

"You're up late, Merran. What time is it?"

"Mum, something's come up, and I'll have to

postpone coming to you until Sunday night, OK? I won't be late; it's not far." Whoops, she'll be sure to ask, far from where?

But Ruth's too worried to ask questions, and Merran quickly ends the call before her mother puts two and two together. While brushing her teeth, she thinks, Tom Clements and Helen Brown, won't *you* be surprised?

Chapter 4

INTRIGUE

At six o'clock the sun still hasn't finished its march across the sky. A blast of hot air greets Owen as he unlocks the front door and pushes it open.

What's Pat doing with the oven on in this weather? Unbelievable. He calls to her, but the house is quiet. The newspaper and an empty Diet Pepsi bottle sit on the table as evidence that Pat has come and gone, having turned off the A/C on her way. Precise to a fault, she wouldn't dream of wasting electricity. As usual she hasn't left a note, but it's more than likely that she'll be either at bridge, or with Colin, her two loves. Owen flings open windows and the back door to create some airflow and turns on the A/C full blast. Jimmy, their fox terrier, attacks the screen door wildly. Owen lets him in, picks him up, kisses him on the head, then fills Jimmy's bowl with dry food.

"Hello mate, sorry you had to be out in the hottest part of the day." Jimmy gobbles up the food in a few seconds, then licks his master on his way to the couch. Pat doesn't allow Jimmy on the couch. Owen knows he's being childish, even passive aggressive, but he needs a few areas in his life where he can be top dog.

He pours a glass of white wine and sits fondling Jimmy's ears as he reflects on his behaviour. He would never have needed to be top dog in the egalitarian marriage they had going until several years ago, he remembers, until he and Pat attended a Relationships Australia weekend, and the leader, touchy-feely Ralph, suggested they follow up with an activity they could both enjoy. Unfortunately, they chose bridge. Pat took to it immediately, but Owen could never remember the cards. From then on, their paths separated, little by little. Pat went on to train as an accountant—of course—and became so busy that he felt neglected; his sadness eventually spilled over into his work. Then along came Valerie, who'd boosted his spirits. Until today. Gloom descends. Is he back to square one now? No way of knowing yet, but the forecast is probably rain, rain, and more rain. Then he feels a warm tongue on his hand, moving up to his face. He cheers up a little: at least Jimmy still loves him.

A quick scan of the kitchen reveals that Pat has sized up the heat situation and decided not to cook. She'll be out eating salads, no doubt. Oh, well, it's his turn to throw a meal together tonight anyway.

"How about an omelette, Jimmy?" His bouncy little friend jumps up approvingly.

While he's watching the news and feeding Jimmy scraps from his plate, he notices the mail piled on the side table. On the top he finds a long, thick envelope with his name on it, the return address one of the Sydney suburbs. Why is Gareth using snail mail? His scanner must be out of commission. A note falls out from a photocopied newspaper clipping with the headline, *"Wirrim Mother Kills Self and Three Children."* The date at the top is 20 August 1933.

Owen reads the note quickly:

Hi little brother, Cousin Phil in Melbourne sent this. He found it in Grandpa's stuff in the shed. Read it, and I guarantee you shock and awe. Apart from the big bad family secret, don't you need a publication now and then on your sad résumé? Something about the pressures of the Depression? Since you're going to be at the reunion, you might find out more on the spot. Sorry I won't be there. Say hi to everyone. It's Rowan and Hannah's engagement party this weekend, remember? Hint, hint. Hard to believe that your little nephew is all growed up, huh? Grace sends her love, Gary.

A brief frisson of guilt flies through Owen's mind—he's forgotten a present for Rowan and Hannah—but immediately flies out again. He settles down to read the account, then with mounting excitement reads it twice more, leaving Jimmy to inhale the rest of the omelette.

Chapter 5

ALMOST A STRANGER

After an exhausting fifteen-hour night flight across the Pacific, Merran feels like hell, having been put through the wringer by a screaming baby behind her; its sibling kicking her seat; a video screen which doesn't work; sitting in an aisle seat next to a person who visits the toilet every hour; and a bumpy ride, made worse by being near the back. A conjunction of the worst kind.

Next, the rental car. She walks up and down for twenty minutes until giving up, and lurches into Hertz, where the amused staff tells her that the GoFar agency exists only in the States. Her reservation must be in the default city, Melbourne, Florida. It happens all the time, they tell her. Hertz only has sub-compacts left; the road noise will be a pain.

She's dreading the long drive to Wirrim. But there's no option but to get it over with. Stay on the left side, stay on the left side, she tells herself as she drives onto the freeway. Easy to do while already on the highway, but not so easy after she's pulled off for a break. An hour after starting out, coffee in hand,

21

she steers from the petrol station into the right lane and barely avoids a head-on collision. More than one driver gives her the finger as they barrel past. She imagines that the lips opening and closing silently through car windows are yelling "bloody idiot." After that, she takes extra care, and tries to take in the scenery, which is vaguely familiar, though freeways now skirt the smaller towns.

Three hours later she reaches Budgerong and the ninety-degree left turn to Wirrim. Now that she's on the home stretch she relaxes a little and decides to stop and walk a bit. For a moment she wishes she'd stayed in the car, as the heat hits her like a dry sauna. She should have known; the mirages on the road are a dead giveaway. It's completely silent. Hundreds of sheep graze in the distance but are too far away for her to hear their bleats. A few kangaroos watch from scrubby trees but do not move. Siesta time. She's too tired to notice much and decides to keep driving. The AC dries her sweat during the last few k's, as she passes Coopers Lake and several farms. Finally, Wirrim's familiar wheat silos appear, looking like those on her computer, except that these are not painted. Too bad. As she crosses the railway line and drives right into the sun, her breath catches, and she notices with surprise that her cheeks are wet. Damn sun!

Chapter 6

RECONNECTION

Helen Brown's home is abuzz tonight. Her fridge creaks ominously. Her two garage freezers are packed after weeks of baking quiches, meat pies, and cakes. Now her daughter Megan, and daughter-in-law April, both in their late twenties, are helping her separate the piles into Saturday breakfast, buffet lunch, and sit-down dinner, and Sunday breakfast, barbeque lunch, and buffet dinner. Every surface is covered with containers and freezer bags. Two weeks earlier, Helen was shocked when Tom called with an estimate of the numbers.

"Looks like a healthy turnout, maybe a bit shy of eighty." He sounded thrilled. "I'll send you a list. You'll love who's coming."

Helen couldn't match Tom's enthusiasm. Better check with Betty, Dorothy, and Anne to see what they can bring. And Wendy too. They'll all be needed to fill in any gaps left by Dale's catering service. Dale's food borders on gourmet, but Helen knows it can be skimpy in volume.

She scans her spacious country kitchen and says to Meg and April,

"We should all be proud of ourselves. I don't know about you, but I think it's time for a nice glass of white wine." Meg walks quickly to the fridge and pulls out a New Zealand Sauvignon Blanc. But no sooner has she screwed off the top and found three glasses, than her mobile clatters. It's not one of the family's ringtones.

"Daryl from the motel here. Have a lady here who says she knows you." Then, dropping his voice, "What's your name again, luv?" Back to Helen. "Merran Scofield, was Provenzano. D'you know her?"

Helen's hand flies to her mouth. It's several seconds before she can speak.

"Ask her what she's doing here." As if it isn't obvious.

More background conversation before Daryl comes back on the line.

"Says she's here for the reunion."

"Bloody hell!" Helen whispers to April and Meg. To Daryl she says, "Well, you'd better tell her to come over. Point her in the right direction. Has she had tea yet?"

After a pause, Daryl comes back on the line. "No, she says she's starving. She'll drive over now."

Helen turns to April and Meg, unable to say anything except, "Just so you know, she's an old school friend. Lives in America now. Quick, pop one of those pies in the microwave, Meg—one of the steak and mushrooms. The oven is better to keep them crispy, but she'll be here soon. Merran always had a man-sized appetite." She realizes she's babbling: this is such a shock.

Soon there's a loud knock and, before Helen can organize her thoughts, there's her old schoolmate on the doorstep. She takes in Merran's greying hair, the customary bad haircut, the ill-fitting clothes, and Merran's piercing look, and more than thirty plus years roll away in an instant. Helen's struck anew by how awkward she feels around this smart, critical person. Merran is the one who should be awkward, landing on her without warning, but that's not how relationships with Merran work.

After a few moments she realizes that neither of them has said a word and remembers her role for this evening.

"Merran, welcome. I'm sorry, I was reminiscing. It's such a surprise to see you. Come in, come in." She's about to give Merran a hug, stopping herself as she remembers the latter's dislike of physical contact.

"Sit down over here. Meg, pour the wine, would you please? We have a meat pie ready for you, Merran. I know you always liked them and complained in your letters that you couldn't get them in the States."

"That's true," Merran says, "We just have chicken pot pies, but they're not a patch on Aussie meat ones." As she's speaking, Helen notices Merran's eyes on April and Meg, and introduces them. She's still babbling, and realizes that Merran has said little since she arrived. Better give her an opening.

"How did you find out about the reunion? We haven't corresponded for years." Merran smiles and tells the story, making herself the heroine, the one who came from afar at the last minute to visit her dying father, and save—at great inconvenience to herself—Australian studies at Clare College. April and

25

Meg are at the table listening and asking questions, so Helen makes an excuse, and leaves them to keep Merran busy while she escapes to the bathroom to put on some lippy and brush her woolly curls into something resembling woman rather than sheep. In the mirror she notices that her flowered housedress is spattered with flour and various anonymous food stains but decides that it will do.

She hears Danny stir in his room and wills him back to sleep. Last thing we need, *you* stumbling around, my darling.

The back door slams. Mike. Sounds of boots clattering to the floor; sighing and muttering. Of course, he's seen the car outside. From two rooms away, she knows what he's thinking—Who's this? Not visitors. I'm too tired to be polite.

Returning to the kitchen, Helen looks sideways at Mike and catches his eye uncertainly. He looks done-in after his three-day truck-driving trip. He reeks of sweat as he carries his small cooler to the sink and dumps the contents. The aroma of stale fish and chips and overripened fruit fills the room. His T-shirt, stained with sweat, announces "Coffee = Buzz. People = Buzz Off."

He notices Merran, then walks right past her with a throw-off line.

"G'day, long time no see," is all he says as he peels off his shirt, drapes it over a chair, pulls a six-pack of beer from the fridge, opens one, pours the liquid straight down his throat, then heads for the TV room, the box in hand. Helen and the two young women go quiet. It's an unwritten rule in the Brown household that everyone keeps out of Mike's way until he's recovered with a few beers and some time staring at the box. Helen knows. April and Meg know. Merran does not. She tries to catch Mike's attention.

"How about a shower first? With a big bar of soap." She holds her nose, and laughs at her own joke, but Mike stops in his tracks and, without turning, says,

"It takes a stinker to know one." He disappears.

It's obvious to Helen that Merran has never caught on as to why Mike can't stand her. During their years of communication back and forth after high school and well into their years of marriage, Merran regaled them with dozens of photos of herself and Richard, taken in Europe, Asia, and wide swaths of the States. Pictures of her home in San Francisco, looking like a fairy-tale castle, with its pink-and-white facade. Merran's bragging about her wonderful life got to them eventually. Mike is not about to forgive her anytime soon for her lack of compassion after Danny was born and their lives took a downturn. In fact, her letters and photos stopped not long after the diagnosis. She never once mentioned Danny.

Merran has now turned her attention to April and Meg, telling them between mouthfuls about her plans for study in Melbourne and what she hopes for in the coming semester in San Francisco.

"The students will be impressed that I grew up here. Jess didn't, you know."

April, holding a frozen leg of lamb, looks at Meg with a puzzled expression. Who's Jess?

"Oh, and I'll brush up on my Aussie idioms; they'll go down well. I'll tell them I used to surf at Bells Beach and Bondi. In a bikini. That'll impress them." This time April turns away, choking with mirth. Merran is still not getting the point, but Helen does and has to get busy with the dishes. A bikini would barely cover one of Merran's legs now.

Realization dawning, Merran concedes: "It doesn't matter whether I surfed or not, really; the image is what matters." April makes a quick exit to the bathroom; they hear small explosions of laughter through the wall. Merran listens for a moment, expressionless, then turns to Meg.

"Melbourne is so much more cosmopolitan these days than when your mother and I were young—do you find that?"

Meg looks puzzled; to her Melbourne is just Melbourne. They go there practically every week for footy games, shows, and shopping. Distance is nothing these days. Finally, Helen sees Merran catch on and shut up. Helen has adjusted to many changes over the years, but to Meg and April, Merran might as well be a dinosaur.

"Cup of tea, Merran?" As she fills the kettle, she remembers—again— Merran's need to impress. It must be such hard work. She looks at the back of Mike's head, notices that the TV has gone quiet, and asks, "How's Richard?"

Instantly, Merran replies as though reading from a script.

"I have no idea of his whereabouts. Gone the way of philandering husbands everywhere, I suppose. Up and out he went last July, without so much as a good-bye. I did hear a rumour that he's moved to Australia. Probably Brisbane. That's where Miss Jezebel, the gorgeous Felicity, was from. Isn't that ironic? He made it here at last."

As Merran delivers her speech, Helen is not only shocked, but doubtful. Of course Richard would have said good-bye. It's clear that Merran has added that detail to protect herself from judgment. In Helen's eyes, Richard was a saint to have stayed with Merran all those years. It was obvious, reading between the lines of their letters, that he was neglected, while Merran rose ever higher in her profession. He wouldn't have left unless the marriage was beyond repair. Sooner or later, it would have been inevitable that a Felicity, a Jane, or a Laura would help fill his lonely life. Good for him. Helen studies Merran's face, sees strain and bravado, and feels suddenly sorry. There's no point in questioning her version of events, and nothing else to be said now, except, "You need to skip the cuppa and get to bed, Merran."

"Yes, I am knackered."

"See you at the reunion. Can you find your way back to the motel?"

"Yes, nowhere is far away in this town. Shouldn't be too much trouble."

"Well, goodnight."

"Goodnight, and thanks for the tasty grub. It sure brings back memories."

As Merran drives off into the early dusk, and April and Meg walk to their homes in the other direction, Mike says, "Huh. I wonder if that's what really happened," and heads off to the bathroom. Helen looks after him. If she had a magic wand right now, she'd zap Merran back to San Francisco where she belongs. But absent a magic wand, she can only hope that some of Merran's toxicity will stay contained.

Merran lets herself into her motel room. She turns on the light, sits on the bed, and opens her handbag to find a tissue but instead draws out a photograph she'd found behind the dresser after Richard left, and thought she'd destroyed. Here he is, bright-faced, his right hand holding a glass of wine in an apparent toast, the other hand entwined in a woman's fingers. She in turn is gazing at him with an unmistakable look of love. Merran turns the photo over. On the back her husband has written, "Richard and Felicity, March 26th. In love."

When Merran first found the photograph, she was shocked. In her imagination, Felicity was young and gorgeous; now, two different words come to mind. Ordinary and dumpy. She appears to be younger than Richard, but not by much, and almost certainly is past childbearing age. Her hair is fine and needs a good cut. Her gaudy orange dress doesn't suit her pale skin and makes her look ill. On a scale of one to ten, Merran would even place her below her own score, and that's saying a lot.

By the time Merran found the picture, though, she'd already spread her story about the Jezebel who'd lured her husband away. She decides to stick with it. The real story would put her in an unattractive light, and besides, who really cares one way or the other?

Chapter 7

FACES FROM THE PAST

On Saturday morning, Owen's excited to be on his way to Wirrim, despite his earlier doubts. But the universe seems to be conspiring against his departure. As he bounds out the door, he's brought up short by the empty space where the Corolla should be. Pat's obviously forgotten about his reunion and has gone shopping. The old Fairlane isn't much good for distance driving these days. So he has to call her and play nice.

She rolls up in the Corolla twenty minutes later and surrenders it without a word. As he fastens his seat belt and turns on the ignition, Pat gives him a brief wave and walks towards the house carrying her shopping bags. No real goodbye. He looks after her, stung by memories of prolonged farewells. Everyday kisses, hugs, I love you's, whether it was for a half-hour trip to the bank or a three-day conference. There've been no affectionate goodbyes for years. No use crying about it. Concentrate on what comes next. But he's hurt once more when he discovers the fuel tank almost empty.

By the time he reaches Wirrim, the reunion breakfast is over and there's no one in sight. Munching a few small sausages he scrounges from the kitchen, he consults his itinerary and catches up with the group at the town's new sports building. He slips in at the back, noticing briefly a young man, probably a footballer judging by his uniform—they're crazy about the sport in these little country towns—who is proudly showing off the building's extensive amenities. Owen pays little attention to the lecture, which is focused on features which the "oldies" on the tour could not have dreamed of all those years ago. There's a store which sells refreshments and memorabilia on sports days; fancy showers; a large dining room. Owen hears clapping, but he's more interested in identifying faces from the past, especially the women.

He notices Marian first, feeling his face grow hot as he remembers licking her ears after the dance in eighth grade. Why on earth did he do that? It's repulsive. As though his gaze is boring a hole in her back, she turns and gives him a quick grin. She's forgiven him at least, or perhaps she doesn't remember. She looks terrific, dressed in white casual pants and a loose, orange silk blouse, a floral scarf draped attractively around her neck and shoulders. In contrast, a scarecrow of a guy is hanging on her arm and clutching a walking stick in his other hand. He looks to be in his late sixties to mid-seventies, so Owen assumes she's married a much older man. He's not long for this world. Then perhaps Marian will be available again. He moves back as he imagines his face turning red.

32

It's embarrassing that he can't stop thinking about sex. Are all men like him, he wonders? From what he's heard, most women in their mid-fifties are through menopause and are glad to be done with the mess, the emotions, and the risk of pregnancy. There are exceptions, though: Valerie has given him quality sex for a good while now, with the emphasis, sadly, on *has*. And what Pat does with Colin is a mystery he's not about to inquire into.

He notices Sandra slouching against the wall, looking bored. She was a troublemaker who loved to upset people by inventing wild rumours. He was shocked on arriving at school one day and finding himself a hero of sorts. Sandra had told the gossip mill that he'd Father-Uncle-Cousin-Kinged her out at the cemetery. The news was passed along like a game of telephone, with Owen's sexual prowess growing by the hour. Of course, it was a lie. He'd been a virgin when he left school: a miracle really, considering the girls he'd fumbled with.

At first, he'd adamantly denied Sandra's story, but when he found that his status had risen with both the boys and the girls, he stopped protesting. On the other hand, Sandra's reputation plummeted. That's how it was in the bad old days, and still is, he thinks—the double standard. He notices that she's alone and has the lined, hard face of a smoker, a drinker and an abuse victim toughing out life. At first all Owen can think is that it serves her right, but then judgment turns to sympathy. He keeps very still, watching her and turning over the memories in his mind, until she senses his presence. Her eyes open wide with alarm. She turns heel and immediately leaves the building.

Then there is gentle Helen, standing on the edge of the crowd. Owen didn't notice her much at school. It now occurs to him why that was: she preferred to work behind the scenes, as organizer of dances, parties, bake sales for charity. She steered away from intrigue and gossip. She avoided the vices of the time—alcohol, tobacco, and sex. Now she's checking a clipboard; no doubt she's part of the reunion team. She has never hogged the limelight, and it appears that she will not do so now.

Who's the lucky guy standing beside her? Owen is startled as he recognizes Mike Brown, a rough type he remembers as someone who did the minimum at school, waiting to reach leaving age and get out into the real world of machines and working with his hands. Owen notices that Helen and Mike are standing a little apart, not smiling or whispering together as other couples are. As Mike gazes around the room with a bored expression, Helen is darting nervous glances in his direction, as if to hold him in place. Owen frowns, then forces himself to look away. It's so unfair, but he can do nothing. And he's making assumptions that might be totally unfounded. He resolves to keep an eye out, though, to make sure Helen is not being mistreated. What he would do to stop it is a hurdle he'd deal with when the time came. Mike would be an intimidating opponent. "Brave history professor attempts to save fair damsel from bossy, controlling 100-kg husband." That headline would boost the circulation of the local paper. On the other hand, he could be totally wrong. Perhaps Mike is merely bored with the tour, which wouldn't be surprising as he lives in Wirrim, so Helen is looking for something to interest him.

Forcing himself to turn to another part of the room, he feels eyes upon him. Omigod—Merran. So, the fears he poured out to Valerie weren't exaggerated after all. The prickly, competitive, and wholly unwelcome blast from the past is actually here. But wait a minute, he thinks. Perhaps Merran was merely ahead of her time—a girl wanting equal opportunity, equal recognition. The thought makes him uncomfortable. Had they all misjudged her? There've been such monumental changes in societal views. Back then it was no holds barred. Ridicule a woman's appearance or intelligence—especially a blonde—and you'd get a free drink. Tell a dirty joke on a woman, and they'd ask for more. Now you'd probably get a punch in the nose, by the woman herself. None of this fair damsel stuff. These thoughts flash through his mind as he and Merran exchange glances. She gives him a nod of recognition. He half-smiles back, his heart thumping.

Everyone is walking away. The tour has ended without his absorbing any of it. His lack of interest in the sports building doesn't surprise him. Now if Wirrim had had a decent library—with a big collection of history books— that would have been be right up his alley. Nevertheless, he thinks with pride, he did manage to borrow books from teachers, and his parents bought him history books for his birthdays. After finishing school, he enrolled for a degree majoring in Australian studies, then the Ph.D., and shortly after was appointed to Bendigo University. His timing was spot-on, he remembers: Australian Studies had recently taken off as a discipline and was gaining in momentum year by year.

Early on in his career, his classes and research were exciting, but a growing sense of failure disguised as boredom exacted a toll on his energy and interest. That was the academic blow, but it was not the worst blow. Pat's cooling of interest in him had a far greater impact.

Walking slowly back to the school for lunch, he's hit by the reality of what is to come over the next two days. Merran might not be the only one who will interrogate him about his career. There might be others who've been successful. This could be a gruelling weekend.

A sudden rustle in his jacket reminds him of the photocopies from Gareth. He quickens his steps and throws back his shoulders. Almost hugging himself, he's thrilled to have a terrific story to tell. Come Monday, his new project will begin. Gary's suggestion that he write a paper has come at exactly the right time, and it just might save his bacon.

It's a tight fit in the school's lunch room; a good number of Helen's food packages have already been unwrapped and devoured. Making takes far longer than eating, she thinks, hoping that her creations will be tasted and appreciated, not just gobbled down. She, too, has been scanning faces, and recognizes more than she'd expected to: old girlfriends, and the naughty boys she'd admired from afar but whose reputations had scared her. She spots Merran near the far wall and turns away, but Merran is already making a beeline towards her with a determined expression.

Helen pushes herself onto a complete stranger and hurriedly introduces herself. "Judith from Mildura, partner of James Bradley" wears a friendly, inviting smile, which encourages Helen to use her as a buffer against Merran. The latter is not to be denied, however, and she arrives at the same time that Helen's son Danny does.

"Mum, you should taste one of these lemon tarts. Out of this world. Beary loves them too," Danny says.

"Yes, I know, Danny. We made them together. Remember, you rolled out the crust for me? Judith, this is my son, Danny. Merran, you already know about Danny, though you haven't met him." Let them form their own opinions. She's sick of explaining what everyone can see with their own eyes.

Both women stare at Danny, startled to see such a large young man clutching a teddy bear and a toy racing car in one hand and a dessert plate in the other. Judith recovers quickly and engages Danny in conversation about both bear and car, but Merran pulls back, ignores Danny, and starts talking about the people she's recognized. As Danny leads Judith to the lemon tarts, Merran whispers none too quietly,

"I didn't know Danny had grown so big."

"He's seventeen now, and as tall as Mike."

Helen's embarrassed as she and Merran see that Danny, after presenting Judith with one tart, quickly stuffs several more in his own mouth. She looks away, waiting for a tactless comment. She doesn't have to wait long.

"He must be a handful. Do you ever think of sending him away someplace he can be better cared for and educated? There's not much for him around here, is there?" Having delivered her opinion, Merran catches sight of someone—Owen?—and dashes away. Helen's chest tightens and her hands clench. She could happily throttle Merran at this moment.

She looks around to see if anyone else has heard. Mercifully not, it seems; the noise level is too high. So far as she can tell, the town is pretty evenly divided on the issue of what to do about Danny. Since he was a toddler and recognized by everyone in town as "different," "handicapped," or "slow," she's heard every pro and every con for putting Danny into a care home.

Judith has disappeared. As tears spring to Helen's eyes, she feels Danny's arms around her neck, inhales his lemony smell, and turns to give him and Beary their favourite three-breath bear hug. Danny, smiling contentedly, wanders off, leaving Helen to muse on what she sees playing out in the corner.

Even after all this time, it's strange to see Merran and Owen together. She can't imagine two more dissimilar people. Owen was the dark horse, going quietly about his business. Merran wanted recognition, and it seems that her career has been successful. Was all that struggle worth it to her, though? Recognition, even fame, is so ephemeral. It almost certainly cost Merran her marriage, Helen thinks. But who is she to judge? Her own marriage is no great shakes either.

As she stands leaning against the wall, she turns and notices that Mike has left the room. Though her husband would never admit it, whenever Danny is around, especially in public, Mike finds a need to be somewhere else. Helen knows he is secretly ashamed, especially now that Danny is older. She and Mike were a team earlier in Danny's life, pulling together amidst misunderstandings and criticism from those around them. Lately, though, all that has changed. Mike signs up for longer and longer road hauls, and when he's at home he's chronically irritable. Her calming and civilizing influence on Mike, so admired in their small community, has become diluted. People have noticed and commented. She feels under siege, forced to the role of middle mother between Mike and Danny. The thought 'I want out' has crossed her mind more than once lately, but until now she has squashed it as she would a cockroach.

Now, watching Owen and Merran talking together, she recalls the ways she tried to calm and civilize Merran, the smart one with little comprehension of social niceties. Why did she do it for her, and why did she do it later for Mike? Perhaps it's her need to protect these two difficult people who need smoothing and soothing. But according to some psychologist writing in a women's magazine she read recently at the supermarket checkout, there must be something in it for her too. But what? Is it recognition, something akin to what Merran strives for? Helen's face colours with embarrassment now as she realizes that her reputation as a peacemaker pleases her very much. It occurs to her that Richard may have felt the same way. Reading between the lines of Merran's Christmas letters years ago told Helen plenty about Richard's role, so similar to her own. Finally, it seems, he grew tired of being praised for trying to manage Merran and decided to bail. Again, the revolutionary thought comes to mind, but she forces herself to put it aside and moves closer to the two in the corner.

Chapter 8
Tall Poppy

This is the first time Helen can remember Owen and Merran talking about anything civilly, and she's astonished to see Owen at ease. Merran is listening for once, head cocked on one side.

Owen is summarizing his long career at Bendigo University, and Helen is not surprised when she hears him admit that he teaches mostly engineering and medical students these days. Though she has not heard it from Owen, she knows it has the ring of truth because it's a modest story. She and Owen both know the unwritten rule that forbids Australians to boast: The Tall Poppy Syndrome. It's not that Aussies resent high-flyers; it's their attitude of superiority that rankles. Show-offs are quickly put in their place.

But this time Helen is alarmed. You fool, Owen. She'll eat you alive. Have you forgotten what she's like?

"So," she hears Owen conclude, "That's it in a nutshell. And what have you been up to since you left Wirrim? Married? Kids? I have a wife and two kids, incidentally. A daughter in Greece, a son in France,

40

a few foreign grandchildren whom I never see. Talking about France reminds me; you liked French at school, right? Did you do anything with it?" Helen moves closer. Owen, oblivious, has given Merran an opening on a platter.

Merran's amazing career takes longer to cover than Owen's—she's not afraid of being a Tall Poppy, not at all—and the lunch is over and the crowd has emptied out before she releases him and bids farewell. Owen's expression is not as abashed as Helen expects.

"She doesn't know what I've got up *my* sleeve."

Chapter 9

STANDING OUT

After a tour of the school and a talk by the principal, James Pollock, there's some free time for guests to stroll about the town, meet with old friends for coffee, and in Merran's case, have a nap. At six o'clock they all assemble for dinner. We don't do much except eat, Merran thinks. She sniffs the air. At least there are some compensations for living in the country— the food is definitely a plus.

People are searching for their assigned seats. A child about ten years old makes neatly written place cards for Merran and two others who've turned up without an RSVP and brings table settings for the three of them. There's a squeeze up the line. Merran notes with surprise that the place card opposite hers belongs to Tom Clements. What a transformation. Pimples no more. Stylish frames. He's turned fat into muscle and is more talkative too—in fact, he's the life of the party.

She turns her attention to the woman by his side, who obviously worships him and is attractive in a dyed-blond sort of way. She's wearing a sequined top in midnight blue, earrings that dangle and sparkle. She has a girlish voice, though Tom holds most of the conversation. A window-dressing kind of woman, Merran decides.

Tom and Vera, it seems, are about to host a contingent of twenty Japanese teenagers on a cultural exchange. Later in the year, a group of Wirrim students will visit host schools in a suburb of Tokyo. Merran deduces from his conversation with other guests at the table, that this has been going on for several years. Although Tom describes the programme with appropriate modesty, the locals in nearby chairs seem anxious to fill Merran in with the details.

"He and Vera have created liaisons with our sister schools in Tokyo."

"They run the Japan Club after school. It's very popular."

"The student evaluations over the years have been excellent."

Merran realizes that Tom still hasn't recognized her. Not a reader of place cards, which she finds a bit annoying.

Tom sits back, smiling. "So, there you have it"— at last reading her name—"Merran Provenzano that was! Haven't seen you in a million years. We thought you'd moved from your address in San Francisco, as we hadn't heard from you for so long, and we didn't have your email address."

"I have moved, actually." Not true. "Just happened to find your website a couple of days ago." True. "And I've been so busy since I left Wirrim."

She decides to switch to Japanese, so she can test Tom's fluency, and launches into a detailed description of her research into Sino-Japanese relations in the late nineteenth and twentieth centuries, and her position at Clare College for her entire career.

There is silence as the others take it in. She can't tell if they understand or not. Tom looks thoughtful, then replies in impressive Japanese.

"I've done a bit of reading on the subject, but not much, I confess. Most of what Vera and I do"—he smiles at Vera and squeezes her arm affectionately—"is to expose the students here to as much language and culture as we can, through the club and via visits to Tokyo and further afield. They also learn Japanese in school, of course. We've had positive results since we started . . . oh, about ten years ago, wasn't it, Vera?" She nods, replying with a few quick words in Japanese, which Merran does not catch. Vera's Japanese is probably less fluent than Tom's, which would be understandable, given her sequins and sparkle.

Tom switches back to English. "It's a bit different from the days when we all had to learn French in Wirrim, hey, Merran? Fat lot of good that did us! Though on our last trip to Paris, I was able to dredge up a few *parlez-vous*." He smiles at the others, enjoying the general laughter.

"Well, that's enough about me." Tom notices a trolley being pushed to the table. "Ah, here's the roast lamb. Bet it's been a long time since you had prime Aussie lamb, Merran."

She opens her mouth to tell him that Costco has

it all the time, but plates are being passed along, and she chooses to just shut up and eat up.

After dinner, Tom makes the speech of welcome, followed by principal James Pollock and a Mrs. Phelan, who taught sewing and cooking in the relevant years. She must be in her late eighties by now, Merran thinks, but she looks pretty well preserved. On the outside, but not on the inside, as it turns out. Mrs. Phelan stands at the microphone mutely for a whole minute, then says a few quiet words before being led off. Tom looks embarrassed, and quickly turns to the next item on the agenda, a gift to the person who has travelled the farthest, Lester Simpson from Western Australia. Lester limps slowly to the microphone. What's wrong with him? He's not *that* old, Merran thinks.

Lester reads his life history from a script. In excruciating detail, he describes his years growing up on the farm outside Wirrim—the cows, the wheat, the chickens, the sheep, the hard physical work before the school bus trundled to his gate. By the time he's reached third grade, twenty minutes have passed, and the crowd, including Merran, is growing restive. Tom whispers in his ear. Lester shuffles his papers and gives them the rest in five minutes. They don't learn much about why he ended up in W.A.— something about his deceased wife, Florence? A job? He accepts Tom's gift and totters back to his seat.

Merran has been trying to catch Tom's eye, but his attention has been worriedly fixed on Lester for the past fifteen minutes. Now Tom looks around, sees her waving, and goes back to the microphone, raising his hand to ask for silence.

"We have someone here who travelled even further than Lester, but as she arrived at the last minute, we don't have a present for her. Merran Provenzano that was, now Scofield, would you please come up and say a few words?" With mock seriousness, he turns to Lester and says,

"Don't worry. We won't ask you to give up your present." Lester clutches his box of chocolates, his face grim. Merran pushes through the coffee crowd for the mic and begins to talk, but nobody seems interested in another speech. Too bad. This would have been an ideal time while everyone is listening, to let them know all she's done since leaving Wirrim. A little disgruntled, she gives up and follows a few of them to several trestle tables set against one of the walls.

She picks up a thin folder titled, "My Life After Wirrim High School," flips through quickly, and then another called, "What I've Done Since Leaving School." As she browses, she sees that some accounts are very simple, while others are elaborate, containing photographs and drawings. According to a sign on the wall, after the reunion all of the folders will go on display at the Historical Museum in town. She wishes she'd known; her story would be impressive. She finds one that Owen wrote and is reading the first page, when she's accosted by a short man with a prominent belly, who claims to have been her athletic rival in the old days. She stands long enough to establish his identity, Mark Cody, and exchange a few hazy—even fictitious—memories. It's hard to believe that this lardy specimen could ever have run a metre, let alone the hundred. In her recollection, she was not only the fastest runner but also the champion long jumper in her final year. When Mark tells her he's been Wirrim's foremost insurance agent for over twenty-five years, she loses interest and, noticing a small crowd in one corner, walks over and pushes through.

Chapter 10
A Story

Owen is the centre of attention. He's sitting at a table and pointing to what looks to be a photocopy of a newspaper article. He's animated, talking quickly. Merran interrupts.

"What's this about?" A nod to the paper.

"As I was telling these people, it's from the *Wirrim Trumpet*, 20th. August 1933. My cousin recently discovered it in old papers in his shed and passed it on to my brother Gareth, who sent me a copy. The story's about my grandfather Dave Enright. It says he lost his entire family when his wife shot herself and their three kids on their farm outside Wirrim."

Merran does a quick calculation. How can he be Owen's grandfather if there were no wife or kids left? A woman standing next to her asks the question, to Merran's annoyance.

"That's the shocker," Owen says, "He went right back to Melbourne and married again. His new wife, Thelma, was my grandmother. Don't know if he told her about it, but I have my doubts. In all the years our family lived in Wirrim, there was never any mention of the farm. The way my parents settled here was pure luck."

"What do you mean, luck?" asks a young girl, probably a grandchild.

Owen continues. "My dad met someone in Melbourne who said there could be work for an electrician here in Wirrim. That's the only reason they had for coming here. My mother was the Enright, but she was such a quiet person that her maiden name never came up. It's such a pity that my parents both died young and never knew that Grandpa Dave had lived here and lost a family. It might have made them feel a bit more sympathetic towards him." He's excited, just hitting his form.

"We knew that Grandpa was a secretive devil, but this borders on the extreme. He never did come to visit us in Wirrim, and now I see why. He probably sold the property to someone after the tragedy, but I remember that it wasn't occupied. I've been racking my brains as to which farm it was, and the nearest I can come is that it might have been the O'Donlon hobby farm. As a kid I noticed that nobody lived out there and often wondered why."

He grins. "How's that for a skeleton in the family cupboard?" He takes in the quick drawing-in of breaths. "And now I've decided to write it up, use it as an example of desperation and hopelessness during the Depression."

He sits back, obviously lapping up the attention. Flattering comments rain down: "You always were a smart kid," "We thought you would make good," and "What have you published so far?"

They fall so easily, Merran thinks. He's not the success you think he is. But her curiosity is piqued. "Can I read it, Owen?"

He pats the seat next to him. "Here, sit by me," he says and goes on talking to the group, which is now beginning to drift away, eager to renew lost ties from the past.

Merran is transfixed, her mind working quickly. Four shots—how could Dave's wife have brought herself to do it? Her own children. Merran never wanted children herself, telling anyone who asked that she was just not the nurturing type. Deep down, though, she knew there was another reason.

Whenever she and Richard had talked about having kids, up would come a fear that, in a fit of anxiety or loss of control, she might harm them, though at the same time she realized that her fear was irrational. Richard did want children and became bitter over the years when she refused, until she went through menopause, and that was that—for her and the marriage. After Richard left she came up with the explanation that Richard was having another go at becoming a dad with someone younger, more beautiful, and without doubt sexier. This was certainly hurtful enough, but her discovery of the photograph had been an even bigger blow to her self-esteem.

Turning her attention from this painful line of thought, she continues to read the article. Who was this young woman? Why on earth would she kill her children, and then herself? As she reads, Merran is drawn more and more into the story.

What a tragedy for Dave Enright, Merran thinks, but how fortunate that he was able to find a new woman and have another family. She asks Owen about his grandmother.

"Grandma Thelma was a wonderful woman. The kind of grandma every kid should have. She and my mother were a lot alike. I don't know what Grandma saw in Dave. He had a quick temper, got into fights, drank a good deal, and died of liver failure. There was a rumour that he'd been jailed for assault when he was young."

"How did he treat you? After all, your mother was his daughter."

"We kids were afraid of him because of his reputation, and kept out of his way, though we probably didn't need to because he was not at all interested in us. Now I wonder if he never got over the loss and just couldn't talk about it. After his three kids died it's likely he couldn't bring himself to see us as family. I suppose he might have been angry with himself that he hadn't been able to stop it, or angry with his wife for doing it. Both. The result was that he was angry all the time."

Merran picks up the copy for a closer look. There's a photograph of the farmhouse. It's a bushman's hut, really, built of what looks like wooden slabs—probably eucalyptus—and a tin roof. The door is open, and she can just make out a passageway in the gloom. She's seen these little homes before, so-called "shot-gun houses," in the American south. Two rooms on each side of the hall; a kitchen and a sitting room in the front, the latter used for guests; and in the back, two bedrooms. Cramped conditions. A water tank stands by the house. There would have been a dam as well, but it's not in the photograph.

The second page shows a wedding photo of Dave and Colleen Enright from 1929. She's a pretty, slight figure in a long white dress with a lace bodice, barely reaching her new husband's shoulder, her expression hard to read—blank, resigned, or just holding still for the camera. And she's just slightly looking away to the side, at a wedding guest. He, with a determined look, pulling her close with his arm. Possessive, Merran thinks. She doesn't like him already.

Already? She surprises herself. What has Dave Enright to do with her? She glances at Owen and finds him looking back defiantly. He opens, then closes his mouth. Finally he says, "It's my grandfather, Merran. It's my family. I'm going to write this up myself. You have plenty on your plate. Leave this one to me."

Deliberately not catching his drift, she carries the copy to a brighter patch in the room. Owen follows, grasping and pulling until he has it back. He looks around and notices eyes upon them.

"We can discuss this later." He stuffs the pages into his pocket and storms off. Merran decides to do her own investigating. She'd only meant to tease him, but then again, a diary *would* be a find.

Chapter 11

AFTERMATH

Out on the street again and preoccupied with her exchange with Owen, Merran doesn't notice that she's driving back to the motel on the wrong side of the road, until loud tooting from an oncoming car makes her swerve just in time. Shaken, she lets herself into her room and turns on the light, which is so dingy that it barely reaches the corners of the little space. She strips off and turns on the shower. A light trickle of lukewarm water and the absence of soap soon drive her out again. She dries herself with a thin towel and is soon in her pyjamas and in bed with the light off, expecting to fall asleep instantly. And why not? Jet lag and the events of the day have hit her body hard. But her mind is not yet ready for sleep. Images and questions from the murder-suicide keep intruding.

Apart from the deed itself, how could Colleen Enright have pulled it off, logistically? The children wouldn't have sat in a row outside, dressed in their little romper suits, waiting to be picked off one by one. Only the baby lacked mobility. No, Colleen had to have put the three of them into a room and shut the door firmly, then taken them out one by one, telling the others she would come back. The thought that these children's last look at their mother was down the barrel of a gun is greatly disturbing.

She throws off the sheet, turns on the bedside lamp, and begins to take notes, but her hands shake so much that she has to stop writing, and her breath comes in shallow, panicky bursts. She tries to stand, but her legs won't support her. She's suddenly shivering all over. The vision of a rifle pointing at her forces her to collapse on the bed. She can see her father's red face, his eye in the sight, his hands taking aim. He is shouting. She hears her own high child's voice screaming. Two people are pulling her apart and she hears a bang, which is so loud it mutes the voices for a good while.

Finally, she hears sobbing, herself or someone else—she isn't sure. She falls into the arms of someone who seems familiar, but she isn't sure who it is. She is being put to bed. Then she's aware that her mother is sitting by her, quietly crying. The trembling gradually subsides but is replaced by such a strong desire to annihilate her father that it takes her breath away. She paces up and down, her hands balled into fists. Finally, she picks up her mobile and rings her mother. Ruth is surprised and annoyed to hear that Merran is so close by and it's "only a reunion" that's kept her.

"He's very weak, Merran. I don't think he'll last the night."

After the flashback, Merran's at a loss as to what to say. 'Good' comes to mind, but she restrains herself.

"I really am tied up here, Mum—ideas for work I need to follow up on. See if you can stall him another day." Whatever that means. "But I am looking forward to having a good natter very soon." Her voice is unsteady; she'll have to cut the call short. Then, more forcefully, she says, "We'll definitely have something to talk about *this* time." Leaving her mother to sort *that* out, and with a faint sense of guilt, she cuts off the call.

She lies down, still jumpy, and leaves the light on while trying to sleep. Hero has been such good company since Richard left, and without his warm body close to hers, here in the silent countryside, she is acutely aware of how alone she feels in the world.

Sometime in the night she wakes to the sound of footsteps outside.

"Who's there?" Her nerves are still frayed. A dog barks far away. A key turns in the lock next door. There's a thud, then Owen's voice mutters "damn." Sounds of entering the room, the door closing, and muffled noises, are soon replaced by snoring, which Merran finds strangely comforting.

Chapter 12
THE INEVITABLE

Helen is still smarting over Merran's tactless comments about Danny, and it hasn't helped that some big ear told Mike about it. Now they are whispering together in bed, trying not to wake their son, the subject of the lion's share of their worries, as well as their disagreements.

In the dark, Mike's voice is irritated.

"Much as I can't stand Merran," he says, "She does have a point. He's getting to be too much for us, and for the town as a whole. I know they care, but there's only so much help they can give us." He props himself up on his elbow. Mike is a large man who prides himself on being in control. Danny can meet Mike eye-to-eye, and Helen often wonders if Mike is beginning to fear him.

"It's not a new thought for either of us, but we really need to do something soon," Mike continues. "He's getting into fights, and he's so strong he might really hurt someone. That punch-up with Paulie Rogers—it took three of us to get Danny off. He could have killed Paulie."

56

Here is Mike's fear, Helen thinks, plain as day. There's nothing to be said: it's all true.

"People are avoiding him now. They used to try to be friendly. And the little kids tease him. And yet you resist doing something about it. I don't think you're facing reality, Helen. I've told you this time after time, and you just don't listen."

And, predictably, here arrives the blame. Mike always has to find a culprit, and it's never him. Helen is silent in the dark.

"Don't you agree with me?" Mike asks, gripping her arm, urgency in his voice. Helen takes the safest route.

"You're right of course, Mike. Then the only option is a sheltered workshop, and they're thin on the ground. That's what I've been hoping for, somewhere he can be safe and useful, earn a few dollars, make some friends, even stay in one of those special housing places where a few of them can live together under supervision. We could see him often, if it's not too far away." Mike's hand on her relaxes. His voice takes on a hopeful tone.

"I've been meaning to tell you something that Jim—you know, Henderson, works at the post office—told me last week, just before I headed out on my trip. He says there's one of those places opening in Bendigo. Just because Danny can't do the jobs we have in Wirrim doesn't mean he can't be useful if he has skilled help. Can you make some inquiries?" He sits up suddenly, and she senses rather than sees his eyes upon her.

"Sorry, Mike, but he also told me about it. I checked, and it's already full, even before it's open.

And there's a long waiting list."

"Then we've got to keep looking. The bottom line is that he can't stay in Wirrim much longer." He turns away mumbling, "We'd better get some sleep—big day again tomorrow."

Helen rolls over and waits until Mike's breathing slows in sleep, then sobs into her pillow, tears of anger at Merran and Mike mixed with sorrow for Danny and the separation that is only a matter of time.

Chapter 13

An Obstacle and an Opportunity

Owen is up bright and early in his motel room on Sunday morning, feeling unusually buoyant. Gone is the emotional millstone he's been carrying for far too long. At last he has a project. His one concern is Merran's interest in the story. Given what he remembers about her and noticing the previous day that nothing seems to have changed, he's worried that she might try to barge in, even steal his idea, for no other reason than because she can. Was she teasing, or was she serious? He can't tell, but he'll have to be watchful. Fortunately she has trouble keeping her mouth shut for long.

By the time breakfast is over, however, he's relaxing. Merran is nowhere to be seen, so perhaps she's decided to leave it to him. It's quiet in the shire hall. There's a lot of food going begging. Al Norton makes a joke about the churches not knowing what hit them. So that's where she is, Owen thinks. He's surprised that someone as critical as Merran would have held onto all of that mumbo jumbo. But he's realized from observations over many years, that there's no accounting for many people's ability to hold fact and fantasy in their consciousness at the same time.

Just then his phone comes to life—Pat's "Ride of the Valkyries" ringtone. But it's a stranger at the other end.

"Mr. Griffiths?"

"Yes, this is Dr. Griffiths."

"Dr. Yeomans here from Bendigo Hospital. I'm afraid your wife has come into Emergency this morning."

His heart lurches.

"Mr. Griffiths?"

"What's happened?"

"Do you have a cat? Well, doesn't matter . . . seems that a cat has scratched her badly down the right side of her face. There's been a lot of bleeding, and of course she's in shock but in no danger. She says you're in Wirrim—can you get here by lunchtime?"

What to say, except as graciously as possible, "Yes, I'll do my best."

Walking towards the car, he whispers, "Bloody cat."

Thinks, bloody Pat.

Merran is not in church but sitting on her bed, trying to settle down from the shaking that began again when she woke up and recalled her flashback from the night before. She remembers suddenly a news item concerning a technique for calming oneself down after a traumatic event. It's very simple, consisting of tapping on one knee and then the other back and forth, while thinking of a pleasant memory. She's found it useful, so she tries it again now.

There's a false start when she taps on her knees back and forth too quickly and finds her heart pounding, but she's able to calm herself down using slower taps. A pleasant memory comes to mind of her sixteen-year-old self sunbaking at the pool in Wirrim, gossiping about boys with some of the girls, though now she can't think of any boys she would have been interested in. Actually, that isn't quite true. There was someone called Tony Lawson, a sheep farmer's son. His sister Amy had invited her to the farm for a weekend, and she was impressed to see Tony feeding the lambs with a baby bottle. *He* wasn't afraid of being called a sissy. And then there was curly-headed Brendan O'Neill. She remembers that he was often out in the paddocks and along the highways collecting wildflowers, had a butterfly collection, and did his parents' gardening for them. Unusual for the time and place. Both boys were a year ahead of her, and she'd lost track of them after they'd left for university. In any case, Tony and Brendan were unattainable by someone like her, who most people regarded as prickly, aggressive, and direct. She knew also that she was not thought of as pretty. It's a pity that neither of the boys—now men—is at the reunion: it would be fun to see how well they've aged.

After a few sets of tapping, she feels calmer. This is crazy, she thinks, but it works.

After a lukewarm shower and more tapping, she feels calm and capable enough to face the day, which might very well be the last of her father's life. Now she knows at least part of the reason why she's never felt at ease with him. Was that the only incident where he threatened her? And what would make him do it anyway? Was she that bad of a kid?

61

While driving to the shire hall for a late breakfast, she spots Owen speeding past, going back out of town. Strange, why would he do that? As she meanders along, she realizes she's a little lost—how could that happen when there are so few streets to choose from? She soon finds the wide main street, its dusty centre divider planted with a few struggling shrubs and half-dead flowers. It's already dry here, she thinks, and the extremes of climate change will only make it worse. There'll be devastating floods and droughts, with no moderation in between.

She turns a corner and discovers the historical museum, an imposing brick structure from the pre-World War I period. She doesn't remember it well, but she does recognize the old bank next door, because she had an on-again, off-again friendship with a girl named Lynne whose father was the bank manager. Merran had loved the building's coolness, its usual quiet broken only by hushed voices and, occasionally, shouting, even sobs. Farm loans would have been granted and refused in this place. Lives built, and lives shattered. Now it's empty, probably yet another casualty of efficiency. A large sign announces For Lease. She hasn't noticed Lynne at the reunion. Wonder what happened to her?

She climbs out of the car and reads the museum's sign, which says that it's open by appointment only. She calls the listed phone number. There's a fumbling sound, then a voice kept low asks her to wait. Seconds later, at normal volume, the woman says, "Sorry, I was in church. May I help you?"

Merran introduces herself and learns that the voice at the other end belongs to a Mrs. McLaren.

"Any chance of getting a look inside the museum today, Mrs. McLaren?"

Hesitation. "I'm serving at the barbeque at twelve. Can you come over at three? I could be there for an hour, no more."

Merran calculates. She'd be in Rylands well before five—that wouldn't be too late, though for what she isn't sure. To please Ruth, or to be in time to witness the death of Johnny Provenzano? Meanwhile, she can get directions to the O'Donlon farm from someone at breakfast and fit that in ahead of three o'clock.

It's a beautiful, clear morning, soon to become hot. Merran decides to leave her car parked outside the museum and walk to breakfast; she gets so little exercise these days. The main street is all but deserted, apart from a few customers going in and out of the bakery and the newsagent. She can't resist a stroll, reviving memories of the businesses that were there over thirty years ago. The furniture and the fabric stores had thrived in the era when most furniture was Australian made, and it was still cheaper to make one's clothes rather than buy imports. Both are now empty storefronts. A faded sign on another bank's branch window informs the public that its office has moved to Rylands. A newish looking gift shop has replaced the old grocery store, probably because a trendy supermarket opened not far down the street. A little further on, she comes across a painted board covered with real estate listings, and is amazed at the low property prices, a fraction of those in San Francisco. But then most places are cheaper than San Francisco. She reads every listing, imagining what it would be like to live back in Wirrim.

The pace would be much slower here, of course. She'd have to retire or find a university position with flexibility. Some teaching and research on campus and writing to be done at home. She might look into it. Just as quickly, though, she has to laugh at herself. What is she thinking! She has a tenured position at Clare College; she has a beautiful home with a dog in one of the loveliest cities in the world. Why would she give all of that up? On the other hand, will she soon be forced to move anyway, to a less expensive city? It's all so confusing. She doesn't do well with confusion.

Chapter 14
DORRIE (1)

Merran's stomach is rumbling. Time for breakfast. As she walks away from the real estate board, she's startled by a tap on her shoulder. She turns and finds a diminutive figure who looks from the lines on her face, her stooped body, and her walker, to be well into her nineties. "Thinking of moving here, are you, love?" she asks. Merran is surprised to find herself drawn to this bright-eyed woman, and even more taken aback when she accepts, uncharacteristically, "Dorrie Richardson's" invitation to sit and chat on one of the benches nearby. She assumes that Dorrie is just looking for social contact and will fill the conversation with inanities such as weather analysis, and remarks about how Merran has some American sounds in her speech. It's become tedious over the years to notice Australians listening hard to detect signs of Americanisms and accent. It's a mark of inclusion, of belonging, if they can say, "You still sound Australian." Merran knows she failed that test long ago.

Dorrie, however, proves to be an interesting conversationalist. After determining that Merran is a historian, and therefore an educated woman, she abandons small talk in favour of politics. It soon becomes obvious that she reads widely, not only *The Melbourne Age* and *The Australian* newspapers, but the latest books on topical subjects.

"I don't drive anymore," Dorrie says, "but from time to time I get a ride to Bendigo with my neighbour. That's where the big bookstores are. And I can order online.

"In the past I tried writing books, not like yours; mostly fiction, but I was never published. Now it's too late for that."

"How about television?" Merran asks. "I've heard that older women watch a lot of TV."

"Oh yes, I watch some shows. But I'm pretty selective. I love the British mysteries: Inspector Morse, the P.D. James mysteries, Agatha Christie, that sort of thing. Most BBC programs, if they're not too violent. How about you, Merran?"

"I'm a bit of a sucker for the rougher series like 'Game of Thrones," and 'Breaking Bad,' I'm afraid. Surprisingly, they help me sleep better. It must be all that adrenalin release."

Dorrie laughs. "That would be too much for me."

"Have you always lived here?" Merran asks. "I don't remember seeing you when I was a kid."

"No, only for the past twenty years. In my early life I lived in Melbourne until I married. I was a schoolteacher then. After World War II my husband and I bought land outside of Wirrim, nearer to Budgerong, and were farmers together for almost a decade. He died early from chronic health problems. Then I stayed out there by myself for a long time. I've been a widow for nearly sixty years, can you believe that? He was quite a bit older than I was, but it was love at first sight."

Merran calculates. "So you farmed until you were into your seventies? That's quite a feat."

"Yes, and after my husband died in 1959, I did it alone while my son was in Melbourne at high school, and later at uni. Later on, he would come to visit with his wife and two daughters, and after his divorce he took over permanently. I moved into town. I never thought I would live so long, because I've had health problems too, but as you see, I'm still alive and kicking."

At this point, Merran expects the conversation to be over and stands up to leave, but Dorrie grabs her arm and surprises her with the question, "Have you ever been in love?" Merran hesitates. Dorrie picks up on her mood quickly.

"Loved and lost, eh?"

Merran nods weakly and looks away.

"I'm sorry I've struck a painful chord." She searches Merran's face. After a long moment she takes a breath as though having made a decision. "I was asking because, as a historian, you might like to look at the letters George, my late husband, wrote to me from the Middle East in World War II."

Merran sits down again. Here's that familiar feeling again: the wish to be there first. The outlandish concern that if she says no, Owen might step in and take over. But good sense must win out.

"Dorrie, I'd love to, but I'm only here for a short time, and am at this moment following up on an incident that happened decades ago outside of Wirrim. Are you in a hurry, or could you save them for me if and when I come back? Though honestly, I don't know when that will be."

Dorrie's face, so eager a moment ago, sags with disappointment. She leans heavily on her walker, then says, "Well, they've been sitting at my place for donkeys' years, so I suppose they can sit a bit longer."

"I'll keep you posted on my movements. Do you have an email address?" Surely not, she thinks, but Dorrie smiles and replies, "Of course! I like to keep up with the young ones. The teenager next door set me up." She rummages in her purse, pulls out a grocery receipt, and writes down the address.

"And Dorrie, could I ask you not to mention the letters to anyone else in the meantime? Give me first dibs?"

"Of course. I'll write a note that you're to have access to them. I like you and trust you to treat them with the care they deserve."

Chapter 15

Keeping Watch

Ruth is holding Johnny's hand. He's now drifting in and out of consciousness. His skin is almost transparent. He's now in a hospice a short distance from the hospital, where his dying can be made as comfortable as possible for both patient and family. Ruth has been on a steep learning curve as to what the hospice will and won't do, as she sees the staff nurses come and go, discuss the patient, and replace the bag that sits quietly filling at the end of his bed. An orderly brings her food and cups of tea.

She agrees with hospice's philosophy: no heroic measures will be made to keep Johnny alive; the care will be palliative only. He suffered so much during his first go-around with cancer, she told them; it seems kinder to let him go now that the cancer has spread. At eighty-two, he would say he's had a good innings, and Ruth has to agree. The energetic optimism which drew others to him has disappeared; he's told her he just wants to go, like so many of his friends before him.

As she keeps watch over him, a host of memories flashes by. Johnny's been a complicated man. He had high standards for himself but wasn't critical when others failed to hit the target. No one needed to be on guard around him, which was why he was so admired. It had always puzzled Ruth that her daughter did not seem to be one to value his generosity of spirit. Ruth knew that he didn't want to be a burden, physically or financially. It's likely he didn't want to burden Merran with his emotional needs either. Whenever Ruth thinks about Johnny and Merran, she is filled with sadness. The little girl he adored had, from an early age, erected a wall between them, and sealed the deal by settling seven thousand miles away without a backward glance. Ruth and Johnny have not talked about Merran's absence in these final days, but Ruth would be astounded if Johnny is not disappointed.

Now he has moved on, closer to death. As if preparing himself for his final adventure, he has refused food and water over the past several days. The nurses have shown Ruth how to keep Johnny's mouth moist, and he is on pain medication. Dr. Singh tells Ruth that death might take several days but will be as painless as possible.

Ruth realizes she's in denial but hasn't yet called the hospice's Catholic priest. She knows that Johnny would scoff at the notion of last rites and was dismissive of the priest when they met for the first and only time at the hospital. To Ruth's mind, though, there is a procedure to be followed, steps along the way to the grave. But not yet. Maybe tomorrow, after Merran has arrived. Surely he will hang on until then. She's heard stories of dying people who've waited for a relative or friend to arrive, before taking their last breath.

She wonders if Merran would follow such steps for her. As an Anglican, Ruth doesn't expect last rites, but a touch of confession might help her feel more at peace as she's about to slip away towards the light.

Her phone goes off under the layers of detritus in her handbag. Too late, she sees that it was Merran. Calls back, no answer. Johnny stirs, and a dark yellow stream trickles down the tube. She wonders what Merran means about having lots to talk about. From her tone, it sounds as though it's something other than the weather.

Chapter 16
DARN CAT

Pat is propped up in her hospital bed, looking like a half-finished mummy. She tries to smile as Owen walks in briskly. He hopes to get this over with quickly and be on his way but is shocked to see how pale and exhausted she looks. Not at all the attractive, fashionable woman he fell in love with so long ago. The thought jolts him: how long has it been since he really looked at Pat up closely? He forces himself to meet her gaze, but Pat looks down quickly and smooths the sheets.

"I was taking care of Rose's cat for the weekend. You know, the black one, Midnight? Rose Erikson from bridge?" She's having difficulty forming the words.

Owen says nothing. He's never met Rose or Midnight.

"He's a feisty little devil. Fights the neighbourhood cats, so Rose has to keep him inside. Of course, he hates that. She should declaw him but hasn't the heart to do it. She will now," she says, then stops with a look of anguish.

"Are you in pain?"

"Not right now, but I will be soon, when these pills wear off. I must look a fright," she says.

Owen detects a veiled question. He ignores the impulse to meet her halfway, and instead says dismissively, "Well, you're strong. You'll heal fast. Will you need plastic surgery?" Thank God for medical coverage. The bills will be astronomical.

"That's to be decided," she says. "But now you're here, the doctor says you can take me home. I'll need some care and rest for a couple of days. The district nurse will change the dressings, so you won't have to worry about that."

He feels panic rising. "But I have to get back to Wirrim for the last part of the reunion."

"Why are you so interested in Wirrim all of a sudden? You haven't been there for years."

"I have to do some research. An idea I have for a paper."

Her eyes open in disbelief.

Within an hour, he's had Pat discharged and has driven her home. He sets her up in a leather chair in the lounge room under the ceiling fan. He puts her pain pills, a cup of tea, and a sandwich on a small table within reach. Finds the book she wants. Gives in to her request that he leave her the Corolla, even though he knows she'll be over at Colin's in a flash, that's if his wife's away. And before she can guilt-trip him any more than she already has, he's back on the road in the old Fairlane. Less than three hours and he'll be there.

Chapter 17

CLUES

Merran is on the road too. Owen drove east, while Merran is now driving west. The old Enright farm is about twenty kilometres out, first along a gravel road off the main highway, then a turnoff onto an unmade section where tyre tracks have worn deep. She stops and rolls down her window to take pictures that she could include for her class and is suddenly transported back forty years. This is one of the roads where she and Helen would go exploring on their bikes. Now she notices red soil swirling behind her car, and there's a particular odour of dry dust in the air. It's so unmistakably Australian and is a part of her sense memory as surely as the dank smell of fog in San Francisco. Then there is the silence, broken only by birdcalls, something that is both alien and utterly familiar at the same time.

She and Helen had ridden their bikes together often during their teen years. They had little in common, but there wasn't much else to do when there were no sports scheduled for the weekends. Merran's mother insisted that she have a companion for the longer rides, and Helen was usually willing to oblige.

Another couple of k's, and Lou Hogan's directions have brought her to a rusty barbed-wire fence surrounding the property on three sides. She can't see the back fence; it will be over the small rise which could be the bank of a dam. She stops and gets out. In the blinding sunlight, she can just make out the ruin of a small bark hut resembling that in the photograph. The she-oaks surrounding it have grown considerably taller since 1933. A small flock of sheep scatters as she walks closer, then settles back to grazing on the meager grass. Their "maaaa" sound blends with the low grunts of pigs whose large covered pen is on one side of the house. A chicken coop sits on the other side, its inmates strutting in anticipation near the wire. Humans equal food. She has none to give them. The granola bar in her handbag just won't cut it.

She's about to unlatch the wide gate when a young woman appears from the stand of trees on her right. Sunburned and energetic, with a large basket on her arm, she draws closer and looks at Merran with surprise. The latter decides to begin, hoping to make a positive impression.

"Hello, I'm Merran Scofield, formerly Provenzano. I used to live in Wirrim. I'm back for the reunion. I heard about this place and a shooting here in the thirties and came to look. I hope you don't mind." She realizes that the young woman might not have heard about the tragedy, but there's no reaction.

"G'day, my name's Jenny Grogan," the young woman replies. "My husband and I bought this piece of land from the O'Donlons. Then we bought the farm next door." She gestures towards the cottage. "As you can see, we use this place for sheep grazing and the pigs and chickens. Nobody wants to live in the house anymore. Apparently, there were some goings-on there a long time ago, but I never heard anything about a shooting." She seems unperturbed, and continues, "We built a new house just a bit further on from the dam." She points; a large white farmhouse is just visible through the tall eucalyptus trees. She shifts her basket from one arm to the other. With Merran's thoughts on the couple's domestic setup, she notices that Jenny appears to be several months' pregnant.

"When's it due?" she asks in what she thinks is a friendly way, pointing at Jenny's stomach.

Jenny's face shows a mixture of embarrassment and annoyance.

"Never. After my three pregnancies, the weight just stayed on."

Whoops, Merran thinks. The proverbial foot in mouth disease. Never ask a woman if she's pregnant, unless she's wearing one of those modern tight-fitting belly spandex things, which announces it to the world. Wait for her to tell you. On the other hand, Jenny should really lose that weight. Still, this isn't my business.

"I hope I haven't offended you," she says. Jenny laughs.

"People ask that question all the time, but I like food too much."

There's no more to be said on that subject. Merran shades her eyes with her hands. "You can see forever out here. Looks like a lonely place, so far out of town."

"It would have been, in the early days. The old couple we bought it from owned it for well-nigh fifty years. The property had been going begging for a long time until they decided to buy it in the '50s." She turns, taking in the dry, flat landscape, with its dotted stands of eucalypts, and continues:

"The O'Donlons lived in town. Just used it as a hobby farm. By then, though, there were cars. In the old days, they would've used a horse and cart. In winter the roads would've been so bad that they'd have had trouble getting to town at all." She smiles. "But, of course, for us now the distance is nothing." Merran remembers her earlier conversation with Meg and April. The times have certainly changed in this part of the world. And why wouldn't they? Surely she hasn't become a city snob.

The hens are losing patience. Jenny scoops pellets out of a storage container and adds greens and table scraps from her basket. Then, amid the feeding frenzy, she invites Merran to help search for eggs. It's such a simple task, but Merran experiences it as intensely calming, here amid the warm smell of chicken feathers and the pungency of straw. She has to drag herself back to the real reason for her visit.

As Jenny latches the wire gate, gently pushing unruly hens back inside, Merran takes a few steps towards the house. The bodies might have been right here where she's standing. The rifle, the blood. Her legs suddenly turn to jelly, and she grabs a corner of the doorway, causing alarmed grunts from the pigs. She takes a few deep breaths and brings up her pleasant memory of sunbaking by the pool. The weakness subsides. Jenny's keen eye is upon her.

"Are you feeling all right?"

"Yes, it's the heat. I just flew in from San Francisco, and it's winter there. I'm a historian and thought I might look around some of the farms out here, possibly write about this area. It must be a hard life in many ways, even now." She's not sure if she's asking a question or offering an opinion. Jenny has moved to the pig pen now and seems to have little interest in Merran's musings. Not an academic, it seems. And not easily impressed. Merran experiences a sinking feeling in her stomach, akin to emptiness. She's like a fish out of water after so many years away. Country people are matter-of-fact, realistic, and skilled in facing adversity. There's not a lot of time to philosophize.

As she observes Jenny feeding scraps to the pigs, all the while talking affectionately to them, she notices that their grunts have calmed. She feels soothed herself. A few minutes later, and a little more in control, she drives back to Wirrim in plenty of time for Mrs. McLaren at three.

Chapter 18
A Find

Mrs. McLaren is turning her key in the museum's lock as Merran pulls up outside. A petite woman who appears to be in her late forties, Mrs. McLaren exudes efficiency as she bustles about, turning on lights and the portable fan. Merran's impressed. If anyone can help her with research on the tragedy, this woman can.

"My goodness, it's hot in here in the afternoons now, since the shire council chopped down a few of the trees out front a month ago. I don't know what they were thinking. They said something about branches hanging over the building. Nothing that a bit of trimming wouldn't have fixed."

Pulling back heavy curtains, she asks, "Did you come to the barbeque? So many people turned up that we had to go back and raid our own fridges. Young children running around—not what you expect to see at a reunion for oldies. Oh, sorry!" She blushes.

Merran mumbles something about having had another engagement. She was asleep, actually. Jet lag is a bummer . . . no use fighting it.

"I'm sorry about the mess," continues Mrs. McLaren, raising her arms in a gesture of surrender as she contemplates the large room. Built-in desks line two of the walls, and these are covered with stacks of old books. Tables chockablock with newspapers and other documents take up most of the centre space. Tall bookshelves stand in rows on one side, crammed with document boxes. Merran notices a few steps leading up to another room which appears to contain artifacts from days gone by. She glimpses an Aboriginal shield on the back wall, and glass cases with fossils, sheep skulls and the like. Of course, in a small town like this, the building functions as a museum as well as an archive. Too bad there's no time to have a good look around.

Mrs. McLaren sheds her jacket, switches on a personal fan on her desk, flaps her arms in the air to cool off, and says (by way of justification for the mess, Merran thinks), "I recently took over the museum from Betty Grayson, who is a lovely woman but, just between you and me, has no sense of organization. Of course, she was a willing volunteer only, no training on how to run a place like this." Merran has lost interest in the history of the museum's staff and moves restlessly in her chair. Mrs. McLaren ploughs on.

"Records have been lying around uncatalogued for years, newspapers out of order, specimens not preserved properly. It's enough to make a curator weep. Still, I'm making inroads, and it's not as if many people are interested in the old stuff nowadays. We don't get many visitors." Then, turning to Merran at last, she asks, "What can I do for you?"

"Mrs. McLaren—"

"Call me Fiona."

"Fiona then, I'm looking for some records from the early thirties: newspapers, diaries, shire business, anything pertaining to the Depression. It's written accounts rather than artifacts that I'm after." Finding Colleen's diary will be a long shot, but at least she can begin with records which will provide a flavour of the times.

"I just might be able to help you. As a matter of fact, I've gathered the early years of town settlement in the 1840s up to the Federation celebrations of 1901, so that's put away." She points proudly to several document boxes on a high shelf. Not that I'm up to the 1930s, but at least what's left isn't so daunting." Fiona points to one of the overflowing tables. "You might start there. In fact, you might help me if you could try to put some of the papers in order." She smiles. "No pressure though. So go for it. I'll be here, just checking Facebook, and I have to ring my son in Patterson. He wants me to babysit tonight. Remember, I have to leave at four, though at a pinch I can probably stretch it to four-fifteen."

There's no time to lose. Merran peels off her light jacket and begins sorting, putting anything from the 1930s in a pile on one table, everything else on another. The minutes tick by as she gets bogged down in news from the past, much of it outside of her dates. The fire at the Reynolds' in 1922; the new tractor at the Pearce's; a fiftieth anniversary celebration, with a wedding photo of happy twenty-somethings next to a sheepish-looking couple, both holding walking sticks and excruciatingly conscious of their seventy-

something bodies. Well, they did give permission—
what did they expect, she thinks. She lingers over
obituaries of people she knew. A surprising one was
Merv Rankin, killed at a railway crossing. Sometimes
there were boom gates, but not always. She recalls
that collisions with trains in those days were not
infrequent. Merv was only twenty-four.

She remembers the time he'd fought Owen
behind the shelter shed after school. Everyone
was there except the teachers, as they'd missed the
whispering and note passing during the latter part
of the day. "Be there for the fight." As expected, it
didn't last long. Owen dodged around, avoiding
punches, but was unable to land one of his own. The
next moment, Merv punched him in the nose, which
bled dramatically. It was an unwritten rule that blood
stopped everything. She didn't like Merv, who was a
sneaky mischief-maker, but is sorry he died so young.

This won't get her anywhere. She presses on and
soon has a decent collection of papers from the '30s.
Fiona might agree to come back tomorrow. Better
look at the boxes on those shelves. Then, behind a
cardboard storage box, she discovers a small collection
of diaries, tied together with a ribbon. Thank you,
Betty Grayson, the disorganized volunteer. But the
dates could be from any time at all.

She sorts through the bundle carefully—
fortunately the custom was to write one's name and
year on the title page. She finds Bridget Monaghan,
1876; Elizabeth Sampson, 1921; and Mary Hunter,
1892. After several more, she holds her breath as she
looks under the cover of the last one. It is thicker
than the rest, and signed Beverley Roberts. Wasn't

she Colleen and Dave's neighbour? She picks up Beverley's diary for a closer look, hoping to find an account of the shootings at the Enright farm, and is astonished when a smaller one falls out. Merran's hands are shaking as she opens it to find, in tiny, beautiful cursive, the words Colleen O'Callaghan, 1929. Below that she'd written Colleen Enright. Hooray for Beverley! She takes a quick look inside and is stunned to see the beautiful cursive, page after page. Irish nuns must have schooled her; they were the only ones who taught handwriting like that. By reputation they were very strict, patrolling their classrooms, rulers at the ready. You had to hand it to them though: their students wrote perfectly. It's a pity that cursive, even handwriting itself, is on its way out.

But neat handwriting isn't all the diary has to offer. On several pages scattered throughout the writings, Colleen has drawn exquisite small pictures with coloured pencils. Who would have guessed that a young woman in her situation—time, place, and responsibilities—would have the tenacity to develop her natural talent to produce such lovely works. Had she been born in a different time, place, and with different responsibilities, she may have been a successful artist. But Merran suspects that her efforts, in this part of the world where people on small farms are frequently one crop away from disaster, would have met with little appreciation. Lucky are those whose families support, or even participate in, a child's attraction to a certain path. She's noticed this particularly with those in the arts—painting, music, writing, among others. To be born into an artistic family is a great gift, one which Colleen did not receive.

Merran turns the pages quickly, noting that there are large gaps in time between many of the entries, and that the diary is only half-filled. The final entry is dated 2 August 1933. Out of the corner of her eye, she notices Fiona putting her phone away and begin to gather her things together. She looks hurriedly through Beverley's diary, and is disappointed to see that the dates don't match. Beverley had stopped writing well before Colleen's arrival at the farm. She feels a gentle hand on her shoulder.

"I'm sorry, Merran, but I have to go. Stuart wants me there with the girls a bit sooner than I'd expected."

"Would it be possible for you to come back tomorrow?"

"I wish I could, dear, but it turns out that Stuart and Alison would like me to stay for a couple of days. They need to help Allie's parents in Mindie with a move to assisted living, and it'll be much easier without the baby."

"When will you be back?" Merran wonders why she asks that. She has to get to Melbourne very soon.

"I could be here about four on Wednesday if you're still in Wirrim."

"OK, I'll see. I'll ring you if I leave beforehand."

Would she really wait three more days? Almost certainly not; so as Fiona strides towards the door, Merran slips Colleen's diary into her pocket.

Chapter 19

PASSING OVER

Ruth is drifting off, but a sudden sigh accompanied by slackness in Johnny's grip wakens her. His eyes have opened, but he shows no recognition when she calls his name. Panicked, she runs to the hallway and shouts for a nurse. Two of them come quickly, but instead of trying to resuscitate him, one sits and holds his hand while the other checks the pulse in his neck.

"No response," said Nurse Josie, passing her hand over his face to close his eyes. Then Ruth remembers—again—that she agreed to no heroic measures for Johnny. Part of her rebels for an instant. He hasn't had the last rites. He should have been kept alive to see Merran.

Josie comes to her, hugs her, then takes her hands. "I'm so sorry, Ruth. He's gone. Would you like to sit with him for a while? Just let us know when you're ready for us to transfer him to the funeral home. Take as long as you like."

"My daughter's coming soon. I'll wait for her."

"Would you like me to ring and let her know?"

"No, I'll do it. I have my mobile here."

Chapter 20
DOINGS

As Merran is pocketing the diary, Owen's in a panic.
With fifty k's still to go before Wirrim, he glances
down at the fuel gauge for the first time and is startled
to see it almost empty. The old Fairlane drinks fuel
almost as fast as it's pumped in.

He and the Fairlane limp into tiny Wheatland,
only to find that the petrol station he expected to
find is permanently shuttered. It looks as though the
632 people living there, according to the population
sign, can no longer support it. Damn! He pulls over
and almost cries, then notices an old car parked in
front of him. He wonders if it has the same unlocked
tank as the Fairlane and gets out to check. He looks
around carefully and sees no one. These towns are
dead on Sundays. Everyone's cooling off under the
fan, playing computer games, having sex. He unlocks
the boot, takes out a siphon and a can he hasn't used
for years, transfers fuel from the old car into the can,
then pours it into the Fairlane.

He's accelerating onto the highway when he
hears revving behind him. It's the old car, its owner

hunched over the steering wheel, looking fierce even in the rearview mirror. He's gaining on the Fairlane but suddenly pulls back and fades into the distance, the car out of fuel. Owen hopes the driver didn't get his number plate. He feels the tightness in his chest give way to new energy. He should have taken more risks in life.

Just as Owen is making his escape, Merran is backing out from the museum and onto the wide main street. Her mobile rings. Ruth. She steers the car back into the parking space, grateful to be given a second chance to pull into the left lane.

"Hello, Mum. I'm on my way now. See you in less than an hour." She hears a catch of breath, then a sob.

"Merran, I'm sorry to have to tell you that Dad passed away a few minutes ago. I'm still here at the hospice. Can you come straight here?" She gives Merran the address. Rylands is a small city, quite a bit larger than Wirrim, but the GPS will get her there.

Although, in the recesses of her mind, Merran was anticipating this, the reality hits harder than she expected. If she's honest with herself, she will admit that the anticipation has been not with dread but with relief. But now she's not so sure. It's more like frustration. There's no way to obtain a confession from a dead man. No way to look into his eyes and finally say *j'accuse*.

She finds her mother sitting by Johnny's bed, holding his hand. She hugs her quickly, then, as much due to obligation as to desire, moves to her father and plants a kiss on his forehead. "Good-bye, Dad."

The body has not cooled much, but it's enough to give her a shock. He's really gone. She half-expected him to open his eyes and reach for her. She isn't sure what her reaction would have been if he had.

After an uncomfortable pause, Ruth says, "I know he was trying to wait for you." Merran is skeptical.

"Well, I'm here, and perhaps he's still here in spirit. Isn't that what the Buddhists say?" She doesn't believe it for a second, but her mother cheers up a bit.

"Even though we expected him to pass away within the next few days, it still seemed sudden," Ruth says, still sniffling. "It was like he stepped from the shore into the boat and disappeared. There was no time to say a final goodbye. I hadn't even called the priest."

"Well, Mum, he's where he needs to be now." She's noncommittal as to where and, assuming that her mother has only optimistic thoughts of Johnny's whereabouts, she finds herself, with some surprise, leaving it at that.

"Have you had tea, Merran?"

"No, I haven't eaten since breakfast."

As Ruth kisses Johnny, her teardrops fall on the sheet.

"It's hard to leave him here all alone, but let's go home. I'll boil you an egg. Do you still like your toast cut into soldiers?" She takes Merran's arm, and they walk slowly to the car park, each with her own thoughts.

The hospice network moves fast. Hugh Wilson, the Anglican minister, arrives just as they are getting out of their cars, and says he's here to ask what kind of service Ruth wants for Johnny. A funeral or a memorial? Is there to be a cremation? Not that Hugh ever met Johnny—he makes this perfectly clear—but Ruth is in his congregation, and he owes it to her to offer his help. He smiles brightly—inappropriately, in Merran's opinion. "After all," he says, "the funeral is for the living, not the dead."

Merran butts in. "Shouldn't he have a Catholic funeral?" She can't care less which branch of Christianity will preside, but she's put off by Hugh's condescending manner. They must teach that in seminary, she thinks, or it just goes along with knowing yourself to be closer to God than the rest of us.

Hugh fingers his white collar, which appears too tight for him. Or is he wanting them to notice it? He moves his chair closer to Ruth, in an attempt to exclude Merran.

"No cremation!" exclaims Merran. "He was a Catholic and should be buried with those of his own faith, in a coffin. There must be some Italians here in Rylands, Mum?"

Hugh interrupts before Ruth can answer. "Today, Merran, many Catholics are choosing cremation, and their ashes go into the lawn area, which is for everyone. And burials are not according to denomination any longer. But I know you've been away for some years." He grants her a small smile. Unctuous bastard! she thinks, then insists, "But the Catholic priest should do the service."

Hugh and Merran both turn to Ruth at the same moment. Ruth's face is ashen. She looks about ready to collapse.

"Sorry, Mum. Let's get you to bed. We can decide on the details tomorrow. I'll help you write the obituary if you like." She almost pushes Hugh out the door. He might be praying for her right now, she thinks. Or more likely consigning her to hell.

The final reunion dinner is underway. It's a smaller turnout than before. Many had to leave before the new workweek. Helen isn't sorry. She has a cadre of friends around her and is sick of worrying about the food supply. All she wants to do now is relax and chat about old times.

The conversation comes around to Owen and his heated exchange with Merran. There's some curiosity about their rivalry over the Enright story, though Helen can tell that their interest is merely food for gossip. So she doesn't mention what is the main point: the importance of a publication for Owen. After listening to him yesterday, she realizes that his career is desperately in need of a boost. If Merran is really serious about following up on the events at the farm, she looks either unnecessarily provocative or just plain greedy.

Just as Helen is on her way to get coffee, someone in the kitchen calls to ask for advice about what to do with the few leftovers. When she returns, she sees that Owen has arrived, looking worried. Geraldine is telling him she saw Merran driving on the Walangie Road at about ten - thirty that morning.

In a flash, Helen knows where Merran was headed. She sees the same realization on Owen's face. He sags in his chair, then stretches and asks, "Is there any food left?" Helen disappears into the kitchen.

Chapter 21
COLLEEN'S STORY

Colleen's diary is just begging to be read, but Ruth is in no mood to be pushed off to bed. Merran braces herself to force down the light meal her mother promised—a boiled egg and toast, which she'd enjoyed as a child but now strongly dislikes— and to listen to outbursts of sobbing and hints of recrimination at Merran's failure to arrive in time to say goodbye to her father. When they hear the mantle clock strike eight, Merran again suggests as gently as she can that Ruth make her way off to bed.

"I'll warm some milk for you Mum. That should help you get to sleep; and I have an extra sleeping pill here that I didn't use on the plane. How about it?"

"All right, but I'd like a shower first."

By nine, gentle snoring sounds from Ruth's room alert Merran that she'll be uninterrupted for several hours. She retrieves the small diary from her pocket and begins reading.

Colleen writes her first entry the day after she met Dave in late 1929.

Susan Curry

October 14, 1929

Dear Diary,

I have some exciting news but need to tell you first how it happened. My cousin Kevin brought me in the buggy from Boolong to Wirrim for the dance last night. It was quite a long way, but he wanted to come because he fancied a girl, Evelyn, he hoped would be there. So I went along to keep him company. Mam and Da told him I had to be back by midnight and that he had to watch that I didn't get taken outside by any strange young men. After what happened to Bridget, being in the family way and having to move to the city, they are careful with me.

Here is a picture of what I saw when we arrived at the dance.

Merran studies the drawing. Colleen used a basic yellow for the bales of hay all around the fire-brigade hall, and brighter yellow for the flames inside the kerosene lamps hanging from the rafters. A darker yellow for the fresh, clean sawdust spread on the floor so their boots wouldn't stick. She's drawn four small black figures placed in the back of the large room, three with fiddles raised, the third sitting behind a drum, and labels them 'Irish fiddlers and a drum,' then lets loose with a riot of colour when she depicts ribbons in red, blue, green, yellow, tied in bows and hung all around the room. It's an attractive picture, showing impressive skill for a young woman who, Merran assumes, has had little or no instruction.

The diary continues:

I heard one of the ladies say that the band of Irish fiddlers was from up Colley way. It's my favourite music, and I was dying to dance, but had to stand along one wall of the room with the other ladies, waiting to be asked, and trying not to get nervous. Out of the corner of my eye, I could see that the men were looking up and down the line, and one by one they would walk over and pick one of us. I'd counted on Kevin for at least one dance, but he spotted Evelyn right away and stayed with her all night, which upset me a bit because I had to sit out a few of the early dances. There must have been more girls than men there, because there were always a few girls on the sidelines, but the men all had partners. I was wishing Mam and Da could have been there to enjoy the music too, but later I was glad they weren't there.

After a while, the leader of the band said it was supper time. The local ladies had made several different kinds of cakes and scones, and for drinks we had ginger beer, with real beer for the gentlemen, of course.

I was just sitting down with my plate of supper when in walked the most perfect man I've ever seen. There was quite a commotion when he came in. Nobody knew who he was. I will try to draw him for you, dear diary.

On the next page Merran is confronted by a stunning head portrait of a young man looking straight at her. She recalls her reaction to him after seeing the photograph in Owen's newspaper article. This person appears confident; he gets what he wants. He would make a formidable foe. Colleen has drawn his eyes a bright cornflower blue. His hair is black and thick, curling around the ears. She writes under the portrait that he dresses nicely and is the best dancer she's come across in her life, concluding with the caveat, "not that there have been many."

He danced with Mary Evans after he arrived, but after he spotted me, he stayed with me all evening long. His name is Dave Enright, the loveliest name in the world. And he's twenty-two years old. He was surprised that I am only

93

seventeen; he told me I look older and experienced in the ways of the world. I don't know what he meant by that, but I suppose it was a compliment. I told him that I'm good at farming but haven't seen much of the wide world. I didn't mention that I love to draw, because around here people think you're wasting time if you're not doing something useful. I wondered why he pricked up his ears when I told him about the farming, but soon found out.

He's inherited from his Uncle Alf a small farm a few miles out of Wirrim. So fortunate. He's very wise, because he's from Melbourne. He says that he's sure he'll make a good farmer. I listened to him talk all night about his ambitions and plans. He has nobody left in all the world. His mother died when he was born, and his father and grandparents are all dead too. He has an older brother in Sydney, so far away it might as well be nobody.

Mam and Da shouldn't know about this part. He kissed me good night, full on the lips. My first kiss. He was making for my bodice as well, but I laughed and pulled away, and he laughed too and said, "Until next time." The kiss and his words sent a strange burn all through my body, just like Bridget told me. By this time we were outside, waiting for Kevin and Evelyn, who were behind the hall, probably doing the same thing or worse. Kevin didn't talk at all on the way home, but I could tell he was very, very happy. We arrived home much later than we should have. Mam and Da had sat up waiting and were so angry that I don't know if I will be allowed to go to Wirrim again for a long time. I don't want anyone else to read this, dear diary, so I'll hide you under my mattress.

4 April 1930

Dear Diary,

My wedding day is tomorrow, and I'm excited, I suppose, but I'm also unhappy that Mam and Da are not happy with it. Dave's a Presbyterian, or was, and Mam and Da are worried that I'll go over to the other side, and our coming children as well. When we talked to the priest a couple of months ago, he told us he could do the service only if Dave vowed that our children would be raised Catholic. Because there were more of us there—Father Ahearne, Mam and Da, and me, Dave finally agreed to it, though I could tell that he was very angry. Mam, Da and I had made a special trip to meet Father Ahearne, and it was a relief to me when Dave said he would do what we asked. Best of all, Mam and Da seemed happier when Dave agreed, but I don't think they like him much and suspect he might not keep his promise.

While they were walking towards our buggy, Dave kept me back and let out a whole lot of nasty words about Irish priests and their control over people's lives. It worried me, because I don't see the Church in that way at all. I go to Mass and confession whenever I can get to Boolong, say the rosary every night, and pray to Mother Mary and the saints whenever I need help with something.

So the result after all that kerfuffle is that we are going on with the wedding. I'm glad we are, because Dave has taken liberties with me, more and more each time we meet. I've told him that he has to wait until our wedding night, but I worry that I won't be able to hold him off if we don't marry now. But I'm sorry that Mam and Da don't like him.

13 April 1931

Dear Diary,

I'm sorry I have neglected you for so long. Brian is taking up so much of my time now. He's a bonny little baby, three months old, smiling and making us happy, though Dave doesn't like him waking us up in the night. I don't mind feeding him when it's all quiet, though. I can feel the warmth of the stove now that the summer is over, and the nights are getting cooler. Dave has done a lot of good work around the farm. He built a small shed for storing things. We bought a cow. Dave also made a chicken coop, and now we have fresh eggs and milk every day, even butter. Those things have made me very happy, but the one thing that upsets me is that Dave likes to work by himself, or he gets help from Doug, our next door neighbour. He says that women's work is inside and the man's outside. Apart from the kitchen garden, of course, which is always the wife's job. I do have a lot to do in the house, though, with keeping the fire alight, cooking, baking, washing and ironing, and, of course, looking after Brian.

Dave goes to Wirrim once a week for whatever we need, but he hardly ever takes us there with him. He says he wants me and Brian to be safe and sound here, but it makes me nervous, because Dave told me about the swaggies who are roaming around to get handouts because of the hard times. We had them up in Boolong for a while, but not as many as there are here. Da used to send them packing, so the word must have got around, and they went past the farm from then on.

Dave scared me when he said that some of the swaggies are also looking for women. He said that I should have my rifle loaded at all times and not hesitate to use it. I'm even more nervous now after Bev, our neighbour, told me she had a nasty character demanding food a couple of weeks

ago. He asked to come in, but she told him to eat outside.
He left quick smart when he saw Doug riding up from the
far paddock.

I have to stop here, as Brian is waking up, and Dave
should be home from Wirrim soon. We are getting very short
of money, but our sheep are due for shearing soon, and the
wool should fetch enough to keep us going for a while. I've
found a better hiding place for you, dear diary. Dave saw
me writing to you one time when he walked in suddenly. He
would be angry if he read this; he might even burn you up.

2 May 1931

Dear Diary,
Well, the wool didn't fetch much money at all, because the
fleeces were in smaller pieces than they should be, and most
had blood on them. It was Dave's first time shearing, and he
wouldn't listen to me when I told him he should get a real
shearer to do it. Even Da does that. It's hard not to nick the
sheep with those sharp shears. Dave scoffed at me and said
how hard can it be. He soon found out. After he'd finished,
every sheep looked like a bloody mess. I had to put tar on the
poor things, and of course they hated that. Dave was angry
when the sheep tried to get away from me, and said I was
hurting them, but he was the one who started it.

I'm expecting again, and this time I've been feeling
sick most of the time. Brian lies on the floor watching me
and plays with the couple of wooden animals Dave made.
Dave doesn't like it when I have to rest, or rush outside to be
sick. He complains about having to bring in the buckets of
water from the tank and having to keep the stove stoked. He
doesn't like changing Brian's nappies, or doing washing, or
anything else in the house, so I have to get up and do it all
and cook him something to eat.

Sorry, I have to stop, feeling sick again.

22 July 1931

Dear Diary,

Brian sat up without falling over for the first time today, and it won't be long until he's crawling too. Dave has put a fender around the stove. He is quiet more and more and doesn't play with Brian much. He stands outside looking at the sky.

He borrowed two horses and a plough and sowed some wheat, which came up nicely, but then the dry spell arrived, and the shoots all died. I told him he should buy some hay for the animals, like Da does in dry years, but Dave wouldn't hear of it. He's counting on rain.

27 December 1931

Dear Diary,

Christmas is over for another year. Mam had been sick earlier in the year when they planned to come, then farm work got in the way, so they waited until Christmas to see Brian. Mam brought some clothes she made for him and for the new baby, who should arrive next month. Our little man took his first steps while they were here and laughed when we clapped our hands. Even Dave smiled, and said he was proud of Brian.

Da walked around the property with Dave and told him a few things about what improvements he could make. But when they came back, Dave's face was red, and Da looked upset too. I heard him say to Mam, "He won't listen to anything I say. He's a know-all. He doesn't know the first thing about farming. It's worse than I thought. But Colleen has made her choice, and she has to live with it." They didn't even stay the night, even though Bev had loaned me a bed for them. I cried when they left. It makes me sad that I won't see them again for a good while. Dave doesn't want me to travel, and Mam and Da don't seem interested in making the journey either.

27 January 1932

Dear Diary,
Our dear little baby arrived a few days ago. The labour was longer and more painful this time. She was breech, and it was touch-and-go, but Dr. Hoskins arrived well before the end and helped me through. Bev came over and kept up the hot water and towels and played with Brian when she could.

Dave was pacing outside, and I didn't want to upset him by screaming, so I tried to keep the noise down and grin and bear it. Dr. H. said I was very brave. When it was all over, and Bev had bathed and swaddled the baby, he called to Dave, who came in and said, "About time." He gave me a kiss and looked at the baby. "Boy or girl?"

"You have a little girl, Mr. Enright," said Dr. H. "What are you going to call her?"

"Elizabeth," said Dave. "My mother's name."

"Oh!" I said. "I want to name her Bernadette."

"Another Mick name," said Dave and walked out.

Dr. H. looked at me and asked, "Is everything all right here?" I knew Dave could be listening, so I said yes. Dr. H. said he was sorry that these were hard, unhappy times for everyone. Of course, he meant us right then, and I felt like telling him what was on my mind, but then we saw Dave just outside the window. Dr. H. packed up his things and left in his buggy without saying another word.

28 March 1932

Dear Diary,
It's been such a hot summer. We hope for rain soon, but right now the grass has turned up its toes. There has been so little for the animals to eat. Dave finally bought some hay. He had

99

to, so the cow could give us milk. There's not enough for me to make butter, though. Brian has less energy in this heat. He so wants to follow his Da around, but Dave walks so fast that Brian can't keep up, so the poor little boy comes back crying. Bernadette is fussy a lot, probably because my milk is a bit less than last time. I'd like to start her on cereal soon, so she'll be satisfied, but it might be too early. I'm not sure what to do. She's harder to please than Brian was at that age.

I hope I don't get in the family way again too soon, but Dave wants what he wants as often as he can, and I'm worried because the money Mam and Da gave us is almost gone. Dave says he still has some credit at Ryan's store, but I don't think he'll be able to charm them much longer. Everyone is in trouble with money, even the Ryans, who used to have lots of it. Bev told me this. Dave never brings me news from Wirrim. He doesn't have any friends there.

Dave has started calling the children "BB" and says, "That's the name of a gun. Did you know that, Colleen?" I don't like his teasing moods and just ignore him. I used to be a good shot at home, but now I'm out of practice. I still have my rifle though. Dave bought one just like mine, even though we can't afford it. He says he's a good shot, though he won't tell me where he learned. He does target practice outside but misses most of the time, so he doesn't like me to watch.

30 July 1932

Dear Diary,

Well, the worst has happened. I'm expecting another baby in February, and though I love babies, I'm worried I won't be able to take care of it properly. Ryan's General Store in Wirrim told Dave he can't have any more credit. Dave didn't tell me this, Bev did. She gives me all the gossip whenever she's been to Wirrim.

It's a mystery to me where Dave is getting money to buy things now. We have kept the cow, but Dave shot two of our ewes for food. I told him not to do it, because their lambs would help the flock grow, but he did it anyway. He wouldn't let me butcher them, even though I told him I knew how. The cuts turned out to be very strange, not what I'm used to, but they tasted good anyway, until they went rancid. The Coolgardie safe wasn't big enough to keep the meat from two sheep all at one time. It stank to high heaven, I'm telling you. It was such a waste of good food that I cried, but then I laughed. Dave looked at me, and then he burst out laughing too. After that he kissed me and said sorry, and let's go to bed. What else could I do? Crying would not bring the meat back.

On the following page, Colleen has drawn her kitchen table covered with bloody chunks of meat, and Dave and herself surveying it, their hands in the air in a gesture of helplessness.

Merran's astonished when she reaches the final entry, from early August 1933, without an answer as to why Colleen lost her mind. Instead, in the few entries prior to the end, she is appealing to the Virgin Mary and the saints for assistance in being a better wife and mother, and for Dave to have a change of heart and love her and the children. She's upset on noticing that Dave has visited the Roberts' several times after Doug has ridden out on his horse. She knows that Bev is at home. It's a bleak picture, but what can she do? She chooses to look on the bright side. She writes that she was heartened one day to see Dave glance approvingly at their latest arrival, Bridget, who looked the most like him. At dinner he fed her cereal for the first time, and actually smiled at them all. She

101

believed that this was an answer to her prayers, and that Dave may have turned a corner.

In a burst of optimism she draws another picture, the last she will ever draw. It shows in painstaking detail her three children sitting all together in their best clothes, smiling for their artist mother. Merran feels her cheeks wet. This picture has been drawn with love.

Then the diary peters out, with no indication that Colleen has any plan to kill herself and the children. In several entries, even in the worst of times, she writes with affection of her children's milestones: first steps, the pushing through of teeth, first words. And, most striking of all, she writes that she knows she will get through this difficult period because she feels strong. She believes that once the hard times are over, life will improve for them. If not, she will do what Dave wants, and move to Melbourne. Not once does she sound like a woman on the verge of losing her mind or will to live.

Merran is about to put the diary in a drawer when a she notices a final page, past what she thought of as the ending. Colleen's bright side has faded.

17th August 1933.

Dear Diary,

I can hardly believe my luck. I'd written to Mam and Da a week or so ago to let them know that we were all right, despite the hard times. A little skinnier than we should be, but alive. I hadn't planned this, but I supposed I was feeling desperate, so I mentioned that Dave is planning to move back to Melbourne, and that I don't want to go. I told them that he doesn't hit me or the children, so they don't need to rescue me, but that if they saw it in their hearts to take the four of us in, I'd be very grateful. It would be temporary, until Dave and I can sort out our differences. Maybe I'll decide to go to Melbourne with him, or we could move into Wirrim and he'd get a job.

Given that they don't want anything to do with Dave, I was excited when a letter came back saying that the children and I would be very welcome, for a limited time of course. Dave will have to drive us there in the buggy, but they are willing at least to talk with him when he drops us off.

Now I'll have to pack. We have so little that it shouldn't take long. I'll be ready when he gets back from Wirrim. My plan sounds good, and I think he will go along with it. He might be happy with time to himself. But he can be moody and unpredictable, so I suppose I need to be ready for anything.

Chapter 22
WHAT NEXT?

Owen sits with his head in his hands, feeling defeated. A phone call to Daryl at the motel is fruitless. How can every room be full?

"He's probably taking the night off after our busy weekend," Helen tells him, and invites him to stay the night. There are some awkward moments when Danny invades the room set aside for the visitor, but Owen has learned about Danny and is quite prepared to engage him in conversation, mostly about cars. Owen is surprised that Danny knows more about cars than he'd expected.

After the boy has gone off to bed, Owen hears noises from the kitchen and finds Helen standing by the sink, with a glass of wine in one hand and a half-full bottle in the other. It's clear that she's planning to down the lot. When Owen complains about not knowing where Merran has gone, she frowns and says, "I thought you knew where she is. Sorry. She's driven up to Rylands. That's where Ruth and Johnny moved a long time ago. Nice people, as I remember them. She pauses. I've often wondered," she says almost as an aside, "how Merran turned out the way she is." Then, to cover up her guilt at uttering these words, she suggests that they both head off for a few hours of rest.

Owen lies awake for hours, his mind a jumble of racing thoughts, but at dawn he finally falls asleep, and it's ten o'clock before he stirs at the sound of Danny's knock at his door. He pulls on his pants, deals with Danny as politely as possible, and makes his escape with a quick explanation to Helen that he'll be back in the afternoon.

Chapter 23

Revelations

Although Merran was up late the night before, she still wakes to the sounds of warbling magpies. Reading that small cursive the night before has left her with a headache. The sun is just rising, adding colour to summer roses waving in the breeze outside.

She hears noises from the kitchen and wanders out to find Ruth pouring tea, her face as white as the teapot.

"How did you sleep, Mum?"

"Not well. I woke a few times crying."

She runs her fingers through her short white hair, and stares at the puddle of tea on the counter where a cup should have been. Merran mops it up quickly and leads her mother to a chair. Then, against her better judgment—the timing is lousy, but she needs to get this over with—Merran takes a breath and says,

"Mum let's eat our breakfast. After that, I have some questions for you."

Ruth looks curious but obeys. When they've finished their cereal she looks at Merran expectantly. "What do you want to know? By the look on your face, I can tell it's serious."

"It's a painful subject, Mum, but, I do need an answer." She hesitates, then plunges in.

"Did Dad ever threaten me physically?" Should she mention a gun? Not yet, too soon.

Ruth looks embarrassed. "What do you mean? Did he smack you? Yes, from time to time when you were young. You were an little imp, and sometimes we'd had enough. He said it was natural to smack, and that his parents did it to him. But I was against it, and over time he stopped."

"I'm not talking about smacking. It's worse than that. Did he ever point a rifle at me?"

This time Ruth looks shocked. "Of course not. What gave you that idea?"

No way to back out now. Merran tells her mother about the flashback and the effect on her of Johnny's angry face behind the rifle, becoming more and more agitated as she talks. Ruth stares at her as though she's speaking in tongues.

"And you believe he could do such a thing? Of course not. The only times I can remember him pulling out his rifle were when there was a snake coming around the house." She stops. "But wait a minute." Merran waits, on tenterhooks.

"And there was one other time. Our house was broken into one night after a big footy match, and someone must have talked about Dad having all the money. He was standing in for the team treasurer that weekend. We were just about to go to sleep when we heard a noise, sounded like our back door opening. We never locked the doors in those days, it was a different time. Dad suspected a robbery right away, because of the money. He jumped out of bed shouting and fetched his rifle out of the wardrobe. You woke up and started crying. You ran down the hallway, right into the arms of the masked robber. You made a perfect shield for him. Dad shot the rifle into the air, and the fellow escaped. No money was stolen, and no arrests were ever made."

Merran puts her face in her hands. Stop, Mum, she thinks.

But Ruth goes on, her voice rising. "It's outrageous you think he'd do something like that. He was always so protective of you."

"Why didn't you tell me?"

"We never thought to bring it up. Remember, we lived on the outskirts of Wirrim, and no one seemed to have heard the shot, so after the investigation came to a dead end we decided to just forget it. We were all OK. You never mentioned it either, so we assumed you'd forgotten. So we just went on with our lives, and when we moved to Rylands, it just faded away."

Merran can't think. Her brain feels as though it's being rerouted, the way a GPS adjusts the route when you go the wrong way. Dad's arms are around her, holding her tight. The sobs are both his and Ruth's. They are his arms that carry her off to bed and tuck her in.

Then, unbidden, memories of interactions with her father take on a totally different tinge. She's in the pool, and Dad is trying to teach her to swim. She feels so independent that she pushes him away, dog paddles to the other side of the pool, and turns, proud of herself, to see a look of puzzlement and hurt on his face. At the time, it didn't seem like a big deal. She was seven or eight, what did he expect?

"Did Dad and I actually fight? I remember laughing with him when he was teaching me to drive. I used to bunny hop all over the railway parking lot."

"Yes, that's true, but don't you remember what came afterwards, every week, like clockwork. Just as you were nearly home from your Sunday afternoon lesson, you'd find some way to needle him, and you'd both be shooting daggers at each other for the rest of the day. You'd lock yourself in your room and demand dinner in bed. And I did it, to keep the peace. He would sit at the table fuming that you expected me to wait on you. You passed the driving test the first time, and I always thought you should have said thank you."

"I thought I did, but then, maybe I just assumed that it was his job to teach me. Don't all kids take their fathers for granted?" Merran's getting desperate. Time for a change of subject.

"I know he lost his parents when he was very young. Car accident, wasn't it?"

Ruth nods. "The family had immigrated from Sicily not long before, and one day drove on the wrong side of the road. The children, four of them, were farmed out to relatives. He told me he was very lonely. Though his aunt and uncle were kind to him, they lived far away from his other relatives and siblings."

"It often seemed to me that you took the place of his mother in some ways. You know, he needed your attention. Did he resent me when I was little and took a lot of your time?"

"Yes, for a while, but as the years passed he came to value our little family more and more. He often said you look so much like his mother. Your dark curls, the colour of your skin, even your voice and mannerisms: all this brought back painful memories for him, but as time passed he came to believe that you were her spirit back from the grave."

"Wow, that's big, Mum."

Ruth smiles. "But his mother was stubborn, according to him, and both of you inherited that too. I sometimes tried to get in the middle to break up your arguments, but it was intimidating. You know how I hate conflict. I should have done something, though, because you pushed Dad away more and more."

She sits, lost in thought, then says, "Now you've told me about the memory—don't they call it a false memory?—you carried for years and years, it goes a long way towards explaining why you rejected him so completely. It was more than just stubbornness on both sides." Merran's chest is tight. She takes Ruth's hand.

"Here I was, delaying coming here, planning to give him a piece of my mind last night, when I should have been busting my guts to get here in time to say good-bye, and to thank him for being a good dad."

Tears roll down Ruth's cheeks, tears of relief. As for Merran, she feels guilt and sadness, but is too overwhelmed to cry.

Chapter 24
WHAT HAPPENED?

Owen's in Rylands, searching for a phone book to look up the Provenzano address. Phone boxes are rare these days, he thinks. After twenty minutes, he finds one, covered with graffiti, but the book is missing. He sits in the gutter, watching pedestrians go by and feeling hopeless, then notices an elderly man wearing a black suit and a Catholic priest's dog collar. Provenzano? It's an Italian name. Might this priest know the family? He catches up with the priest and asks the question.

"What a coincidence!" the priest says, introducing himself as Father Boyle. "I not only know the family, but I'm on my way to discuss a funeral mass with Mr. Provenzano's widow. Would you like to walk with me? It's not far." This puts a whole new complexion on things for Owen. Merran didn't mention anything about her dad on Saturday, and had certainly been to the old farm yesterday, so he'd died as recently as last night.

Father Boyle notices Owen's hesitation and suggests that he might pay a short visit to offer his condolences in any case.

"I think Merran might be at home," Owen says. At least, that's what he's hoping for. "I saw her at our school reunion in Wirrim just this weekend."

Merran answers the door and invites them in. She looks shocked and a little embarrassed to see him. As well she should be, sneaking around, doing field research on *his* story. After introductions, there's an awkward silence. Now, face to face with Merran, the daughter of a man so recently deceased, he suddenly doesn't know what to say, except to mumble condolences to her and her mother. Noticing the priest turn to Ruth, Owen makes his exit, hoping to convey sensitivity to the family, but in truth hoping Merran will follow him out.

She does, but she's not the same woman he saw only yesterday. She's pale, and looks preoccupied, not the attack dog he's used to seeing. She blots tears with a damp tissue. "Remember I told you that my father was at death's door and I chose to go to the reunion first? Because of that I arrived too late. I feel awful."

She looks vacantly around the garden, trying to pin down some thoughts.

"I know I need to apologize to you for something, but my mind's gone blank."

Owen's happy to take the lead for once.

"First, Merran, I'm so sorry you lost your dad. As for what you need to apologize about, did you by any chance go out to the farm yesterday? You know, where Colleen killed herself and her children?" It's not fair to hit her with this right now, but her betrayal has to be named sooner or later. She avoids his eyes, and colour comes back into her cheeks.

112

"I'm sorry, Owen. I did go out to the farm yesterday, and I also went to the historical museum to look for primary sources from the period." The latter piece of information is a shock. He knows she went to the farm; the museum is a complete surprise.

She continues, "I came across something at the museum that's puzzling. See if we can put our heads together to come up with an answer. Would you take a walk around the block for about twenty minutes while I talk with the priest? Or you can just sit here if you like. Mum isn't really with it this morning, and I need to make sure that Dad's funeral is something he would have liked. He deserves a good send-off."

Owen sets off, walking quickly. He needs the exercise. For the first time, Merran's admitting she needs help from him. She actually sounds *nice*. On arriving back, he sits on the attractive wrought-iron seat in the Provenzano garden and looks around slowly. Someone has taken great care to create an oasis in this unforgiving climate. Every one of the raised flower and vegetable beds, and the many shrubs and fruit trees, has been watered, trimmed, and is almost weed-free.

It comes to him suddenly that his own garden in Bendigo is as neglected as his marriage. Years ago, when he and Pat actually did things together, they had planted Australian native shrubs which should have tolerated the heat, but even they have been put under such stress due to inattention that most have died. Pat is guilty too. Neither is interested in maintaining this symbol of domesticity any longer. Death appears in different forms. He slumps on the garden seat.

A few minutes later, Merran shows Father Boyle out the door, then sits next to Owen. She takes a small book from her pocket and passes it to him.

"Here, I found Colleen's diary in the museum. You can read and return it in a few days while the custodian's back is turned, and she'll never know. And since it's part of your family history, you could decide to keep it. It'll never be missed in that mess of a place."

Owen pages quickly through the diary, noticing the drawings.

"It looks like a work of art. I hope it also tells us how she came to commit a murder/suicide."

Merran holds up her hand to stop him. "I just wanted you to see this bit near the beginning. Remember that in the newspaper article Dave Enright said his parents told him to come back to Melbourne right after the shooting? Well, Colleen says here that Dave's parents died even before she married him."

Her words disturb him, but he doesn't know why. He says slowly,

"What are you implying?"

"Colleen says in her diary that Dave was visiting a female neighbour—you know, Beverley Roberts— while the husband was out. And she says here that he wanted to go back to Melbourne, but she didn't want to live in the city. It's possible that he had an old flame in the city as well; he sounds to have been an unfaithful devil."

Owen's words are heated. "The old flame, if there was one, couldn't have been Grandma Thelma. She'd never have been part of a deception like that. In any case, there's a big leap from an affair to murder."

Affair? Valerie springs to mind. He blushes, and his voice rises.

"Come on, Merran, you're way ahead of yourself."

"OK, I'll slow down a bit. Let me check if Mum needs me, and if not, we could walk down to the coffee shop and have a think." She has no sooner returned with the all clear than Owen's phone pings. He looks down at the text. It's Gareth.

"Hang on a minute, Merran. My brother might have something else up his sleeve."

Hi, little brother, thought you'd like to know that cousin Phil is still cleaning out the shed—it's about time. Most of the stuff is worthless, and damp too. But guess what he found this time? A rifle, among Grandpa's bits and pieces. Didn't the newspaper say that the police took the rifle away with them? I'll leave you to sort this out. The party was great. Gareth.

"Colleen writes that there were two rifles in the house—his 'n hers," Merran says. "I wanted to find out more about that anyway." As they arrive at the coffee shop and order Long Blacks and lemon cake, Merran's face shows intense concentration. No chance of a relaxing break, Owen thinks. She's recovered remarkably quickly.

"OK, let's continue," she says. He has no choice but to go with her agenda, as always.

"We still haven't established a motive for the murders," he says.

She looks at him hard, pauses for dramatic effect, then drops a bombshell.

"Well, Owen," she says slowly, "what if Dave came home to find her in bed with a swaggie?"

"A swaggie? What swaggie?" Shit. Where'd that come from?

"Colleen says in her diary that there were lots around at that time. She was terrified of them. Dave would go to Wirrim and leave her alone with the kids."

"Yes, I know about swaggies; don't you call them hobos in the States?" Owen says, frowning. "But how do they come into it?"

"You know that some of them wanted not only food but sex as well. They took advantage of women alone in the bush."

"Not many, Merran. Most of them just wanted food."

She ignores him, twirling a greying curl with her finger, an old habit while thinking.

"Maybe the swaggie was raping her," Merran goes on, "and Dave arrived and tried to shoot him but missed and hit her instead?"

"But what about the three kids? He had no reason to kill them."

"The swaggie might have tried to escape with one or two of the kids as hostages, and Dave shoots again and kills a kid. He was a lousy shot, Colleen says."

"So he keeps picking them off while trying to get the swaggie? That's far-fetched. I think we'd better think this over some more. You're going too fast for me, and there's a risk of getting this all wrong." And, he thinks, she's trampling all over my territory. Swaggies . . . that's unbelievable. He buys himself some time by cutting his cake in half. He offers one half to Merran, who has already finished eating her whole piece.

"Here's another thought," Merran says, her mouth full of cake. "With one or two kids dead, Dave

116

sees this as an opportunity to get back to Melbourne unencumbered by a grieving wife. It's a gift he can't refuse. She won't be much use to him from then on. So he shoots her and any remaining kids with his own gun, carefully puts *her* gun beside her—taking out a few bullets of course—and drags the swaggie off somewhere. Hides his own gun somewhere out of the way. Lets her get the blame, so he won't be found guilty of killing anyone."

Owen can't resist opposing her. It's now obvious that she's intent on solving the mystery, just for the intellectual challenge. She's like a dog with a rag in its mouth.

"But wouldn't the police find clues that he'd killed the swaggie?" he asks. There's a silence. He waits for the next volley but instead, she sits back in her chair and sighs. Owen notices, to his surprise, that all the oomph has gone out of her. She picks up her coffee cup and says,

"Owen, it's all too much, too quickly. Trouble sleeping, my father's death, this investigation, it feels like a mountain I can't climb right now. I need to focus. My Australian history class at Clare College begins in ten days, and I need to get to the State Library."

Owen's ability to form words has left him.

"This is what we will do," she says, appearing to pull herself together, "I think I could solve this pretty darn quick, but I'm too close to the wind. If you don't like the swaggie theory, it'll be up to you to do the footwork and follow this up. Read the diary yourself, see if it convinces you that someone other than Colleen killed those kids. There's lots to follow up

... swaggies' remains—yes or no. One or two guns?—can we be sure?" She jots down each point on the coffee receipt. "Did the police search the property? Should they do it again? Your take on Colleen—loving mother or murderer?"

She passes the receipt to Owen.

"After Dad's funeral I'll be out of here. I can't say I'm giving up my belief that Colleen is innocent, but it's going to have to be you who gets the evidence that takes it to some sort of conclusion. Then you can write it up as a bit of social history. Let's talk before I fly back."

Owen turns away, as if to take in the view of the street outside, but in truth he doesn't want Merran to see his look of excitement. He drives back to Wirrim with a smile that won't go away.

Why reagent?
Wouldn't this piss
him off?

Chapter 25

GOODBYE

The funeral Mass takes place in Saint Anthony's Church in Rylands, with Father Boyle celebrating. Although he met Johnny only the once, he delivers what Merran considers a worthy eulogy. Nice old man, she thinks. Someone you can trust, even confess to. Though she isn't the confessing type, she wonders if indeed the sacrament is as effective as seeing a therapist. And there's no charge for it either . . . that's a plus.

An hour later, the hearse carrying Johnny's coffin, covered with flowers, enters the cemetery, followed by an entourage, which includes the black funeral car for Ruth and Merran and a stream of cars sticking close behind, lights on. As they make their way around the paths to the newly dug grave, Merran reflects not only on her father but also on Colleen and the perplexing absence of any mention of intent to kill. She did, surely, love her children with all of her heart. Merran is convinced even more than when she first read the diary that Colleen just couldn't have done it. If Owen is able answer all her questions, it

119

will go a long way towards explaining what actually happened. If the search yields nothing, then she'll conclude that Dave killed them all in the midst of some sort of crisis.

She's jolted back into the present when Johnny's pall bearers approach the grave and loosen the straps holding the carved cherry box, allowing it to descend to the bottom. Just how far down it is, becomes achingly real to Merran as she and Ruth shovel the first dry dirt clods onto the coffin. The thud of soil sounds hollow, and breathtakingly final. Where is Johnny's consciousness now? Her throat constricts. She says farewell in her mind; there are no words. Then while the priest is wrapping up with some prayers, she looks around and realizes that her father's grave is not in a specific Catholic area, just as Hugh Lawson told them. Nearby are McCallums, O'Donnells—the Macs and the O's. In her wanderings around the Wirrim cemetery years ago she'd often wondered what happened to people who had no religion at all . . . rarer then, but what of those who left the church, or were excommunicated? Would that have happened to Colleen? Merran wonders if Colleen's parents took the bodies to Boolong for burial, or if Dave kept them in Wirrim. Another question in her mind is if all four of them were buried together or, more likely for the times, if Colleen is in unconsecrated ground in a different part of the cemetery. How sad if she were innocent, and she and her children were separated in death. Part of her scoffs at notions like these: they're all dead and don't know or care. Still….she looks up and notices Ruth and the funeral guests walking slowly away, chatting. Now she herself is crying—for Johnny or Colleen, she can't be sure.

Chapter 26
A Search

Owen's question to Merran is still nagging at him.

"Why do we even need a swaggie? Dave could have done all this. He was a callous character, and he was certainly looking to get away from the area, but I don't think he would have just killed them all in cold blood." But Merran insists there needed to have been someone else present, some commotion, to have made Dave act in such a violent manner, and he finds himself coming around to her idea. In his imagination, the dog (Merran) still has the rag in its mouth, but now he realizes that the rag has been passed to him.

He decides he's ready for a search of the farm. If his head was spinning with new information and questions on Monday, by nightfall on Wednesday, it's doing cartwheels. He's read the diary several times and, like Merran, finds it difficult to imagine Colleen as a murderer. With Helen's coaxing, he's arranged that Wirrim's interim policeman (the permanent one is on holidays) and some helpers should search the Grogans' property—with their permission, of course.

While this is being carried out, he pays a visit to the Wirrim cemetery.

The final resting place for Wirrim residents is on the Walangie Road and enclosed by a wire fence. As Owen remembers it from his childhood, there was nothing but graves. Now, a well-cared-for lawn area is devoted to cremains. Despite the small size of the grave section, Owen wanders for an hour before giving up. There's no grave labelled "Enright." He rings the caretaker listed on the sign at the gate. Joe Taylor is a quiet-spoken, friendly man who tells Owen he's retired and has plenty of time on his hands. Ten minutes later, he rolls up in an ancient Holden, skids to a halt in the gravel, and waves.

"Over here. I'll look in the records for you."

A small room smelling like old dust contains the death records for Wirrim and its outlying areas. Owen recalls Wirrim's funeral customs: black ribbons fastened to shop entrances, along with notices of funeral arrangements, and corteges passing slowly by the school on their way to the cemetery. They were not elaborate, but were customs nevertheless, and faithfully adhered to.

Record books from the last century are high on a dusty shelf. Joe retrieves a ladder from the corner, climbs up carefully, and pulls out one labelled "1930–1939," rubbing his handkerchief so briskly over the cover that Owen steps to the ladder to catch him. As if he could: Joe is heavyset and would crush him. He backs off. There's been enough death here already.

"1933, you said?" Joe opens the volume and runs down the columns with a nicotine-stained finger. "Looks like there were a lot of deaths that year." He sounds surprised. "Could have been the effects of the Depression. Not influenza—1918 was the big year for that. I don't know about 1933, but it would be interesting to find out." He glances at Owen, who's having trouble disguising his enthusiasm.

"I'm a historian, Joe. Questions like that get me going."

"To each his own," mutters Joe with a grin, and returns to the record. "There's a grave with a Colleen Enright in it, but it's in the old unconsecrated part, over near the north fence. Did she kill herself, or somebody else? There's another grave called Enright, from the same date. That's strange." He backs off, looking shocked. "It says here that there are three small children buried in it."

"Yes, that's them. A boy and two girls," Owen says.

"No headstones were ever put on the graves." Joe muses, "They must have been Catholic, as the children's grave is in their section. So what did the mother do to deserve unconsecrated ground?"

"Her husband said she killed herself and the children, but I have doubts about that." He can hardly believe he's come around to this idea so quickly.

That evening, Constable Ross Walters calls Owen with a report on the search at the farm. The young man is tripping over his words in excitement, as he tells Owen that there's not only one grave, but at least nine, on the Grogans' property. Owen calls Jenny, who is surprised but tells him that the previous owners mentioned they'd found a mess when they'd bought the farm after it had been abandoned for several decades. They'd disposed of loads of swaggie castoffs: shredded bedrolls, billies with holes in them, old boots and packs. There'd also been a small collection of rough wooden crosses in the shed.

The role of one identifiable swaggie—if indeed there was one present on that fateful day—in the death of Colleen and the children would therefore have to remain inconclusive. Owen imagines the terrible scene where a desperate and frustrated Dave arrives home to find a stranger threatening his wife and holding her and the children hostage. It strikes Owen that Colleen and the children were killed by men's wars and financial greed, not as the result of a mother's despair. Here is his paper.

Owen stays with Helen and Mike a little longer. He and Danny have been getting on like a house on fire. Owen takes it upon himself to investigate sheltered workshops in Rylands, much closer than Bendigo, and soon he's able to come to Helen with exciting news. A new facility is about to open. So Danny will be off very soon to earn a bit of money, making crafts for sale and doing other useful jobs, and to share an apartment with several young adults with various disabilities, under the care of a young woman whom they've heard is "not only experienced, but all heart." Danny is so excited he can't stop talking about it.

Merran puts in several days at the State Library, though not as many as she'd planned. She's feeling nervous, but hopes she has sufficient material for her upcoming class. She and Owen have talked a few times, the final phone call taking place on the day before she is to fly back to San Francisco. He tells her proudly that he's begun the outline of a paper on the social conditions that led to the Enright family's tragedy, as well as similar events during the Great Depression. He will describe the possible scenario leading to the four deaths, he says, and indicate how easy it would be for a fatal confrontation to develop. Colleen and her children could well have died as two strong males confronted needs beyond their control.

"There were incidents during the recent long drought where bankrupt farmers were driven to homicide or suicide," he told her. "So it's not beyond the bounds of belief."

"I'd say go for it, Owen. This might give your career a boost." But as she says this, Owen detects a subdued tone in her typically confident voice.

"Are you OK? You sound different."

"It's just the phone. You sound as though you're in a tunnel. Do I sound worse?" She tries to laugh, but it comes down the line as a croak.

He waits. After a beat, he hears her intake of breath, then a sob. "I'm wondering, Owen . . . if Colleen is innocent of suicide and murder, or even if it's inconclusive, could she be reburied with her children?"

Chapter 27
BRICK BY BRICK

Three events occurred within quick succession a few weeks after Merran's return to San Francisco, enough to shake her to the core.

First, she was terrorized when a disgruntled former student with an automatic weapon roamed the corridors of Clare College over the course of twenty minutes. He'd seemed more confused than intentional, however, and was talked down and captured with no loss of life. The administration brought in a crisis counselor and recommended that all staff follow up with therapy.

Merran resisted at first, but a series of bad dreams and daytime flashbacks became debilitating. And it seemed that every time she turned on the news, there were reports of new school shootings. She searched online and found Catherine Moore, an older, patient, and very wise therapist. After a few sessions she felt better, but when Catherine read between the lines and realized that Merran had been carrying significant psychological burdens for a long time and would benefit from additional therapy, she urged Merran to continue. This was the second event.

126

Over several sessions that followed, Merran rebelled whenever Catherine called her on her competitiveness and tactlessness, such as taking over their time together with boasting or one-upping; or downplaying the need for change; or insulting Catherine when the latter raised her fee. But Catherine identified these actions as testing, pointing out that Merran was pushing to find out the limits of Catherine's tolerance. Would the therapist reject her like most of the people she knew? It took more weeks before Merran began to relax. When Catherine continued to greet her each week with a friendly smile and proceeded with an obvious plan, she hung on with therapy, surprised and intrigued that she'd met her match in one whom she'd come to respect as strong and smart as well as gentle. Once the walls that Merran had built around herself began to crumble, the two of them found a deeper layer in her psyche: her shame. About the way she'd neglected Richard; about her dismissive attitude towards her parents, particularly her late father. And not least, her provocative behavior towards Owen at the class reunion the previous year. The two women discussed ways to repair the damage done.

Apologies aside, Merran was not off the hook. There were swift consequences of her poor behavior. This was the third event. Her sneaking around, trying to barge in on Owen's ambitions to write a paper, had taken up more of her research days Down Under than was wise. A few weeks into her Australian history class she realized that her preparation was too narrowly focused on the Depression, and on one state, Victoria. This was a shock. Even Jess Wallace's

127

notes hadn't helped as much as she'd expected: the elements of her "curriculum" consisted of numbered one-liners. Merran had never before experienced such difficulty filling her lectures: she was known to be meticulous and exhaustive, and often had to pick and choose between too much information. She was mortified when several students expressed disappointment to her and, she assumed, to J.L., her department chairman.

Sure enough, when the class was over, most of the evaluations were neutral to unfavorable. Australian history was only ever offered in the spring semester, and she'd been happy to refocus her teaching on Asia, enjoying the brief limelight when her book was published in late summer, and to put the Wirrim experience into a box tied with a ribbon.

PART II
January 2018

Chapter 28

Off Again

It's a windy day in early January when J.L. calls her to come to his office "urgently." This time Merran is prepared. Through the departmental grapevine, she's heard that Jess has asked for additional time off to continue caring for her mother who is still unexpectedly alive, and has hinted that she might not come back at all. Due to her sessions with Catherine, Merran has dropped her jealousy and resentment against J.L., and now thinks of their relationship as a "friendly standoff." Although her step promotion was approved, she's decided to stay on at Clare College for the time being after all, due to an unexpected love interest.

It isn't hard for J.L. and Merran to come to an agreement which includes a second study trip to Melbourne, but he insists on two conditions: first, that they split the expenses; and second, that she make only a brief visit to her mother in Rylands. Ruth has been reporting worrisome health symptoms and would appreciate some support. J.L. makes it clear that he's expecting a better return on the department's investment this time. If he had done due diligence and checked a map, he would have discovered just how much of a detour Rylands would be: four hundred miles round-trip. He still doesn't know about Wirrim. After all, the town is more or less on the way to Rylands. Less rather than more, but no matter, Merran rationalizes: her visit there will be quick. She simply has to stop there to look at Dorrie Richardson's wartime letters from her late husband. The letters might put a human face on WWII for the students.

Most of all, Merran is curious how her former classmates in Wirrim will react to the changes she's experienced over the past year, both physical and psychological. Will the changes be evident to those she treated rather insensitively at the class reunion— Helen, Tom, Vera, Danny and, of course, Owen? She hasn't heard from any of them since. Perhaps they were glad to see the back of her. She wants to set things right, if she can.

In her rental car and nearing the left turnoff to Wirrim, she knows she should drive to Rylands first, where her mother will be ticking off the hours since the plane landed. Nevertheless, she takes the turnoff. She'll call in on Helen, catch up on some gossip, track down Dorrie to make an appointment for a brief look at the letters, then go on to her mother. Twenty-four hours, tops. Well, maybe thirty-six. The rest of her time will be in the State Library. Sounds like a plan that will work beautifully. She can already picture the students' positive evaluations.

Now that she's on the home stretch to Wirrim she relaxes a little and decides to stop. For a moment she wishes she'd stayed in the car, as the heat hits as it did a year ago. She's a slow learner, she thinks ruefully. It's completely silent out here. Sheep and kangaroos again. Where are the birds, she wonders?

As if on cue, one green budgie flies over the car, chirping, then a whole flock rises from their roosts. The sun's still up but well on its way to setting, and Merran notices that insects have risen from wherever they were sleeping—if insects sleep—and have attracted hundreds more birds. As she watches, transfixed, the daily ritual of the bush plays itself out before her eyes. She recognizes galahs, cockatoos, and magpies. For the years she's been overseas, she hasn't given thought to what she's been missing: the calls of such unique bird species, and especially the complex, cheerful melody of the magpies. Before she can stop herself, she calls, "sing, maggies, sing!" All at once the warbling starts, and she's transported to her little bedroom in Wirrim, where she woke each morning to the maggies' song, so different from that of American magpies.

She gets back in the car, turns on the ignition, which sets the air-conditioning going again, and uses the rearview mirror to apply a coppery-red lipstick, powder her nose, and brush her newly styled chin-length curls, which in the past year have turned back the clock, changing from mostly grey to her original medium brown. She's recently had her colours done, and now wears clothing suited to her inherited southern Italian olive skin. She straightens her knee-length black skirt a little and uses saliva on a tissue to remove a small stain off her gold and black cotton blouse. She checks again that her low heels are ready on the seat beside her. It won't do to emerge from her car in sneakers. Satisfied, she resumes her drive with mounting excitement. She passes Coopers Lake, and a few minutes later the familiar grain silos come into view. She crosses the railway line and here she is, in Wirrim again. She feels a flash of joy. It feels more and more like home.

Chapter 29
The Exchange

She's approaching Helen's street when she sees pandemonium ahead, at the school. Flashing lights, a small crowd. Interesting. As she draws up at the curb, she notices that Tom and Vera Clements, and another couple she's never seen before, are listening to a tall, angry-looking policeman who, in Merran's quick assessment, is a ten in good looks, but a two in tact. He looks vaguely familiar, and when he notices her walking towards them, she catches his look of puzzlement. Those brown eyes, that mop of black curls, now going grey. Who is this? Brendan O'Neill? Since she saw Brendan last, he's grown several inches and is even more attractive than she remembered, especially in his police uniform. What is it about women and uniforms? Brendan is tanned and muscular, but with worry lines around the eyes. At this moment, though, his face is fixed in a frown. She moves a few steps closer.

From what she can hear, he's berating Tom and Vera for negligence, while the other couple stands by silently. Tom and Vera have tears in their eyes and are looking anywhere but at their accuser. What's going on? Merran's eyes sweep the school ground for answers. She's astonished to see yet another couple: Owen's arm is around Helen's waist as he leans on the door of a new bright red Prius, with a "Bendigo: The Gold Rush City" sticker on one of the doors. She feels a twinge of envy, then quickly puts it aside as irrational: she herself has recently purchased a new green Subaru Forester for hiking trips off the beaten track. How is she to account for these complex emotions? She and Catherine, her therapist in San Francisco, have discussed this very topic quite recently. The conclusion they reached is that Merran believes subconsciously that success is a zero-sum game. This insight alone has been life-changing.

She notices Helen's look of surprise to see her. It doesn't look like a welcome. Owen acknowledges her with a tight wave, his expression guarded. Merran hesitates for a moment, then turns back towards the car. These are not gestures of old friends dying to see her. She's half-expected this, but it's still disappointing.

She and Catherine have discussed many things, but not this particular circumstance: an unannounced arrival and its consequences. She recalls what happened the previous year, when she did exactly the same thing, arriving at the high school reunion without prior warning. Fight or flight? No, instead she freezes, keys dangling from her hand. Then, get out of here fast, you idiot, she tells herself. You're not as evolved as you thought.

She makes to unlock the car and drive away, when Owen and Helen untangle from each other, walk over, and hug her.

"I was taken aback when I saw you, Merran. Why didn't you let us know you were coming, and how long can you stay?" Helen asks, patting Merran's back. Helen is one of those people who pats and hugs at the same time. Despite Merran's developing comfort with touch, a little physical affection still goes a long way. She pulls back slightly and changes the subject.

"I'm sorry I didn't let you know I was coming. I need to arrange to see Dorrie Richardson again, to discuss some World War II letters she told me about. But first I need to make a quick visit to my mum in Rylands." She sighs. "After that I'll be on my way back to Melbourne to do penance for my sins at the State Library, same as last year. My chairman has coerced me into teaching the Australian history class again." It isn't quite true. She'd practically offered to do it this time. Historians stick to the facts; at least they're supposed to, she thinks ruefully, but sometimes fiction makes a better story, and it's not exactly a lie. "Thought I'd stop off here for an hour or so to say hello, but now I realize the timing's not good." She turns to indicate the crowd. "What's happened? And why are there kids here in the summer holidays?"

"You remember that Vera and Tom host a cultural exchange of about twenty students from Japan each January?" Owen replies. "Then they take our students to Japan during the July holidays. What's happened is that one of the visiting students has gone missing. Apparently, he went for a walk early this morning and hasn't been seen since."

Merran recoils in shock. It's now obvious why there's such an electric atmosphere.

"And who are the two standing with them?" Merran asks.

"Rhonda and Bill Jenkins. They only moved to Wirrim in the past year. They're the boy's host parents. They were worried when he didn't come home for lunch as usual, and still hasn't shown up by now. It's getting late. That's when Rhonda called Tom and Vera, and then Brendan O'Neill."

"Since when has Brendan been the local policeman? I didn't see him at the reunion last year."

"He had to be out of town that weekend, but said he regretted it."

They stand silently for a few moments, pretending not to listen to Brendan's rant, but when Tom looks over with a scowl they are embarrassed and leave quickly. Helen says, "Let's get out of the heat. All this week has been stinking hot. I can't see that we can do anything at the moment. Brendan will keep us in the loop. The police from Bendigo should be here soon, and I think we'll be able to join in on a big search once they tell us what to do."

"But why all this fuss about a kid being out a few hours longer than usual?"

Owen says, "it's because he's not used to this landscape. There are not many markers, so he could get lost more easily than a local kid. Vera and Tom need to get him back pronto. For the sake of the programme, too."

"He adds, "A lot of us have already been on the roads and just got back before you arrived. Good thing we didn't miss you. Of course we're all very worried, but it won't help if we just stand around here making nuisances of ourselves. How about a cool drink?"

138

"Oh, and you must be hungry, Merran," Helen says. "Have you driven all the way from Tulla again?" As Merran nods, she notices Helen looking her up and down, surprise on her face. Twenty pounds lighter, at least. This has been one of the successes of the past year.

"It's too hot for your favourite steak and mushroom pie, but you will eat a sandwich and some Anzac bikkies, won't you, Merran?"

"Of course, the diet's on hold while I'm in Australia. Too much great tucker."

They're leaving the school grounds when Merran turns and sees Brendan O'Neill watching her, and then suddenly punch his forehead in a gesture of recognition. He smiles and waves, sending her heart thumping. She's waited nearly forty years for that smile. She'll make sure to talk to him very soon. But not until the boy is found.

Chapter 30
Catching Up

As they cool off under the fan in the dim lounge room, Merran notices Owen's arm around Helen's shoulder. With a start, she realizes that her arrival might have interrupted their plans for a romantic tryst. How unexpected to see them as a couple, she thinks, but forces herself to say nothing. She knows that Owen and his wife Pat had problems in their marriage. At the reunion last year, she'd overheard Owen tell Tom that he and Pat were married in name only, and each was involved with lovers. Helen and her husband Mike had held their relationship together over the care of their son, Danny. It's possible that now Danny is safely in a care community in Rylands, there's been nothing to keep the relationship intact. Merran thinks she approves. She'd never got along with Mike, and his dislike of her was patently clear last year.

Helen and Owen are unaware of her recent 180-degree changes, so Owen's glance is cautious, as though he's afraid of a tactless comment.

"You must be a bit surprised seeing us here together," he ventures preemptively.

"I can guess," smiles Merran. "Congratulations." Owen certainly looks fitter and happier than when they met the year before. His then-skinny body has firmed up; his arms even have muscles. He stands straight rather than stooped. He's had his hair cut short, and it suits him.

Helen takes his hand. Her hair is brighter, not woolly grey any longer. She's had it thinned, and dyed to its original auburn, which complements her pretty heart-shaped face, the sparkle in her hazel eyes, and her clear, smooth skin, unusual for people in this harsh climate. Merran wonders what brand of moisturizer she uses. She looks for rings but there are none. She thinks of asking if Owen has plans to make Helen an honest woman, but catches herself just in time, adding merely, "I'm happy for you both." Owen and Helen look at each other with surprise.

"Seems that a lot has happened in your life as well, Merran?" Owen says.

"Oh, yes, I hardly know where to start," Merran says, smiling. "But I want to hear your news first. Owen are you still teaching at Bendigo Uni?"

"Yes, but I can do some writing here, and only have to show up for three days out of the week for teaching. You knew last year, of course, that my career was in a slump."

"Yes, Owen, and I'm sorry I was such a pain in the...."

Owen cuts her off with a dismissive wave. "Let's put that behind us. Once you'd found Colleen's diary and passed it on to me, I was free to write my paper

141

on the deaths at the farm. That publication was the beginning of a turnaround for me—though of course one success can't make me rich and famous."

"What have you been up to since?"

"I'm developing a specialization on the social effects of the Great Depression. I've taken up running. But the biggest life-changer of all has been sweet Helen here."

Merran takes in Helen's look of pleasure. She is saying that she still works at Cody's insurance agency but is thinking about buying a dress shop whose owner wants to get out of the business. "I'm a bit more aware of style these days," she says shyly. She glances at Owen and blushes. Hmmm, those two are really in love. She checks herself—not a trace of jealousy, only happiness for them. Now that's progress.

"Any sign of Richard?" Owen asks.

"I've seen neither hide nor hair of him, but I heard through the grapevine that he's now in Brisbane with his lady-love, Miss Jezebel. No kids yet, but who knows when?" Might as well hold to her original story. Felicity the sexy one is more interesting than Felicity the dumpy one. In actual fact, she has no idea where they are. Owen looks embarrassed.

"Oh, don't worry," Merran says. "He was never going to get a kid from me. But I'm dating again, someone from the hiking club I've joined. Blake's a lot younger than I am and fit as a fiddle in so many ways." She realizes the implications of what she's said, and grins.

They all laugh. How different it feels to Merran now that she has learned to relax when in company, rather than feeling pushed to compete. She can enjoy these old school acquaintances, who might even become real friends. Owen is thinking, his head on one side.

"I know your calendar is full while you're here, but I wonder if you might help the police by talking to the Japanese students. You're fluent, and Tom and Vera are overwhelmed at the moment. Apart from being worried about the boy, they're scared that if he's not found quickly, their programme might be put on hold or even cancelled. You know how dedicated they are. It would be such a loss for them and for the schools involved."

"I didn't see their Japanese chaperone. Wouldn't he or she have to be bilingual?"

"They did have a chaperone," Owen says, "but the poor fellow's wife was rushed to hospital with acute appendicitis, and he flew back to Japan in a hurry. It was only the second day they were here, but Tom and Vera told him they'd manage without him. So it's a godsend that you've arrived."

"Well, I never say no to an opportunity to practice my Japanese," Merran says, rubbing her hands together, then stops and reddens with shame. It isn't about her.

"Just then, Owen's phone rings." He mouths "Brendan O'Neill," and listens for a good minute or so. "He wants us to take the Wilpita road to look for the missing boy. There's going to be about ten cars going down the five roads from the main street. If we can't find him within an hour, we are to come back and meet with everyone else." They all make for the door. Seeing Merran's hesitation, Helen asks, "Would you like to come with us? Make yourself useful?"

Make yourself useful? That's a phrase Dad used to use when he tried to get help in the house or garden. Bloody hell! She looks at her watch in shock.

"I was supposed to be at Mum's for an early dinner. She's used to my being unreliable, but under the circumstances it's unforgivable. She hasn't been too well lately. I'll call her and get going, if you don't mind."

"But you will come back, won't you? We can ring Brendan and ask if you can help question the Japanese students," Owen says. "That's if we don't find him on this swing before dark."

"I'll be back the day after tomorrow," she says, then reconsiders. "But time being of the essence, I could come back tomorrow morning and return to Mum after lunch. I don't think she'll object to that."

Owen hands her his phone. "Here, call her now."

Chapter 31

Ruth

Merran steps outside to ring Ruth and is greeted with an angry sigh at the other end.

"Where are you? I worried about you all afternoon. Your plane arrived on time, so after a few hours I called the police to see if you'd been in an accident. You didn't answer your phone." Damn, she didn't turn it on after landing.

"I should've known you'd get sidetracked," Ruth continues. "Last time you were here you even missed your father's death. You've been telling me you've changed. I don't see much evidence of that." Wow, that's so unlike Mum. She used to be such a milquetoast, so much easier to deal with.

"I decided to call in to Wirrim on my way and found out that there's a boy missing from the exchange group here from Japan. You know, I told you about Tom and Vera last year? I got talking to Owen and Helen, and the time just flew. I'll be there in half an hour. OK?" She hangs up before her mother can reply and hopes they won't get into an argument when she arrives.

By the time she reaches Rylands, however, Ruth has apparently had a change of heart. She hugs Merran and cries a bit about Johnny's death. Merran's own tears won't come, but as she rarely cries, she tells herself that it doesn't mean anything one way or another. And yet she did become emotional the previous year when Owen told her that Colleen Enright's grave was a distance away from that of her children. Perhaps it's easier to cry about those she doesn't know, than those she does.

She soon learns that Ruth's angry outbursts are more frequent lately.

"I was an old-fashioned wife. You must have known that, Merran. Dad made all of the important decisions. I trusted him enough not to question his judgment. It's been hard to adjust to being in charge, after sixty years of marriage. At times it feels overwhelming, which is why I need you here now and then. You hurt my feelings when you put your friends first today. I know it's important to find the boy, but you could have rung sooner. I would've understood. How could you have forgotten you were to be here for tea?"

"I'm sorry, I wish I'd come straight here," Merran says, but it's not completely true. The visit to Wirrim has opened up an intriguing line of inquiry. She'll get to practice her Japanese; she's renewed contact with school friends; it looks like she might even get involved in the search for the young boy. Perhaps Mum could do with a good therapist, too, who could help her understand her daughter's priorities. Why can't she look on this as an opportunity for growth? Ruth is looking at her expectantly. Merran feels at a loss to answer. This conversation is going nowhere. She switches to logistics, always her strong suit.

"Well, I'm here now. By the way, is there any dinner left?" Ruth nods and heads for the kitchen. Merran follows her, talking all the way.

"We can get onto your health issues for a bit tonight, but I'm afraid I have to go back to Wirrim tomorrow morning. I might be needed to question some of the Japanese students."

She wolfs down her meal of tuna casserole, carrots and green beans. Her mother always insisted that a meal needs colour on the plate.

"But I'll come back for a late lunch and have dinner with you as well and leave the following morning or afternoon, so I can get back to Melbourne." Best not to mention Dorrie, she thinks. So, all in all, you and I will have a bit of time to come to some decisions about what you should do next. We can always Skype when I get back, can't we, Mum?" Ruth nods numbly, takes a breath, and submits, though not without an uncharacteristic touch of sarcasm.

"All right. So . . . while I've got your attention, Merran, this is what's been happening. I didn't tell you before now, because the changes to my health seem so subtle and random. I can't tell if they're related or not." She hesitates and looks down. "You might think I'm a hypochondriac. Each symptom is not too serious by itself, but I can't help thinking there's something going on that I don't understand. Maybe they *are* connected."

"So, what's been going on?" Merran pushes her plate away and takes out a small notepad and a pen from her bag.

147

Ruth speaks slowly, gazing out the window. "I didn't tell you about this, because I didn't want to worry you, but I've had several falls in the past year. In fact, if I remember correctly, I had the first one soon after you left last January. Nothing broken, thank goodness, but it frightens me because I'm alone in the house now."

"Well, I think we can rearrange furniture, so you won't run into things, Mum." She's deteriorating very quickly, Merran thinks. How old is she—nearly eighty? Now that Dad's gone, her body might be packing up. She wonders where Ruth is in the grief process—anger, bargaining, acceptance, or one of the others she can't remember. It might be best to get her some special phone linked to a nursing agency. Wonder if they have something like that in Rylands? But there won't be enough time to set that up before she leaves.

She's starting to panic in light of all the demands on her time. What about the Japanese boy? What about her research in Melbourne? What about the letters from World War II? Coming to see Mum was not such a good idea after all. Ruth raises her voice.

"You're jumping to conclusions. Just pay attention, Merran. It's not as simple as tripping over furniture. My legs just seem to seize up, and I lurch forward almost head over heels, even when there's no furniture in sight."

"I'm listening, I was just strategizing," Merran says.

"Stop doing that, and just hear me out, please."

Merran feels chastened. She sits back in her chair. "Sorry, Mum."

"And when I go for my daily walk, I've noticed recently that if I don't pay attention, I'm weaving back and forth across the footpath, almost as if I were drunk. My reputation might be shot if this goes on for much longer."

"Wow, how much *do* you drink, Mum? That's not like you."

Ruth bursts out angrily, "I've been a teetotaller my whole life, and you know it, Merran. I left the drinking to Dad, and after he died I got rid of all of it from the house. What do you take me for?"

"Sorry, yes, I do remember. I just wondered if you'd changed your mind about drinking, that's all. Go on."

"Then there's sleeping," Ruth says. "I take hours to go to sleep. At first, I put it down to missing your dad next to me, but now there's pain in my legs, and I can't keep them still."

"Restless legs, I've had that too, Mum. Sometimes I just want to chop my legs off."

Ruth gives her a hard look.

"But the worst symptom of all lately is the tremor I have in my right arm. I can be sitting with a friend drinking a cup of tea, and my arm shakes so much that sometimes I've spilt tea onto the carpet. It's so embarrassing. It's such an odd collection of symptoms, but it was the tremor made me think I need help."

Merran hasn't noticed the tremor. That should be investigated.

"It is an odd collection, Mum. You should see a specialist. I would suggest a neurologist. But you'll have to start with your local GP, whoever that is, to get the referral."

She promises Ruth she'll check in with her regularly. At least, that's her intention. They set off for bed. For once, Ruth falls asleep quickly, but Merran lies awake for a long time. There is something lurking on the edge of her mind: a possible diagnosis. But she can't wrap her head around it. Nor can she settle into sleep when she realizes—too late –how brusque she was with Ruth. She'd made it all about efficiency rather than inquiring how her mother feels about all of her strange symptoms. She didn't ask how Mum is coping alone, whether or not she's lonely, whether or not she has friends she can confide in. She didn't even hold her hand. If wise Catherine were a fly on the wall, what would she say about this behaviour? Dang, she's been thinking she's ready to quit therapy. Now she can imagine Catherine's gentle smile and her words, "Not yet." The mother piece of therapy still has to be addressed.

Chapter 32

TEENS

By the time Merran reaches Wirrim the following morning, there's a crowd of chatty onlookers at the school fence. When she lived here as a child, bad things rarely happened in this little town, except the occasional graffiti or a rare break-in, and those were almost always by out-of-towners. In fact, back then few people locked their doors. Now there's an air of respectful excitement at something new.

As she turns after locking her car (just in case), she spots Tom and Vera in the schoolyard talking to a group of students, a few Japanese among them. Several of the students are crying; others look away stoically. It's obvious that the boy is still missing. Several police cars are lined up on the curb.

At the reunion dinner the previous year, she was stunned by the transformation of Tom from the overweight, pimply, myopic teenager she remembered from school, to a slim, attractive, well-informed speaker of Japanese. She remembers that Vera, a relative newcomer to the town (that is, she'd married into it around twenty years before), looked

151

showy in her sequined top of midnight blue, her earrings sparkling. Merran's assessment then was that Vera was merely window dressing. Now, as she hears her talking to the students, she realizes with some guilt that Vera speaks Japanese even better than Tom does. When there's a break in the conversation, Merran beckons to the couple. They looked worried and exhausted before; now they exchange a glance and give her only a brief three-way cursory hug. They probably think she's still the obnoxious academic climber she was last year. She decides to ignore the obvious and asks them about the missing boy.

Tom catches Vera's eye with a questioning look; she nods and says,

"We need to bring you up to speed, Merran, but we don't know much. His name is Hiroshi Nakamura. We really haven't got to know him. He's a quiet fellow, even withdrawn. No trouble, at least until now. The students have been here for less than a week, but Tom and I have noticed some odd dynamics in the group. Haven't we Tom?" Tom nods and continues,

"I couldn't understand everything they were saying to each other, because they were so surreptitious, and I'll admit that I'm getting a bit hard of hearing, but it seemed to me that Hiroshi was the butt of a lot of jokes, teasing, that sort of thing. I spoke to a few of them about this, and it stopped for a day or two, then started again. I must say it bothered me, because he would look so miserable. The boys only told me yesterday that he'd taken off for an hour or so couple of times already, then came back for meals. He was supposed to be in class, but he's the kind of kid who can stay invisible, you know what I mean? Perhaps each teacher thought he was in the other class. So he wasn't missed." He stops, his face reddening.

That sounds a bit far-fetched, Merran thinks. There are so few kids here. Then again, she's never been a teacher of school kids; they can be pretty sneaky. It's the last she'd ever want. By this time Tom is close to tears and reddens with embarrassment. Vera throws him a worried look; he takes a deep breath and continues.

"We've already spent hours on the road, during the night and early this morning, looking for him, and so has Brendan. The Bendigo Police will be here soon. They already sent helicopters which have been out too, but there's no trace of Hiroshi anywhere. We've also tried talking to the students. It hasn't been easy; I don't think most of them realize how serious the situation is." He looks away.

Vera breaks in. "It's not only alarming; it's unbelievable. Nothing like this has happened before. When we take our students to Japan, there's a lot of fooling around as you would expect from Australians, but from the Japanese we've had only good behaviour. Of course, that's a stereotype, but true nevertheless." Tom looks at Merran and says quietly, "I'm glad you're here. At least you speak Japanese." It's faint praise, but she'll go with it. Tom adds, "We three might be of some use to the police, when they get back from the latest foray."

"Well, I'll help in any way I can," Merran says. And like you, I've had some exposure to teen talk in Japan. I've stayed many times in Hiroshima with friends who have a boy and a girl I've known all their lives, and now they are teenagers. I practice talking with them just for the hell of it. You do have to listen hard, so I can understand that your hearing loss might shut you out a bit, Tom. A lot of it is slang. It's the equivalent of 'omigod,' and 'I'm all, like, get over it.'" Tom looks up at Vera with a faint smile. Merran's relieved. Good, she's won them over. Catherine will be proud of her. Then it comes to her that she seems to be competing with her old self for a pat on the back from her therapist. A year ago she would have been horrified at the thought.

The wait for the police seems interminable. Brendan comes back briefly but has little information. Merran wonders if she will be a puddle on the ground soon, as it's so hot. After a half-hour, Vera beckons Brendan and says,

"I don't see any harm in questioning the Japanese kids while we're waiting. Do you, Brendan?"

"Not at all. I've been wondering why you haven't done it by now. Go for it."

The Japanese students are clustered in the shade near the side fence, eating sandwiches one of the teachers has brought from the café. Tom and Merran watch as Vera goes over and talks to them. Soon she returns with two students, a boy and a girl. Merran takes the girl into an available classroom for questioning.

Her name, she says, is Sachiko. She examines the floor, as Merran expects, and looks nervous. No doubt she anticipates that Merran's questions will be in English. Her head comes up, her expression surprised, however, when Merran addresses her in Japanese.

"How old are you, Sachiko?"

"Fifteen."

Merran can't help thinking that she seems older than her friends' daughter looked at the same age but, dressed in a Wirrim t-shirt and jeans, she would appear older. Back in Japan she would wear the common Japanese royal blue uniform of pleated skirt and jacket, white blouse, and backpack that often advertises Hello Kitty, or something of the kind.

"Do you know Hiroshi well?"

Sachiko says, "No, he goes to a different school. I only met him when I came here."

"You've all been here for a few days now. Is there anything you can think of that would cause Hiroshi to walk away?" She doesn't say "run away," because Sachiko might become alarmed.

The girl hesitates; Merran takes this for a yes and pursues it.

"What have you noticed?"

"Well," she replies, twirling her hair, "some of the boys don't treat him very well."

"Tell me more," Merran says.

Sachiko hesitates again, then appears to come to a decision. Her words quicken.

"They tease him a lot. At least … it's just them, not any of us girls, and it's not all the boys either. Just a few, I think they're from his school."

"What do they tease him about?"

"I haven't heard any of it." She looks nervous. "But some of my friends have. Hiroshi is a little guy, and his voice hasn't broken yet. And his Japanese is not very good either. So they pick on him."

"So bullies are making his life miserable, is that it?" Sachiko nods. Merran's surprised to hear that

155

Hiroshi's Japanese is not good. She'll have to find out why. The scenario is all too familiar. Her mind flashes back to the times she was cornered in the locker room by bitchy girls, called a rabbit because of her protruding teeth (fixed after she moved to the U.S.); laughed at due to her bowl-shaped haircut (thanks to Mum). Her social awkwardness and competitiveness were well known. Unlike Hiroshi, however, she'd fought back by the only means available: both ignoring it and excelling at school. There was no other option, no other school available. Hiroshi, apparently, has not yet found a way to protect himself. Merran wonders why his parents haven't transferred him to a different school. It sounds like they certainly have the means. On the other hand, it's possible that he hasn't told them about the teasing at all.

Sachiko looks relieved to be finished with questions, and glances towards the door. "Yes, I guess all that would make him unhappy," she volunteers. "But I don't know any more than that."

She fiddles with her hair, which is streaked with red highlights. There's a charming innocence about her and other teens that Merran has noticed in her frequent visits to Japan. It stands in strong contrast to the sophistication of teens in the U.S., and it's probably going in that direction in Australia too. Despite the "omigod" equivalents, Japanese teens retain the freshness of youth. She thinks, she's exaggerating out of admiration for a culture which is, even nowadays, still an appealing meld of tradition and modernity. Racial homogeneity has gone far towards enabling that, of course. But she's also aware that it isn't a completely rosy picture. One of the downsides of Japanese education is the unyielding and constant academic pressure put on children from their earliest years.

Sachiko is looking at her expectantly.

"Are you sure there's nothing else you can tell me?" Sachiko shakes her head. Merran has no alternative but to let her go.

As the girl leaves the room, she is surrounded by excited friends, who spirit her off towards the fence, no doubt wanting a blow-by-blow report on Merran's questions. The Wirrim students look puzzled, their Japanese obviously not adequate for this kind of situation. Teachers stand in a group, looking helpless. Merran tries to get other students to talk to her, but there is so much resistance that she gives up. So much for practising her Japanese.

Chapter 33

Professionals

Three cars roll up at the same time. One of them disgorges three uniformed policemen from Bendigo, the big guns of the force. In another is James Pollock, the principal, who's been in Melbourne for a conference and heard the news from Tom on his way back. He looks relieved that the police have arrived. The third contains Helen and Owen, unable to stay away from the action. Merran thinks it amusing that they drove such a short distance. Owen must be in love not only with Helen, but with the Prius as well.

Brendan and James talk briefly to the policemen, then James orders the teachers and students back to their classrooms. The rest, including Brendan, make their way to James' office. Owen and Helen make coffee and pass it around.

After Sergeant Ted Richmond has introduced his companions, Senior Constables Melton and Azawa he immediately gets down to business.

"Of course, you've notified the parents?"

Brendan says, "not yet. We wanted to talk to you first. What do you think?"

Richmond fiddles with his coffee cup.

"Now that he's been gone overnight, I'd say we have to. One night in the bush alone is too much for a city boy like him." He looks around. "Who's in charge of the visit?"

Tom and Vera both speak at once. "We are."

"What can you tell us about him?"

Vera nods to Tom, who says,

"He's from Tokyo, like all the others on the exchange. There are several schools represented. Hiroshi's father is in the National Diet, or government, so he's a bigwig. The boy's mother's address is in Toulouse, France. She's an artist. That's all we have. They could be divorced. It's likely they are."

Tom's face is strained with worry. He continues, "We don't expect he's gone far, but even so we've turned up nothing. One of our fears—not to sound callous—is that if the parents think we've been neglectful, they might make us shut down the programme." He adds a little to describe the nature of the student exchange.

Richmond nods. "I hate to be hard on you, but the parents have the right to complain. Now that you mention that the father is in the Diet, it raises a big red flag for me. We have to err on the side of full disclosure, if you can call it that. Brendan, can I leave it to you to notify both parents as soon as we finish this meeting? You can tell them that we are just beginning the investigation, and that they don't need to come right away. We'll keep them informed, OK?" Brendan nods, none too happily.

There is a wild whistling sound outside. James gets up to shut the window against a willy-willy, a hot wind that's whipping up the dust outside into a miniature cyclone.

"Did he have water with him?" Richmond asks.

Tom says, "I hope so. We've already impressed on all of the students that they need to carry water at all times. I hope he took our advice."

James's white shirt is rapidly becoming damp. He puts his head in his hands. Merran imagines that he's now reflecting on the impact of this event on his own reputation. Perhaps, just like her at Clare College in San Francisco a year ago, he's up for a promotion. In his case, it's the Victorian State education system that will make the evaluation. Could he have been in Melbourne not only for a conference, but to look for a job in the suburbs? According to Helen, it's well known that James hates being stuck in Wirrim, which he calls Woop Woop, or Back of Beyond. His five daughters in Melbourne are giving birth at such a rapid rate—twins run in the family—that he often jokes there will soon be family netball and football teams. He and his wife naturally want to be near all of that action.

Richmond is scribbling notes. Nobody moves, until James lifts his head from his hands and sits up wearily.

"What now?" he says.

"I know you've been driving around extensively, and the helicopter has been doing surveillance." He looks at Brendan. "Have you talked to the local farmers?"

"Yes, we have. Because we had such a large number of police here, we were able to cover all of the farms within a fifteen-k radius. But nobody saw anything."

"Now it looks as though he might have hitched a ride, or been picked up by somebody," Richmond says.

"It's unlikely he'd have hitched," Vera says. "He's

shy and his English isn't good. So that leaves us with a pick-up. Very scary."

"I'm ordering the Search and Rescue squad from Melbourne," Richmond says slowly. "And we need to put out an alert in the media." He stands and heads towards the door, but Vera stops him.

"We forgot to tell you that some of the boys from his school are here, and there's a history of his being teased, back in Japan and also here."

Brendan says, "Rhonda, Hiroshi's host mother, tells us that he's on medication for depression and anxiety."

"How does she know he's on medication?" Tom asks. "We didn't even know that."

"She checked in his bag to see if he had any washing, and saw the container," Brendan says. "It's an antidepressant. Obviously, he doesn't have it with him, so he may suffer a bit."

"Too bad we haven't felt the need to ask about mental illness on our application. It's never crossed our minds, has it, Vera?"

"Even if we did," she says, "no one would let us know. Mental illness still has a very high stigma in Japan. He probably gets his medication from France. Family pride is at stake."

Richmond calls to activate the Search and Rescue team and sends everyone off.

"You're off the hook, folks. Thanks for getting started. It's been a big help, but now you can leave it to the professionals."

Tom and Vera go home for a rest; Owen and Helen walk to the café for lunch; Merran looks at her watch and realizes that she needs to hotfoot it back to Rylands.

Chapter 34
A Diversion

Having extracted a promise from Richmond that he'll keep her up to date on any developments, Merran leaves for the bakery to pick up a couple of their famous vanilla slices—layers of puff pastry, thick custard, and vanilla icing, to share with her mother. The slices are disappearing fast; according to Helen, they're always sold out by lunchtime.

She needs to leave town but can't bring herself to do so quite yet, with Hiroshi still out there somewhere. Perhaps he'll pop out from an alley. She strolls along the main street where she'd met Dorrie Richardson the previous year. As if waiting for her, Dorrie is seated on the same bench. Merran steps over to greet her.

"Let me guess, Dorrie. The grapevine beat me to it. Am I right?"

Dorrie grins."Yes, Alene Bennett was up at the school and told me you'd arrived. I got your email saying you were coming but wasn't sure when it would be. Do you have enough time to look at the letters? After all, I've stayed alive a whole year for you."

Merran is caught. Once again, life has intervened.

"You know I'm involved with the missing Japanese boy?" It's not completely true, but then again, she does have to start reading in the State Library soon.

"But isn't the Search and Rescue team from Melbourne taking over? I heard you others are off the hook."

News travels fast. She misses nothing.

"That's true. We're all extremely worried about Hiroshi, but we're no longer needed. It's a shame, as it gave us something to do. But we haven't been exactly told to stay out of it either." Dorrie's face is expectant. How can she disappoint her now?

"OK, Merran says. I'll try to look at the letters. Can we set a time now? I'm visiting my mother in Rylands for dinner and will stay the night. How does tomorrow suit you?"

"What about three o'clock? Come for afternoon tea, and we can get started. I'm at 56 Sherbrook Avenue. Right over there." She points. "My flat is the one nearest the street."

Chapter 35

STALLED

On her way to her mother's house in the afternoon, Merran decides to concentrate on Ruth's needs rather than be distracted by Hiroshi's disappearance. They Google Ruth's symptoms. They look up clinics, the hospital, find the names of neurologists, call a few of Ruth's friends for recommendations. She teaches Ruth the deep breathing exercises and the tapping that she used herself, which does help curb her mother's anxiety a bit. Ruth seems happy with the short visit and doesn't press Merran to stay longer than one more night.

With time to spare before dinner, they decide to call in on Father Boyle, who officiated at Johnny's funeral the previous year. Merran has a soft spot for him. She knows that he could have refused to conduct her father's service the previous year, but Father hadn't hesitated.

His housekeeper answers the door with a frown.

"No, you can't see him. He's writing in his study and asks not to be disturbed." She moves to close the door in their faces, when Father's voice booms down the passage way.

"I recognize you two; saw you out the window. Ruth Provenzano and Merran Scofield, am I right?" The two women look at each other in astonishment. He walks slowly towards them, limping on one leg, then stretches out his hand. "As a spiritual exercise, I pray daily for the families of those whose loved ones have had funerals in my church."

The word spiritual, when used by those in San Francisco who live on the touchy–feely fringe, usually repels Merran, but hearing it from Father gives it an entirely different complexion. It's practical, it's active. Something like what her Jewish friend Rachel at Clare College calls a mitzvah. She makes a mental note to explore her spiritual side—if the has one—very soon, with Catherine.

Father Boyle notices his housekeeper standing back, looking annoyed at being countermanded by the man himself. In what Merran sees as an act of kindness, he smiles ruefully at Ruth and Merran, and gestures towards the woman. "Mary, you are right. I am trying to write my sermon, and it's getting harder all the time. Sometimes I just need to just sit and wait for inspiration. So, sorry ladies, I'd better get back to it. Thank you for coming and thank you Mary for trying to protect my time."

There's still a half hour before Ruth's roast lamb dinner will be ready. She tells Merran that Helen's son Danny's sheltered workshop is a short walk from the church. From a hundred metres away, they hear loud, excited conversations; as they enter, they see that eight young men are working with wood. Danny isn't hard to spot, having grown even taller over the past year. Merran's surprised and a little

165

touched when Danny bounds over to her, his arms outstretched. This time she returns his hug, almost not believing she feels ok with touch. She and Ruth follow him around the workshop. This day the little group is assembling ornamental bird boxes for an upcoming craft sale. Merran doubts that any self-respecting Australian bird would nest in one of these but notices her mother's eyes light up. A bird box would fit well into Ruth's English garden scheme.

Danny looks proud as he shows them the high-quality workmanship that has gone into the boxes. "Jean says we can use the tools safely now." An attractive young woman, undoubtedly Jean, is sitting at a small desk in one corner. She smiles and waves, leaving the talking to Danny, who is now walking towards a large electric saw. "We don't use this one," he says laughing, as Merran sidles away from the machine's sharp teeth. "Jean does." He looks over at Jean, who is laughing along with him. "We finish off with the small tools over there." Merran can tell that the responsibility has given Danny a huge emotional lift, and no doubt Helen as well.

In the evening, mother and daughter have just finished eating their delicious roast lamb dinner, with chocolate-sprinkled pavlova for dessert, when Merran's phone rings. She signals to her mother that she needs to take the call and goes out to the verandah. It's Helen, sounding gloomy.

"What's up?"

"Hiroshi is still missing. This is the second night, and we're all feeling desperate. You don't need to do anything. I just wanted to vent. Search and Rescue are here, and the helicopter goes out and back every hour or so. They've even got a couple of small planes in the search. It's quite a sight. Everyone is out of their homes talking about it. Some have gone out to check on the smaller roads, but it's just repeating what's been done before." Her voice cracks. "I don't hold out much hope that they'll find him now." Merran hears Owen's voice in the background.

"He's telling me to get off the phone and relax for a bit before bed."

"I'll come and keep you company tomorrow if you like. I've finished what I need to do to help Mum. And at three o'clock I'm meeting Dorrie Richardson to look at some letters."

She's sure Ruth will have been watching television, but when she goes back into the house she notices hurt and sadness on her mother's face. They watch a comedy show on television, but neither of them cracks a smile. By nine-thirty there seems to be nothing to do but hug each other awkwardly and say good night.

Chapter 36
THE MAN AT COOPERS LAKE

When Merran arrives at Helen's home the following morning, James, Tom, and Vera have already joined Owen and Helen at the kitchen table. Each looks sleep-deprived. So this is now a support group, she thinks. Scrambled eggs sit drying, bacon swims in congealing fat, and the toast is cold. Merran pours herself a cup of lukewarm coffee and takes a seat. "Any news?" They look at each other.

Finally, James begins. "I came across Brendan this morning, and here's what he told me. It's true that Hiroshi's parents are divorced. His mother, Mayumi Watanabe, lives in Toulouse, as we already knew; she's some sort of artist, born and raised in Japan. Hiroshi spent seven years with her and attended a French-speaking school until he came back to Japan quite recently. That would explain his rusty Japanese.

"Now he's living with his father, Daichi, who's on a trip with his current girlfriend to the Arctic to see polar bears. No, that can't be right, it's their winter." He consults his notes. "It's the northern lights they're going to see, so it will be another day at the earliest until Daichi arrives. The police haven't heard yet whether or not Mayumi can come. You remember that terrorist attack in the south of France recently? Turns out she was injured by flying glass and has been recuperating. Her best friend was killed. Apparently, the parents can't stand being in a room together, but I'm guessing that she would want to be here if she could. That's all we have at the moment. Not much that's new." James sounds relieved that there will be some delay meeting Daichi, who sounds like a powerful figure and will be understandably angry. James, Tom and Vera will be reamed out, for sure.

Each returns to reverie, then Merran pipes up.

"While I was lying awake last night, I thought of something that might be useful." She looks at Vera and Tom.

"You took the students out to Coopers Lake, didn't you? I wonder if anyone has talked to the students about it. I certainly didn't when I interviewed Sachiko. Now I wonder if we need to check if anything happened out there that might be a clue. The police have searched the area, but nobody else knows Japanese apart from us."

Vera says, "We went there first, to give the Japanese kids time to relax and adjust to the time difference, which isn't much—two hours at this time of year— but we thought that a swim might also be a bit of a break from the heat, and an ice-breaker for all of the students as well."

Tom sits up straight. "I've just remembered something," "I can't believe it didn't occur to me earlier. I suppose Vera and I were numb and couldn't think clearly. Vera, do you remember that he was the only one who didn't go swimming, and spent his time wandering around the campsite? I was busy being lifeguard. Did you notice anything that might be important?"

"No, but we could ask the students. It might be useful." A look of hope comes over James's face. They all walk quickly to the school, where recess is about to end. James has again ordered classes to meet, just to keep their minds occupied. The bell rings, but now the students have spotted James and the other adults, and they rush to the gate, full of questions about Hiroshi. It's plain, though, from the adults' uniformly blank faces, that Hiroshi is still missing. Merran notices that a few of the boys look close to tears, and wonders if they are the worst offenders. Have they already been questioned by the police? She has a quick word with James, who then announces loudly, "We'd like to ask you about the trip to Coopers Lake a few days ago. We know that Hiroshi didn't swim. But does anyone remember what he did to fill in the time? Did he talk to anyone? Were there any strangers around? If any of you has any information at all, please stay. The rest of you go inside." After Tom translates this into Japanese, four boys stay back, looking uncomfortably at their shoes. Tom addresses them tersely and gets nothing in return. Vera takes over, letting them know that any information they can give might be crucial. Whether it's her gentle manner, her gender, or her assurance that they will not get into trouble, one of them begins talking, and the rest follow, until they are all talking at once.

Vera translates. "The boys say that Hiroshi didn't go swimming because they told him they would dunk him in the lake and hold him down. They already knew that he was afraid of water and a poor swimmer. They threatened dire consequences if he told the teachers.

Owen asks, "Why did they want to stop him from swimming, or at least paddling on the edge?"

"No other reason except to spoil his day, it seems to me."

Merran and Tom, who have been following the conversation in Japanese, and becoming more and more angry, look askance at Vera, who signals them to hold their peace. The boys search her face defiantly, but Vera remains outwardly calm. However, Merran notices some clenching and unclenching of Vera's fingers, as though she's itching for a punch or even strangulation.

The boys keep talking. At Coopers Lake, once they were sure that Hiroshi wouldn't be going into the water, they'd gone off to swim and splash. But a few minutes later, when they paddled back to check on him they noticed him talking to a man near the dressing rooms. They describe him as clean-shaven, and wearing red shorts, a navy blue T-shirt, and sandals. One of the boys argues that the shorts were dark green. The other three laugh and tell Vera that Katsuro is colour-blind. The man was carrying a small bag and seemed to be on his way somewhere. He looked old to them. Tom and Merran look at each other, and Merran says,

"He was probably over thirty." Tom gives her a faint smile.

At last the boys have nothing left to say, and leave, their ring leader Akihiro whistling under his breath.

After Vera has translated the whole conversation for James, Helen, and Owen, Helen says, "I wonder if the local students saw the man and knew who he was." Vera makes a quick visit to each of the classrooms, but the effort yields nothing. The few who'd noticed him had never seen him before, which meant that he most certainly was not from Wirrim.

They've no sooner retreated to James' office for some ice water and air conditioning, than Brendan O'Neill arrives to give them an update. As he sits by Merran, she smells after-shave and clean clothes, not the earthy, sweaty body she might have expected from someone so tantalizingly male. She surprises herself by feeling cautious, even mistrustful, rather than head-over-heels excited. Why on earth should she feel this way? He's everything a woman would want. Perhaps he represents a so-called trigger, reminding her of someone from her past. But who? Sometimes she grows weary of her psychological analyses and wishes she could stop trying so hard and just go with her gut, but she already tried that method with her father the previous year. How thoroughly she'd misjudged him. What a waste of a relationship.

Brendan sits down, his expression subdued. He looks around the table at each of them, and says,

"There's no trace of the boy, despite all our efforts. We're putting out an Australia-wide alert."

He stands to leave, but Vera stops him.

"We heard from some of the boys that there was a man at Coopers Lake, and that Hiroshi had a conversation with him. None of the local students recognized him."

Stranger danger, Merran thinks. Here it is, a fear at the back of every parent's mind.

"That's great information. We didn't get that from the kids when we questioned them, though we could only ask the local ones, as none of us speaks fluent Japanese." Merran says nothing, but she's furious. She notices Vera and Tom's look of surprise as well. They could have been called. Brendan glances at her sharply, then changes tack. "Sorry, Merran, but you weren't here, and we called you, Vera and Tom, but there was no answer. Senior Constable Azawa knows a bit, but he's rusty—his parents dropped the ball when they immigrated. Thanks. We appreciate any help you can give us. Keep at it, folks." As he turns to leave, he flashes a smile and winks at Merran. Where did *that* come from? Her legs are turning to jelly. Time to get to know this guy.

Chapter 37

BLAKE

Worries about Hiroshi have made Merran hungry. As she searches along the main street for somewhere to eat, she tells herself that a few more calories won't hurt. The adrenalin will help get rid of them. Hmmm—how scientific is that? Her mind flashes to her new love interest, Blake Bergstrom. Funny, she hasn't thought of him since her conversation with Owen and Helen. Love interest, or something else? They met at a conference last February. Blake is a historian too, tenured at UC Berkeley. He's a fitness junkie, a hiker with a hard body, not an ounce of fat anywhere.

She's wondered why he was drawn to her at the panel on Chairman Mao. Was it her intelligence? Probably: she had been very well informed. It certainly couldn't have been her appearance. It was bad enough that she was a decade older than he was, and she looked it. She thought at first, he'd taken her on as a project. In the months since they met, he'd encouraged her to "tighten up that body of yours." She assumed, therefore, that the condition of her body was as important to him as her mind. At first, she resisted going to the gym, but as the pounds rolled off and her muscles hardened she actually felt better, had more energy, and even slept better—that is, when they weren't making love, which she discovered was as important to her as it was to him.

Poor Richard had tried to spark her interest in sex, to no avail. Her mother's admonition against premarital sex, "The man needs to keep one foot on the floor at all times," rang in her ears every time Richard tried to make a move. Even after marriage, she'd felt repelled by the act itself and, though she'd warmed up a bit over the years, it wasn't by much. And she'd downright refused to have children, arguing that her career would suffer, even when Richard made it clear that he wanted to be a dad.

Richard would be astonished now if he knew that Merran is a student of the *Kama Sutra*, which Blake introduced to her early on. For the first time in her life she's able to achieve orgasm easily. This has translated to her behaviour with others: more receptive, rather than closed-off and suspicious. More relaxed as well. Along with that has come, surprisingly, less need to boast or put others down. People have noticed and commented on the changes, though no one knows how they've been achieved. Catherine the therapist, and Blake the sex tutor: an unlikely but effective team.

With significant force of will, Merran bypasses the bakery this time and keeps walking but, as if to test her resolve, a young man emerges from the only café with a small paper bundle. He sits on the bench outside the shop and eagerly unwraps the contents, releasing fish and chips for himself and a flood of memories for Merran. Since childhood, when she spent her bottle-deposit money on packets of fish and chips wrapped in newspaper, it has been her favourite meal. She visualizes Blake's grey eyes focused on her, feels the sensation of his hands roaming her body, and the pressure of his arm as he lowers her onto the bed. The old Merran would have scoffed at the weakness she now feels in her knees, but now it is real, and she has to sit down to recover. Damn, she can't even eat fish and chips anymore. The young man notices her staring at him and leaves, still pulling chips out of the bundle. Merran takes his place on the bench and waits for the sensation to go away. It's time to visit Dorrie Richardson.

Chapter 38
DORRIE (2)

"At last, Merran," Dorrie exclaims as she opens her front door wide. "Here, come and sit. I've been waiting for you so long."

It's clear that this is, for Dorrie, a special occasion. Every wooden surface is shining in the afternoon light, and a small table is set with dainty flowered cups, saucers, and plates from the days when such items were common gifts from woman to woman on special occasions.

Merran sits in a comfortable chair and looks around the room while Dorrie fetches the tea and cakes. She hopes she can live like this when she's in her nineties, with a picture window overlooking a pretty garden, floor-to-ceiling bookshelves, and within walking distance of everything necessary for life. Does Dorrie maintain all this herself? Surely not, at her age. But whether she does or she doesn't is not important. It's the good taste that counts.

Dorrie pours a little milk into each cup, then pours steaming tea from a gold-rimmed flowered teapot.

"My mother has one very much like it," Merran comments, pointing to the teapot. "She brought it from England. Where did you get yours, Dorrie?" She gulps the tea. These cups don't hold much, she thinks.

"It's very old. I inherited it from my mother, via her mother, who emigrated from Scotland around the 1870s or 80s. It's one of my treasures."

"Then I'm honoured," Merran says. "And I'd definitely like some more of that delicious tea. I guess it's loose-leaf. My family always drank that kind. No teabags!"

Dorrie grins. "I'm old-fashioned that way too. This is a loose-leaf brand from India, but I can't read the name." She hobbles to the kitchen and returns with a box printed in what looks to Merran like Hindi. "I have a neighbour who travels a lot and she brings me some occasionally. I save it for special occasions."

Merran helps herself to a slice of orange cake. Calories again. But afternoon tea is a ceremony. Sampling the food is part of the ritual.

"It's delicious, Dorrie."

"Sorry, it's a bought one. I don't bake anymore, but this brand isn't too bad. Now, Merran, I'd like to hear about your career as a historian. What's your special interest? What are you working on at the moment?"

"Oh, after I left Australia, I took up Asian history, in particular the diplomatic relations between Japan and China, and have taught a range of classes for over thirty years at a small liberal arts college in San Francisco. I've recently finished a book on Chairman Mao." She smiles. "One of dozens on him, of course." Now that isn't skiting, is it, she asks herself. She's toned down the bragging since last year. But Dorrie looks confused.

"Then why are you interested in letters written by an Australian?"

Sharp, thinks Merran.

"I've been asked—at very late notice—by my chairman to teach the Australian history class this coming semester, while the usual instructor takes family leave. The class begins in less than two weeks, as a matter of fact. That's why I'm in a hurry to get to the State Library in Melbourne, to read as much as I can."

Dorrie nods. "Then we'd better make a start."

Chapter 39

LETTERS

Dorrie reaches towards a large plastic storage bin with a blue lid, stowed beside her chair, and drags it between them. Merran is confused for a moment when she sees that it holds a pile of freezer bags. More food? Surely not. But then Dorrie reaches in and draws out one of the bags, opening it to reveal a small pile of letters.

"That's quite a stash. How many are there?" asks Merran, leaning forward in her chair, her heart beating faster. Only a historian would find old letters exciting, she thinks with amusement. Dorrie notices, and her face lights up.

"So, Merran, these are the letters I told you about. I haven't counted them lately, and my memory can sometimes trip me up, but I seem to remember that there are well over a hundred of them." She passes one to Merran.

"See here, these brown envelopes have the official stamp and the initials of the censor on them." Dorrie then shuffles through the bags and brings out one of the longer letters near the bottom of the bin, written on the flimsiest of white airmail paper. Each of its four pages is filled with tiny handwriting, down the page, along the sides, on the back, taking up as much of the space as possible.

"I've sorted them into approximate time periods, because he couldn't date many of them for security reasons." She puts the long letter aside and returns to the top bag.

"There are about a dozen here, which he wrote to me before he left for the Middle East at the end of 1940."

"What was his name?"

"George. George Albert Richardson. He was the youngest of Bessie and Henry's three boys. George never knew whether or not his parents ever married, but they were together for twenty years. Bessie had immigrated from London, and Henry came independently from Newcastle-upon-Tyne." She grins. "No, neither of them had any convict ancestry. Wouldn't that have been intriguing? They were just hard-working settlers who saw an opportunity to better themselves over here."

She sinks into her chair comfortably, and asks, "Would you like to have some background on George's life before we tackle the letters?"

"Oh, yes, please! Biographies and memoirs are my great love."

"It's only what he told me over the years we were together. I wrote as much as I could remember, in the mid-1990s, soon after I moved to Wirrim. It was a few decades after he died, and I may have got some of the details wrong. Still, it's a fair account of the things he'd been through before he met me."

She stands with difficulty, using her walking stick, disappears into the bedroom and returns with a thick file containing handwritten pages. "This is what I wrote. If you have time, it'd be great if we can read it aloud. Me, then you, and so on."

Merran, alarmed, looks at her watch. "I have the afternoon free, and perhaps a little time tomorrow morning, but that's it, I'm afraid. Could we look at the letters first to see how far we get?"

Dorrie's face drops, but Merran holds her ground. It's vital that last year's fiasco with the class at Clare College not be repeated. But she needs to soften the blow.

"I'm sorry, because I'm sure that George's story is amazing."

She's relieved when Dorrie's expression changes at the compliment.

"I've also written about my life and would love you to see both stories," she says. "I could copy them for you and mail them." She gets up to pour more tea, then smiles. "You're right. I did ask you to look at the letters, didn't I?"

Merran hopes her relief doesn't show on her face. That was a delicate negotiation.

"That's generous of you. Now, I'm anxious to see what's in that big bin of yours."

Dorrie draws out the first batch of letters. "In my opinion, George was an ordinary man who lived a remarkable life. I hope you'll think so too. I've already picked some letters out, the ones that have the most information or personal thoughts. There are too many to read today."

"Would you mind photocopying a bunch more of them, Dorrie, to send with the bios?"

"Yes, of course; it'll be no trouble."

"George began writing to me as early as September 1940, several months before his ship sailed. Though we were able to meet at least weekly, he wrote that even a day without communicating with me was a torture. I have a dozen or so from that short time, written from various huts and hostels provided by the Methodist Church and the Salvation Army. I'll read you some bits."

As she listens, Merran wonders if George wanted to make sure that she would think only of him while he was away.

September: . . . I don't know how I am going to do without you when I have to go away. . . . I would have been in tonight only we were out on a thirty-mile march and have only just arrived. . . . We passed three schools on our way, you should have seen the children, they just went mad. . . . I thought what you would have done if we were passing your school. I think if I had been that close to you I would be A.W.L. tonight. . . . This is a poor love letter, seeing as it is the first one. Your most sincere lover, George.

"He signed all of his letters this way, Merran, right until the letters stopped."

Merran suppresses a sob as she remembers Richard's affectionate nature. Just as surely as she'd repelled her father, she'd done the same with the husband who she thought she loved. Too late, her eyes were opened. Her father died without even a kiss goodbye; Richard left with someone whose eyes sparkled when hers met his.

Dorrie notices, but says only, "Loving and losing, it's hard, isn't it?" She goes on to the next letter.

October: I was called to the orderly room today to be interviewed by the signal officer, also the transport officer. I don't know where I will end up yet.

"As the date of embarkation in December grew closer, George wrote more often."

15 Dec: . . . Things are in a mess here again. The first thing we heard when we arrived was that our departure had been put off again. . . . I tried to get leave but couldn't. . . think if I am here for Xmas I will be asking Mother whether she has any objections to us being married, would you like that Darling?

Dorrie puts the little batch of letters back in their bag. "That's the flavour until he set sail. But his plans were not to be. I'd already left to visit my two sisters and didn't get his letter until I got back. And he was whisked away just before the holiday to sail out of Sydney on December 26, 1940.

"He wrote on the voyage too, to let me know that all he could think about was me: my soft brown eyes, my soft curves, my soft curly brown hair, and my warm smile." Merran perks up.

"That must have been a boost."

"Yes, it was the first time anyone had written such things to me, and I have to admit, it was really nice."

Merran notices a look of sadness flit briefly across Dorrie's face.

"But he was safe, wasn't he?"

"Yes, he was, but if I'd known he wanted to be married before he left, I would have jumped at it. A little too quickly, though. Many girls married in haste and repented at leisure, as the saying goes." She reflects for a moment.

"Neither of us knew what we were getting into, married or not. This isn't news, but it's true that our lives were now controlled by cigar-smoking men poring over maps ten thousand miles from Australia."

"For example Winston Churchill?"

Dorrie nods and makes a sour face. Merran decides not to go there. This isn't the time to debate war strategy. Dorrie searches the bin and brings out another batch.

"Here's one from him soon after his arrival, early in 1941. I'm not sure where it was, exactly, but likely Palestine."

I had a very nice trip and would love you to have been with me to enjoy the pretty scenery. We came to some of the most modern villages you could wish to see . . . the people are Jews. I used to read all about them but could not imagine what they were like, but now I know. I will be able to tell you tales for weeks when I get home . . . while I was away I was invited to some Jews' place for the evening and enjoyed a very nice couple of hours. They played some very nice music, some performed Russian dances. They also sang in many different languages. All the time there was coffee and eatables on the table. It was quite a pleasant change after being cooped up for so long. . . . While I was away I also visited Tel Aviv, that is the latest Jewish city in this country, but was only there for a couple of hours.

February 1941.

I was down to see the cemetery where the soldiers were buried last war. It is kept in very good order. There are a few Australians and New Zealanders, but mostly English. The surroundings are real Australian; gum trees, peppercorn trees, and every kind of flower that grows in Australia. There are quite a few new graves there also. I've had a look around the country for a mile or two since I last wrote. There is really nothing to see, only Arab villages and open country. . . . I have been to a place called Gaza, it is just an Arab village not very interesting.

Dorrie stops and says, "Wouldn't he be surprised by what has happened in Gaza in more recent years?"

She stretches and yawns.

"I think we need another cuppa, or would you like coffee this time?"

Merran says, "Coffee and coffee cake will go down nicely. Wake us up. But let me make the coffee. You're looking tired." Merran is fading too. Who knew that listening to wartime letters could make you so weary? She wonders if these letters are really worth working with. There's not too much drama in them yet.

"Here are a couple more," Dorrie says, turning in her chair so Merran can hear from the kitchen.

Early 1941: You were saying they were calling for girls for transport work. I can tell you, Darling, I am pleased to know my sweetheart is not made of that stern stuff, because as I have said, this country is not fit for men, let alone women. If any woman takes my advice, all the transport driving she will do will be in Australia, that is their place. It is not so bad for a man to leave his country to fight, but no woman other than a nurse should be allowed to leave it. Anywhere in this country is no place for a woman. You pass that on to any of your friends who have a notion of coming. There is not much news I can tell you from here, as there is nothing but sand here, that is all for miles, and anything else I cannot write about. I can say a little more now as the Padre is censoring our mail now. He is a lot more broad-minded than the fool of an officer who used to read our mail. . . . Tell Mum that if I came home now I would only have to shake myself a couple of times and I could concrete all the back paths with the sand in my clothes....

Well, Dear, we are in the Libyan Desert well and truly, and having plenty of excitement. The angry bees were here today again, bombers I mean, but they did no harm. We had our first (word scratched out by censor) *today. On the way up here there were a few raids, but luck struck good. You would be surprised to see the gear belonging to the enemy laying everywhere from one end of the country to the other. Motor trucks in thousands. The country I passed through was beautiful, you know what the coloured pictures are like, well it was like that. . . . Whatever towns I passed through were very pretty although they were few and far between. Do you remember hearing about planes being destroyed by our planes? That is also true, I have seen some of them, as a matter of fact they are laying everywhere. . . . Had a shave and a bit of a clean-up today and feel much better. The fleas are here in thousands. I think they are fifth columnists. . . . Darling, you think I do not put too much love in my letters. But never the less I love you more than I ever have. You do not want to worry if this is not full of silvery speeches, things are too serious for things like that. . . . Well, Darling, I will close now hoping this finds you well and happy. So with my very best love, I Remain, Your most sincere lover, George.*

Not looking at Merran, Dorrie puts the letter back in the bag quickly, and has already taken out a new one when Merran interrupts.

"Why were you complaining about not enough love in his letters? They seem pretty loving to me."

"That letter embarrasses me now. I can only say that I was barely twenty years old, and not happy at work teaching five-year-olds. I relied on his declarations of love to keep me going. I couldn't get enough of it. Now when I read the letters I feel like a petty schoolgirl. You might give me credit, though, for reading a letter which paints me in a rather dim light."

"That's true, and it can't have been easy to be you in that time and place."

"Yes, and understand that we had fallen in love, but didn't know each other well at that time. There were bound to be a few rough patches."

She sits with the next letter, scanning it briefly.

"This one is also from early in 1941."

You mentioned Palestine and the Bible, Dear. They don't seem to be connected when you read one and see the other. I think Old Nick must have come from this place. . . . you cannot imagine so many flies and fleas could get in such a small place and then be able to get in yourself. You were asking about water. Well, I get enough to clean my teeth once a day and drink if I go sparingly. Washing myself is almost out of the question. . . . Well, My Darling, I will have to bring this to a close. I love you Dear and am looking forward to the time when we will not have to say good-bye. Give my love to all and with my very best love, I Remain, Your most sincere lover, George.

Dorrie has warned that George's sentiments are repetitive, and Merran notices it too, but there is something endearing and sincere in his words that captivates her. She mentions it to Dorrie.

"Yes, he was a romantic. As you might have noticed from the letters so far, he and I didn't have a lot in common. I was studious, a reader of Wordsworth, Dickens, and the like. George claimed never to have read a book for fun. I had much more education than he did. On the plus side, we did both enjoy gardening." She looked straight at Merran.

"Still, that wouldn't have been enough without the secret ingredient."

Merran raises her eyebrows.

"What secret ingredient?"

"Plain old physical attraction, my dear." She blushes. So does Merran, thinking of both Blake and Brendan.

"Some people call it pheromones, but whatever it is, it worked for us." She turns to her papers again, but no words come. Suddenly she bursts out laughing, and Merran joins in, spitting out her mouthful of tea and cake.

It's several minutes before Dorrie calms down enough to return to her pages.

"On a more serious subject: "Now he was heading towards Tobruk, Libya, prior to a siege that began on 10 April 1941, though he was not able to write about this in his letter."

Tell Mum we went right through Egypt thank God, this place is anything but a picnic, I'm pleased we did not hang around. I did not see any sights in Egypt while travelling through. I mean the usual ones.

19 April 1941: I am writing a few lines again to show that Fritz has not put the wind up on us, or driven us into the sea, as he was skiting of doing a few nights ago. They say almost all censorship has been lifted, and it's about time,

189

as there is very little we can say he does not know already. I daresay you have heard many rumours, but you must not listen to anything you hear, as we are as safe here as if we were back home. Fritz has had a taste of the Aussie and does not seem to be too anxious to trouble us anymore. We left Palestine on the 26ᵗʰ Feb and travelled up through Libya taking in the captured places, El Bayda, Tobruk, Batta, Derna, and Benghazi, including many little places. Some of the places were very pretty such as Derna. It is a little city huddled up in a corner of the coast all by itself. I think it must have been a holiday resort for the Italians. . . . There is not much variety like you see at home, houses all white everywhere throughout the country. . . . We were about two hundred miles past Benghazi, we held the front lines there for about a fortnight, then we were to return for leave, when Fritz turned up. He will not forget that trip in a hurry. Every time we contacted him he was a few less both in armoured vehicles and men. He thought he had us. We had just got here, that is Tobruk, and in he rushed. I think he was going to wipe us off the map in one sweep. What a shock he had coming to him. We never had a hole dug, only just put our gear down when he sent planes and tanks and men over.

Well, I don't think any of his tanks or men got back and very few of his planes. They are laying everywhere here. About four of our planes went up, and he had about sixteen bombers escorted by eight or ten fighters. We saw two fighters get away, that is from here. I don't think too many got home to tell the tale. We haven't seen too much of them since. Of course that was only a little fun compared with what is coming. Everyone is as keen as if they were going to the races. We heard the other night that Fritz was going to either shoot us down or drown us. He was supposed to have dropped some leaflets telling us to surrender as we were done. You should have heard the lads laugh. . . . When it was all over, and the lads were cleaning up, they captured a prisoner. You could not guess what it was. A little black monkey. He belongs to our crowd now. . . . Jerry Lindberg, he is called.

"So was George a Rat of Tobruk, Dorrie? Sounds like it."

"Yes, so you know about them?"

"Not much, apart from the fame."

"Well, it was a group of soldiers who held the port against Rommel's Afrika Korps for months during 1941. You'll see soon why George wasn't there the whole time, though."

That letter was a burst of energy, Merran thinks. And it wasn't bravado either. It was the most optimistic so far.

Dorrie says, "I think you'll find the next letter interesting. It's about the monkey they had at the camp."

Jerry is a nuisance at times, stealing and hiding our possessions, peeing on our beds when he gets upset, among other things. But he's done much to cheer us up. He's given us the chance to take care of a defenceless animal, and that has been good for me and my mates. We get a laugh at his antics. But there are some who take out their frustrations on him and kick him whenever they feel like it. These are also the ones who talk dirty about women and visit brothels when they get the chance. I'm ashamed to be in their company, they're miserable excuses for human beings. Everyone here has been through the school of hard knocks. Why do some take the high road and others take the low road? I don't know the answer to that, do you?

Merran says, "Me neither, but look at the time. Can you believe we've been here so long? You need a rest, my dear." They part, planning to say goodbye in the morning. Dorrie is yawning as she closes the door carefully, leaning on her stick.

Chapter 40

JELLY LEGS

Merran has plenty to think about as she walks the short distance from Dorrie's little flat to Helen and Owen's house. George's letters from the Front were interesting, especially the romantic parts, though not mind-blowing. But what could you expect when the censors were hard at work?

She regrets not having had enough time to hear Dorrie's biography of George, but it'll be something to look forward to later.

Lost in thought, she reaches the house and is concerned to see Brendan's police car parked outside. She notices him disappearing around the corner of the house towards the back door, which is where most visitors announce themselves in the country. This is possibly dangerous, she thinks. Despite her earlier doubts, she still finds herself inexplicably drawn to him. She needs to put Blake at the front of her mind. And for good reason: as she joins the little group at the kitchen table, she notices Brendan's look of pleasure. She knows she doesn't look her best. She's limping due to a blister from one sandal. She's sure there are bags under her eyes. Her mind has been on the twentieth century, not the twenty-first, for hours. In her present state she doesn't want attention from him. She pulls back as he leans forward to look directly at her. It's so obvious that everyone stops talking. Tom and Vera, who have been sitting disconsolately with their heads in their hands, look up and stare.

"I just came by," Brendan says, "to let you all know that there have been no good leads yet. There are always some calls that yield nothing, and pranksters who waste our time. We did have a possible hot lead in a suburb of Melbourne, where a Japanese boy came out of nowhere and tried to enroll in a language programme. The administrator held onto him until the police arrived. But it was a false alarm, wrong boy. Hiroshi's father is on his way, but there's no ETA as yet. His mother is keeping in touch with us, but it's very unlikely that she'll make it here." He stands up to go, and Helen lets him out. There isn't much to say, but O'Neill's smile and wink to Merran across the room as he leaves speak volumes. Jelly knees, darn it, despite her best efforts not to trust him. Fortunately no one else notices. They look about ready to drop. Merran suggests they turn in for the night. In their present state she wonders if she'll be called upon to undress them, read them a bedtime story, and tuck them in.

O'Neill. Danger or not, Merran would give a small sum to have a conversation with him. Too bad she's not prepared. Her psychological assessment is woefully incomplete.

Twilight will soon give way to darkness. Vera and Tom leave. Owen and Helen clean up the kitchen and take themselves to their bedroom. Merran notices a questioning look from Owen to Helen, and her nod of assent. They can't be *that* tired.

A gentle breeze rises and blows through the open window over the sink. She-oaks sigh and sway, lit up by the full moon. Merran stands and drinks a glass of water, relishing the silvery beauty outside and the welcome coolness inside. As she is leaning forward to wash her glass, she notices movement among the trees. Surely there are no prowlers in Wirrim. Now the prowler is waving. She makes out his features: tall, curly hair, his dark blue uniform replaced by a tracksuit. No mistaking Brendan out there in the moonlight. He beckons. She moves quietly towards the door and lets herself out to the sounds of rhythmic thumping from Helen and Owen's room.

"What do you want?"

"I thought that now might be a good time to have a chat about what we've been up to since high school. Remember, I wasn't here for the reunion last year."

"It's not that hard to figure out what's happened to us. I'm a historian, and you're a policeman."

"But how we got here is the question," he says with a sly grin. "I have a hunch you have some interesting stories to tell, as do I. Come on." He turns to walk down the driveway. Merran finds herself following him, hardly believing what is happening. For one makeover, two interested men isn't a bad return on investment.

Chapter 41
WON OVER

They walk along the dark, deserted streets, catching each other up on the paths they have chosen over several decades. After a while, Brendan takes Merran's hand, interlacing their fingers as they walk. Assuming that his advances will escalate, she realizes she isn't ready to move as fast as he seems to have in mind. First, she has to make sure he's trustworthy. He might be married, though Helen would surely have mentioned that. He knows she's returning to San Francisco soon and might be using her for a brief fling, with no obligations on either side. There's something to be said about such an expectation. But it isn't her style.

All of these thoughts pass through her mind like a subterranean river, while on the surface their conversation continues. She wonders if his mind is engaged similarly on two levels. He confirms her thoughts by pulling her closer with his arm while they are recalling days at Wirrim High.

She's just about to throw caution to the winds and yield to brief pleasure, when it occurs to her that she has no idea why Brendan is attracted to her. She has to know; his answer will reveal whether he is sincere or merely using her. But she decides to bide her time and listen to a new story he's about to tell her. After high school in Wirrim, he went on to enroll at a technical college in Melbourne for a degree in plant biology and had barely begun when a friend was raped in an alley while taking a shortcut on her way home from work. During the police investigation, he had managed his anger by finding out as much as possible about their procedures.

"I was a bit of a nuisance, actually," he said, smiling. "But when the rapist was arrested and convicted, I decided to ditch my plans and apply for the Police Academy instead. It seemed like interesting work."

"And what did you think of it later on? I've heard it can be pretty tedious."

"Sometimes writing reports is not much fun, but apart from that I've enjoyed it very much."

"Why did you come back to Wirrim?"

"That's a long story," he begins. Merran waits.

"I hadn't planned on it right away. I found I liked city life at first and, as luck would have it, I went to a dance at St. Kilda Town Hall and met a beautiful Filipino nurse whose name was Lilibeth. She was working in the emergency room at the Royal Melbourne and didn't want to leave. There'd have been no opportunities here in the country for her to use her advanced training, in any case."

"Don't emergencies happen in the country too? All those tractor accidents?"

"Of course, but the helicopter takes them off to Bendigo these days. It's cheaper than setting up an emergency department."

"How did that sit with you, having to stay in the city?"

"It didn't bother me. We were very happy." He hesitates, swallows. "We had a daughter . . . still do." He seems to be trying to control his voice. "Her name is Marisol. She was the light of my life." He chokes up, and Merran ventures to pull him close, fearing what he will say next.

"A drunk driver ran into us as we were on a long trip to a netball tournament in Sydney. It was full daylight. We found out later that the bloke had been drinking solidly all night after the burial of his wife." He gives her a faint smile. "Ironic, isn't it? Lilibeth was in the back seat behind me. She and I had only minor injuries, but Marisol took the brunt of the collision on the passenger side and had serious injuries, including brain damage. She's in an institution, near Lilibeth, in the eastern part of the state. I only see her every couple of months now. It's a long drive. Anyway, Marisol doesn't recognize me anymore. How many times I've wished it'd been me." He trails off. Merran is lost for words.

"What made the pain almost unbearable," he continues after taking a deep breath, "was that Lilibeth blamed me, despite all the evidence, and even after the drunk confessed. She turned into a new person, hysterical and irrational. I'd never seen her behave that way before. The only option was divorce, and that was five years ago. After that I knew I couldn't stay in Melbourne any longer."

Merran suddenly realizes that Helen has told her none of this. Brendan's past would be a juicy topic, for sure.

"How come I haven't heard any of this since I've been here?"

"Because I've never told anyone. You know the gossip mill around here. All this time I've worried that someone will find out and I'll be the centre of attention. My personal tragedy might undermine my authority as the local cop. People around here read the *Herald Sun* every day, but fortunately the tiny piece in one column had no names in it. Marisol didn't die, so there was no obituary. The accident happened in New South Wales, far away. My parents had moved away from Wirrim years before, and I'd been gone a long time as well. There was no link to Wirrim anymore."

Merran says seriously, "I'm so sorry that you've had such tragedy." After a moment she continues. "But now that you're back here, are you finding country policing too much of a contrast to what you were doing in Melbourne? Do you ever get bored?"

"Not at all. I've had some criticism from my Melbourne mates, who accuse me of underachieving, but to me country life and country policing are more about community building. I like that." Merran can tell that he's hungry for someone to listen and doesn't interrupt.

"After I arrived here, I was feeling low for so long that I thought of suicide. But even though I have a gun, I would never do it. I told the locals that a close friend had died and that satisfied them as to why I was often sad. Because they've accepted me back as one of their own, I couldn't let them down. It's taken a while, but I'm feeling a lot better now. It dawned on me when I saw you on the school ground that I'm ready to date again. It surprised me."

"And here I was thinking that you were a jerk!" exclaimed Merran. "Teasing me, winking at me. You had me really confused."

"I'm sorry. My feelings are a jumble. It's like being a teenager again." He takes her into his arms, hesitates for a moment, then kisses her lightly. "Of course, I was aware of you at school, because it's so small, but how could I not have noticed how charming you were?"

Merran laughs. "Because I wasn't at all charming then. My social skills were nonexistent, and I was always trying to outdo everyone academically. I was also overweight, and my mother's haircuts made me look like a freak. Not someone you would have been attracted to."

His voice goes down to a whisper. "But I am now. You're smart, you're beautiful. I admire your feistiness." He smiles. "We're coming up to my house. Would you like to see some of my nature photos?"

Merran laughs. "Is this equivalent to your etchings? If so, I'm not ready for what follows."

He smiles. "Slow and steady wins the race. I would never force you, Merran. But I'd like to show you some terrific photos of kangaroos up close. They were taken by a talented friend of mine from Budgerong, who leaves his camera on overnight at waterholes in the area. The camera takes a photo when it detects movement. He's captured amazing stuff."

A few metres on, they come to a garden gate, which Brendan unlatches, then leads her down a shrub-lined path whose miniature lights end at a bright red front door. Merran wishes she could see the garden, which she assumes he's planted with Australian natives.

"I call this my Red Door hideaway. Since the accident and my divorce, I've decided to turn this into as beautiful a place as I can, a kind of refuge. And I hope that eventually I'll be able to share it with someone I love."

Merran is taken aback by his naked honesty. He's a deeper thinker and more of a romantic than she would ever have imagined. Brendan turns on a low light, and they immediately enter the main lounge room, which is sparsely furnished with a few tasteful Danish teak pieces, the better to highlight the photographs that are displayed, gallery-like, on all four walls. Merran stands in the centre of the room and turns slowly, taking in the nocturnal beauty of each photograph. Shadowy kangaroos come down to drink; other shots show them in full flight. Several depict joeys peeping out of their mother's pouches. A dingo's startled eyes look straight into the flash, and the rump of a wombat is depicted just as it's about to disappear into the scrub. A silvery glow from the moon in its various phases casts an eerie light over all.

"These are amazing, Brendan. They remind me of Ansel Adams."

"Me too. Adams is one of my favourites."

"Has your friend exhibited his work in galleries? They certainly look good enough."

"Yes, he has, in the towns round about, but he's not the only one with photos like these. More and more amateurs are setting up cameras at night. Still, his are the best by far, in my opinion." He smiles. "Now, with your permission, I'd like to show you some of my own artwork."

Merran is astonished but gives him her hand as he leads her to the master bedroom. She gasps at what she sees. The walls are covered with brightly coloured abstract paintings done in oils, some as small as a bathroom mirror; the largest taking up an entire wall.

"Red!" she exclaims. From several metres away, the large painting looks uniform, but when she comes closer to examine it she sees that it is comprised of many shades of red. He's used a trowel in some areas, resulting in three-dimensional effects which are most appealing.

"I'm about to knock out the wall separating this room from the bedroom next door, the better to show these. They're a bit cramped in this space, don't you think?"

"Absolutely stunning. Yes, they do need more space, though." She turns to him. "They're fabulous, Brendan. Where did you learn to paint?"

"Marisol was interested for a while, and I went with her to a few lessons, but other than that I'm self-taught. Painting is for me what fishing is for other blokes around here. It relaxes me." He turns to her and asks, "What do you do for relaxation, Merran?"

She feels caught. Can she say "hiking" and not blush? If her brain contains little boxes, Blake occupies the one labelled hiking. Best to steer clear.

"Oh, I read, and sometimes I get out in the garden. I suppose my dog is a hobby. He's big and active and craves my attention minute by minute when I'm home. Let me think….I go to the gym a few times a week. And, like many historians, I do like wandering around old cemeteries. That reminds me: why weren't you at the reunion last year? Owen and I worked on the mystery of a murder-suicide out in the country, which resulted in the reburying of some bones in the cemetery."

"I did hear about it and was sorry to miss it, but I was visiting Marisol. Lilibeth keeps me on a tight schedule. Your exploits were the talk of the town by the time I got back." He grins. "That's one of the reasons I'm so attracted to you. You've got guts." He gives her an inquiring look. "Now I'm interested in what else you have. Any change of heart?"

Here goes, she thinks, and it's OK.

He takes his time, unbuttoning her shirt slowly, then reaching under her bra to caress the warm mounds beneath. Her response gives him no doubt of her consent. It amazes Merran how enthusiastically she reciprocates his advances. Perhaps it's because of Blake's efforts to waken her sexuality. But not only that: she trusts this man. In the next few minutes she also discovers that Brendan is a very skilled and considerate lover. It comes to her that he began the seduction early, when they were walking. The photographs and his paintings set a positive mood, and their conversation blew away any doubts she had about his sincerity.

Afterwards, they lie in an embrace, talking, lovemaking some more, and occasionally drifting off to sleep, until his alarm goes off at five-thirty. He makes coffee. They quickly shower and dress, exchanging few words. He drops her off at the corner, and she slips quietly into Helen's guest room, to emerge sleepily an hour later as Helen and Owen sit bleary-eyed, fuelling themselves with caffeine to begin their day.

Dorrie has made coffee as well.

"I don't know if you're as sleepy as I am, but I sure need it," she says.

"Thanks, but no thanks," Merran says. If she drinks one more cup, she'll be jittery all morning. "I already had some at Owen and Helen's, and coffee makes me shaky. I need to keep my car on the road." They collapse into a hug, reluctant to say goodbye. As Merran goes out the door, Dorrie looks at her with an unspoken question. What does she know? Who's been tattling? This town has eyes and ears. But Merran isn't ready to talk to Dorrie about Brendan, and leaves for Melbourne right away.

Chapter 42

MAIL

Merran has booked an airbnb across the street from the State Library in the heart of Melbourne, where she hopes to maximize her time. She's a little concerned that Dorrie might be delayed in sending the letters and the biographies to her. The mail between Australia and the U.S. has become slow of late, so she needs it to arrive before her flight. Dorrie doesn't own a scanner and is unwilling to ask any of the townspeople to help. Although very fond of tuning into the town's grapevine, she's kept her own private life very much to herself.

One night Merran is lying awake, listening to a rowdy group of students on the footpath five stories below, and replaying in her mind the meetings with Dorrie. She might have enough material for a book—a short one—rather than a paper. The previous evening, she'd left off when partway through a microfiche of newspapers from the *Melbourne Age* from 1941 to 1942, which covered the worst of the battles in Benghazi, as well as the bombing of Pearl Harbor. She's already viewed a few movies on YouTube covering action by the famous Rats of Tobruk. From what she's read in the library so far, Merran's hoping that Dorrie's materials could be a useful—though small—addition to wartime literature.

If the letters prove interesting enough, that is. Suddenly she realizes something that she's not been able to put into words up until now. Dorrie's story about George's life began with her description of him as an "ordinary man who lived a remarkable life." But so far, what she's heard from Dorrie doesn't quite measure up. Thousands of young men wrote letters home from the warfront. What makes George remarkable? It feels like there are puzzle pieces flying around in her brain, but she can't for the life of her make them come together.

At seven am, two days before she's due to fly home, she's woken from a deep sleep by a knock at the door. It's her affable Indonesian landlord, who hands her a fat package and leaves before she is conscious enough to thank him. Darn, she meant to ask him something, but can't remember what it was. Something about the hot water running out? Too bad, but she's leaving soon anyway. After a quick cold shower she crosses Swanston Street and is soon ensconced in her favourite chair.

This building holds such happy memories for her. She studied here on weekends while at university, loving the calm, studious atmosphere created by its green-shaded lamps and comfortable wooden chairs set in radiating lines from a central pool of light pouring from the skylight above. There've been many changes over the years, including the addition of a genealogy room, and upgrades on lighting and furniture, but to her it is still the place where her love of Australian history was nurtured, until she moved across the Pacific and her interest shifted to Asia and a new set of libraries in Japan, China, and the United States.

The packet from Dorrie is a couple of inches thick and comprises several sections, each of which is divided by a sheet of paper on which Dorrie has made brief notes. "I think he was in Palestine at this time; these are from Benghazi, though he wasn't able to tell me that until after he'd left; these are after he'd been released from hospital after his injury." Merran jumps: Dorrie didn't mentioned an injury. "These are from the Casualty Clearing station in Palestine." "These were written just before he boarded the ship to return to Australia." She's added approximate dates when she thinks they were written. On the final page she writes, "These are representative, and I think I have chosen pretty well. Good luck, and it's been delightful talking with you. It certainly livened up my days!"

Two file folders lie under the letters. One contains George's biography; the other is a shorter account of Dorrie's life until she met George. On flipping quickly through the pages, Merran feels relieved. Dorrie has done exactly what she asked her to do; it will save her a lot of time.

With all of the self-discipline she can muster, she decides to put Dorrie's packet aside until she's on the plane to San Francisco. Each morning she requests a pile of biographies and memoirs, as well as general histories; every evening she has to return unread ones to the trolley and request them again the following day. It's a tedious process. She has broadened her understanding of several of white Australia's major events and is now thinking that if J.L. offers her the class next year, she would love to gain more understanding of aboriginal history, both pre- and post-white contact. For years she's noticed the paucity of knowledge of Americans about Australian history generally, let alone the dark period which followed the British Invasion of 1788: the First Fleet arriving with its prisoners. It isn't just a devastating story from the eighteenth century, though; her students need to know about ongoing injustice towards aborigines ever since. It doesn't surprise her that Americans have little knowledge of these dramatic events, though. Australians don't know much about the treatment of Native Americans either. Invaders are good at hushing up atrocities.

As she puts Dorrie's pile of copies aside, she feels a surge of pride that she's reining in her impulsivity. It's still difficult, but at least she's making progress.

But her mind is wandering. Back to work. Over the next several hours she endures more stints at the microfiche machine, which she has always thought a special kind of torture. When she isn't scanning newspapers, she's reading musty books, which make her sneeze and wheeze, but overall, she feels encouraged that her course content will not only be more in-depth this time, but broader as well.

As she reads, she's distracted by an impulsive promise she's made to Brendan, that she will email him. But now she's regretting it. Blake will be waiting for her. Does she want complications like that? It's one thing to have a lover on each of two continents.

To have them encroach on the other's territory, even via email, could be disastrous. Though she came to enjoy—and even fall for—Brendan during the brief time they had together, she's concluded that, viewing it in the cold light of day, her intense liaison with him has no future. Now, as she remembers the pleased look on his face, she knows she's gone too far. Email would be only the first step. Next, he'd be asking to visit her in San Francisco. That would be unmanageable. Her actions would make a good book, she thinks, titled *How to Ruin Your Life in Three Easy Steps*. Step One: Confuse a fling with the real thing. Step Two: Imagine that a fling can continue across continents. Step Three: Ruin another relationship with said fling.

PART III
LATE FEBRUARY 2018

Chapter 43
YOUR MOST SINCERE LOVER

Merran stands before her class of twenty-five students.

At five weeks into the course, she's had to admit to herself that this particular group is not necessarily here for Australian history per se. Eavesdropping on their conversations, she imagines that most of them are outdoor types who enjoy surfing and their weekend parties, Several appear to be friends who've signed up for the class as an excuse to be together for a couple of hours each week and get credit for little work. News of last year's problems with the curriculum have filtered down; they hope she might have to lower her grading standards a second time. Not a chance, she thinks.

As she's expected, the unit on convict transportation was very popular—especially if the offender was sent 10,000 miles on a cramped, smelly, unhealthy ship for nothing more than a small infraction such as stealing loaf of bread, or a handkerchief—and they lapped up the novels she suggested: *The Secret River*, and *For The Term of His Natural Life*, as well as excerpts from *The Fatal Shore*. And they were intrigued by the close parallels between the California and Victorian Gold Rushes in the 1850s. In fact, they have been gradually warming to her class overall.

Consequently, she finds herself liking these students more and more. Of course, she'd categorized them at first as a bunch of like minds which, she knows, is not true of any group. It's just the vibe. Over many years of teaching, it's surprised her how classes each semester can feel so different from one another. Some years she coasts; others, inevitably led by a student who challenges everything she says, feel like a siege.

These kids are so young, Merran muses as she notices the tension beneath their bravado, the searching look they give their friends after telling a joke. They're so unsure of themselves, desperate to be seen as cool. In or out, a constant worry. No way would she go through the young adult years again.

Over the first few weeks of the class, Merran has noticed a shift in the vibe. Her reputation in the past, she knows, was that she was a tough grader, impersonal and inclined to demean her students before their peers. Apparently, the word is now getting around that she's nicer these days. She's heard whispering: "She's smiling!" or "An A might be in the works after all." Something to crow about to her therapist, Catherine?

The room is suddenly quiet, then Merran hears giggling. She pulls herself back from her reverie, to find twenty-five pairs of eyes upon her, waiting. She's told them that the topic for today will be Australia's involvement in World Wars I and II. She's jumping ahead in the curriculum but is anxious to discuss

George's letters. As a way of warming them to the subject, she's shown them the previous week the bundle of photocopied letters she brought back from her research trip. This impressed them, and it didn't hurt that she'd written a title for her upcoming lecture on the board, "Your Most Sincere Lover." Never has the entire class arrived on time before, especially on such a cold, rainy day. They might be uncomfortable, but they are certainly expectant. She has a captive audience for the next two hours.

She's read both George and Dorrie's biographies by now and decides to begin with George's. For the next few minutes she recounts some of the details of his life from Dorrie's written account. She then continues with Dorrie's story of her own life. She's chosen several passages from George's letters that she thinks will interest the students, and begins her lecture with the words, "This is the story of an ordinary man who lived an extraordinary life." Whether she believes it or not, she's not sure, but she'll be interested to hear what the students think.

As she comes to the end of the two bios, there's not a sound in the room. She continues by passing out a summary of war details: why Australia was involved in the Middle East, Turkey, and France in WWI, including a few details about Gallipoli, which only one student, Scott, has heard of. He saw the movie a few years ago but claims not to remember much. Then on to World War II. She doubts the students know which countries comprised the Allies, and which the Axis. They might not even know much about America's part in it, unless they're lucky enough to have grandparents or even great-grandparents who participated and would be an endless fount of war stories.

"Now who would like to read an excerpt from when George was at sea, heading for training in Palestine?" She passes the page to Violetta, whose voice is clear and expressive. As she reads, Merran can hear Dorrie's voice in her mind.

I cannot put too much in this as it may fall into somebody's hands also, but still I can tell you how much I love you and miss you, it seems like a lifetime since I saw you Darling. . . .

I have not received your letter or your parcel, at least that would be something. . . .

We have had a wonderful trip up to date. The food is very good, and weather is wonderful. I do hope they put some mail aboard; I feel as though I have been cut right out of my world and dumped into a strange one. Darling if I ever come back from here I will not roam any more, this lot will cure me forever. . . . Well, Darling, I hope this finds you loving me and in the best of health, it may not be too long, but I cannot risk saying anything about the voyage, will tell you when we get to the other side, dear. . . . do not worry Darling, as we are safe.

Violetta stops reading and looks up. "I thought Dorrie says in her bio of George that he left school when he was twelve. He's a good writer for someone who left school so young, don't you think, Dr. Scofield?"

Merran nods. "Children in those days were in very large classes with as many as sixty kids and learned by rote. Their education was very much focused on the three R's, and not as broad as it is today. George learned the basics well."

215

Next, she draws out a small brown envelope printed with the word *Telegram.* "George also sent one of these from the voyage. Do you know what it is?" No answer. Merran isn't surprised. "I checked on Google, and the service does still exist, but in miniscule numbers compared with the custom in George's time. From the 1840s until even the mid-1970s, they were the fastest method of delivering important news, especially births and deaths, and at weddings it was common to read from a large pile of congratulatory telegrams, many of them quite bawdy. Here's George's telegram from January 4, 1941:"

All's well best love George.

"As you may have guessed, you paid by the word. Sorry, no bawdiness here.

"Here's a letter from the end of January 1941, soon after he'd arrived in the Middle East. Would you like to read it, Eric?"

Eric, a quarterback from the Clare College football team, and rumored to be successful with women, reddens as he begins.

My Darling Dorrie, I am writing you a line or two, as it might be a while before I can write again. I was very glad that you received the cable that we had arrived safely. My last letter was short, but it was the best I could do. I always want you to remember that I love you with all my heart and no other woman will take your place under any circumstances. Love to Mum also . . . I would love to be sitting down to a good square meal with you both right now. I am not allowed to tell you where I am exactly, but it's in the Middle East. . . . With all the love that I am capable of, I remain Your most sincere lover, George.

The class claps. Eric bows awkwardly from the waist, his expression unreadable.

Merran shuffles through the letters and chooses one of the longer ones.

"How about you, Leroy?"

Leroy, who she knows to be in the theatre company, takes a moment to read through the excerpt, and then becomes George right before their eyes. Even without the slouch hat, the khaki uniform, the heavy boots sunk in sand, and the flat, nasal accent, he is worn and tired. His eyes are slits against the desert sun. His expression is one of resignation mixed with remnants of the fighting spirit the Aussies are known for. As Merran watches, she can imagine George's premature wrinkles and peeling skin, the rank odour of his unwashed body. Yet he can write of hope.

My Darling Dorrie, You don't know how happy I am today. I have just received two letters from you. One was written on the first, and the other, 7th April. There is more danger of mine getting lost as this place often gets a pasting from the Huns. Anyway, we will not talk of that. I was pleased to know that you and Mum are well also that you enjoyed your weekend at the seaside. Both Jim and I are OK so far, we have not been swept into the sea as threatened. . . . Darling, one of your letters made me want to be near you, to cuddle into your lovely self, and be content. I know you love me, Dearest, still it makes me happy to hear you say so. I never had as much faith in any woman in my life as I have in you Darling. . . . The weather has been terrible, there is another dust storm here now, this is the third day. It would break your heart. I wouldn't mind the war so much, but the weather is something we did not count on. I have just got a change of clothes but have no water to have a wash. . . . I never thought I would be able to go so long without a bath or a change of clothes, also that I would sleep in my clothes for two months and my boots too many times. . . .

24 September 1941: My Darling, Another one of your loving letters arrived today and I am very happy. I have been a bit downhearted since I received your last letter, you seemed to be in such a mood. . . . You were asking about the engagement ring. Dear, that has always been a sore point in my happiness that I could not get you one before I left, but if you are content to have it that way, why not get one stone in your little ring and get another one made with diamonds plus one Moonstone if you would like it like that. . . . I would sooner have got the ring myself but don't have the money to buy it here, we are paid so little. I should have some back pay coming from June but won't get that for a while. . . .

29 September 1941: This letter writing, I wish I was finished with it. . . . I know you love me even when you are telling me off. I know how you feel, sometimes I feel the same, I just want to pick someone and have a real good fight and then I would be all right for a while.

October 1941: You never miss a chance to tell me of my faults, as far as roaming is concerned, you always have that in the back of your mind. If you keep thinking a thing it ends up poisoning your mind, and of course you suffer quite a lot of unnecessary agony. Just get this into your head, Darling, my life is changed and my love for you is too great for me to ever want to roam when I return. This place is a wild kind of hell. Dorrie when you come to compare yourself and me, you have not really changed your life and I should say your routine of your life. You can still sleep in a good bed and eat what you like, but my life has changed completely, everything we do or eat is at the bidding of someone else. . . . I am not complaining because I came here of my own free will and

*will take what comes my way. So do not misunderstand me
again love. I try to write you a nice letter, but I don't always
succeed. Darling I have only had about six days of pleasure
since I have been over here, and that would not have been
so wonderful had it not been that I was doing something
creative I had in mind for some time, and that was to buy
those Moonstones that you wanted. . . . You hurt me very
much when you said you were glad we were not married
before I left. I don't think you meant that, it was better when
you came to look at it, because you really did not know me so
well did you, Dear, then things might have been much worse.
. . . When you looked at your Moonstones did they shine
love, you never told me, you were too busy telling me off. . . .
Darling do not write like that again.*

Leroy stops and thrusts the papers at Merran. "She
sounds like a bitch, excuse my French. Is she like that
now?"

"Well," Merran says, "she's no pushover, but I
imagine that being free of the worries of war for so
many decades has taken off some of her rough edges.
Nowadays she's a peach-cheeked old lady in her late
nineties."

As Leroy walks slowly back to his seat, he says
quietly, "I bet George wouldn't imagine in a million
years that we'd be hearing these letters in San
Francisco so many decades later. Isn't it an invasion
of his privacy? Of course he's dead, but still..."

Merran says, "Good question, Leroy. What do you
others think?"

A quiet young woman speaks up. Christine has
made very little contribution to any of the classes
before this. How appropriate that she would speak
on a matter of privacy.

"It would be invasive if his next of kin didn't know we were doing it. I suppose that Dorrie knows, does she, Dr. Scofield? Are there any children, and if so, do they know?"

Merran is startled. She doesn't remember Dorrie mentioning her son's name. They have little contact. It's almost certain he doesn't know that Merran even exists.

"Yes, there is a son who still lives on the family farm, but I've never met him. Dorrie moved into town over twenty years ago. You raise an important point; I'll have to get back to you on that. But I don't see any harm from continuing the excerpts now. Let's do that after a short break."

She expects that the break will be, as usual, twice as long as it should be, but to her surprise all are back at the appointed time.

Merran picks Kim to read next. Merran knows her to be a champion surfer who has already competed in competitions at Bondi and Bell's beaches. She's bound to view Australian culture through the lens of surfing. This excerpt will be quite a contrast from what she knows.

"Before Kim starts, here's a bit of backstory," she tells the class. "During those war years Australians were fighting with the Allies far from home but were getting very worried about Japanese encroachment southwards on the Malay Peninsula, closer and closer to Darwin. And George felt stuck in the Middle East, powerless to protect his loved ones, and became frustrated and depressed. By Christmas he was feeling very low. OK, Kim."

I suppose the war has made a big difference over home, I have been thinking of you and loving you more than ever, Dorrie. I am very miserable at present, I only wish they would send us somewhere. What with the way things are at home, and us here hanging around, it will drive us all mad. I don't know why they keep us here in this rotten country when we could be doing some good and protecting our own homes. I just cannot put my mind to anything now. I have been doing some very silly things lately, my mind has been in Australia plenty. I have been losing interest in my work, you will say moaning again.

Kim looks up, opens her mouth, then closes it, and clutches the paper more tightly.

Even though Melbourne is not likely to be under attack by the Japanese for a while—not like Darwin and Brisbane, which are much more at risk—it might be wise to build an air raid shelter, just in case. It should be built as far away from the house as possible, you know, where you and Mum burn rubbish near the back fence.

Merran says, "the Japanese did bomb Darwin in February 1942. In fact, they bombed the city over one hundred times."

"And did he get to fight the Japanese after all?" Kim asks. "Was he able to go home first and marry Dorrie, or did he go straight to fight in Malaya on the way home?"

Merran finds herself atypically at a loss for words. The students sit waiting, while she attempts to come up with an answer.

"Dorrie and I never discussed it," she says finally. "We were very short of time, and my goal of course was to get hold of the letters she'd mentioned." She rushes on, looking for a way out.

221

"There must have been letters from him if he did go back to fighting. But Dorrie didn't mention them, so I suspect that there weren't any. A back injury he had from a bomb released him from fighting. But I promise you that I'll contact Dorrie as soon as I get back to my office, and let you know next week. Kim, you've asked a very good question. Thank you!" But under her breath: damn!

Chapter 44

AFTER THE LETTERS

Dorrie's email response to Merran's question arrives within half an hour.

"I'm sorry that my typing is slower than my mind these days, which is frustrating. In my Olivetti days I could keep up with the best of them.

"*Do you have Skype?*" Merran writes back.

"No, I've never needed it."

"Then I'll call you. What's your number?"

"That's better," Dorrie says. "Now to your question. We were so short of time that I didn't think to mention what happened after he left the Middle East. What a whirlwind we had going, Merran. You were so focused on the letters that I concentrated on those. I'm glad you're contacting me again because I've been wondering if you agree with me that George was a remarkable man? He only became truly remarkable soon after the letters stopped."

Merran is both taken aback and relieved. Sure, George was a good soldier, but so were thousands of others. Now she wonders if her students feel the same way but are too polite to tell her. What makes him remarkable?

Dorrie continues. "Now I need to tell you the rest of the story. There were no letters from him for three-and-a-half years after that. But he wasn't at home with me. Instead, his ship was captured by the Japanese in Java in March 1942, their last stop before arriving in Australia. At first, he was reported missing, but we soon found out that he had been taken a prisoner of war and sent to camps on the notorious Burma-Thailand Railway until the end of the war. We weren't able to see each other until after the war ended, in October 1945."

Merran replies quickly. "Oh no! But why didn't you show me the letters he wrote from the camps?" There's silence on the line. Whoops, she thinks, she should have demonstrated more sympathy over George's capture. When Dorrie speaks again, Merran notices a little reserve in her voice.

"I was a little upset by your reply: it was a little insensitive. Also, you didn't seem to notice that I said there were no letters for years, until the war ended. But then I got hold of myself and remembered what our goal is. So now back to your question. Of course I wrote, at first. But after a while the authorities realized that the Japanese were not delivering the letters, so we were told to stop. We got a few of our letters back. Because there were none from him, I was writing in a vacuum, with almost no information about how he was, or where he was. Over those years it was painful and frustrating. Now and then I would hear that a radio message had been picked up, by somebody somewhere, saying that George Richardson wants Dorrie McKenzie to know that he's safe and well."

Merran says, "But was he really safe and well? I've read accounts of those camps along the Railway that were pretty horrific."

"I found out only after he returned that he was in terrible shape. He brought a medical history card with him that I still have, and just found again in the storage box. Hold on a sec. It's right here in the bin.

"Looks like different people filled this in along the way. His lowest weight was in 1943, at 70 pounds. Here's a list of the diseases he had: malaria, beriberi, blackwater fever, intermittent diarrhoea, pneumonia, leg ulcers. Not cholera, thank goodness—he would have died from that. Let me read ahead a bit."

Merran waits, then Dorrie comes back with the details.

"It says that he was also slightly deaf, probably from the bomb in the Middle East. And his vision was a little blurred. I noticed those when he first came home, but they actually got a bit better after the war."

"Apart from the diseases, did he talk about injuries? I know that beating was rife in the camps."

"Oh yes. He had deep scars on his back and legs but would never talk about how they got there."

"Did he get any recognition from the government? Some sort of medal in appreciation? A stripe, at least, or a promotion?"

Dorrie's reply is so loud that Merran has to hold the phone away from her ear.

"He got bugger all, Merran. Sorry to swear, but it still riles me. I have his Certificate of Discharge here. When I read it I nearly hit the roof. It says that he had

'Nil' marks or scars. I wanted to find the scoundrel who wrote it and give him a piece of my mind. But George wanted to put the whole experience behind him." Her voice is now cracking with emotion. This is a different Dorrie, Merran thinks.

"And here's another sore point for me, which he also ignored. The Certificate states that the Total Effective Period of his enlistment, which included Active Service, was two thousand and sixty days. But he came out of the hellhole of the world almost penniless. No compensation, bloody nothing. We started our marriage on a shoestring."

"After I'd read George's bio that you wrote, I thought I almost knew him. But there's this whole other piece now. What was he like mentally when he came back?"

Dorrie's voice sounds stronger. "He came back, miraculously, in good mental shape. I was expecting the worst, something like shell shock—you remember what happened to his brother Charlie in World War I, don't you?"

"Yes, from George's bio. It's called PTSD nowadays."

"Yes I know. It was a miracle that George escaped it. There was the occasional bad dream, but nothing more. He would sometimes be lost in his thoughts but would snap out of it if I said his name. Of course, Malcolm wanted to know more than George was willing to tell him, and I suspected that a lot of what he told Malcolm was watered down."

So that's the son's name, Merran thinks. Malcolm.

Dorrie goes on. "His greatest problem was his heart, which had been under so much strain in the

226

camps. And he had so many losses when he was young. That would have contributed to his poor health as well."

"True, that comes out loud and clear in the bio. When I read it I thought, poor kid."

"He suffered from angina mostly. We'd moved to the farm by then, when Malcolm was five. There were some loans available under the Soldier Settlement Scheme, and we grabbed the opportunity. It was George's dream to be back in this area, and on our own farm. I wasn't well suited to that life. You read about my sheltered upbringing in my bio, didn't you?"

Not waiting for an answer, she continues.

"But I grew into it, especially working with him. He was an excellent teacher." Merran is about to say something, but Dorrie is on a roll.

"I was worried all the time, of course. Didn't think his heart would stand it. He lived for another seven years and was able to enjoy our son, though he did have some stretches in hospital. Malcolm was devoted to his father. He missed a lot of school, staying with George when the angina would flare up, and ready to hand over his pills when the pain got too bad."

"Where did George die?"

"At home, which is what he would have wanted. Just dropped dead one afternoon, in front of Malcolm. Sorry to be so matter-of-fact, but it was a long time ago. It helped that George had told me often that he didn't fear death. He'd felt it knocking on his door so many times while he was a prisoner, and seen hundreds die, that he'd learned it wasn't a big deal. Just a transition, he called it. So I took on his attitude and kept on looking forward after he'd gone. The farm was a sad reminder of him, but a comfort as well, and I threw myself into it." Shuffling sounds. "I have a few photos here in the box. I forgot to get them out when you were here, but I'll show you sometime."

"What about Malcolm? How did he cope?"

"He stayed here with me until he finished high school in Budgerong. Then he went on to Melbourne Uni to study Civil Engineering. He married and had two daughters, but his wife was a handful and they eventually divorced. He came back to the farm then, but it wasn't good for him. He missed his dad too much and couldn't move on. I feel sorry for him, but there's nothing I can do now. In fact, he's past retirement age. He could easily sell the farm, but probably won't." Her voice is now so quiet that Merran almost misses her next words, "I expect him to die there."

Merran doesn't know what to say, but then recalls a bit of research.

"I'm so sorry. But let me tell you something I think you'll find intriguing. I was recently reading an article about the children of Holocaust survivors, wars, or terrorist attacks. The terrible events that happened to the parents may not have been talked about in the family, but even so, the children pick up on the stress that the parents have gone through. Malcolm seems to have taken on the stress that you and George tried so hard to get over. I tell you this not to blame anyone—it's just a fact."

There's silence on the other end. Merran starts to worry. But Dorrie soon speaks up.

"Thanks for that, Merran. It makes a lot of sense. I was just thinking…Malcolm's ex-wife, Camille, was French. She came to Melbourne Uni on an exchange in her second year, met Malcolm, and stayed. Camille's parents were part of the Resistance during the war; lovely people, but you could sense the way the family functioned—or, didn't function—after five minutes. I only met them a couple of times. It was awkward because they bickered about anything and everything from dawn to dusk but seemed devoted to each other at the same time. And they were afraid and anxious 24/7. Camille must have taken on all that anxiety. She sure was a right-royal drama queen. She just pushed and pushed Malcolm, and he got more and more depressed. I gave up visiting them, it was so ugly. Oh, there's the doorbell, I'll be back."

Merran puts a coffee capsule into her office espresso machine. Time for a break: this conversation is heavy. But Dorrie is back quickly.

"It was just the postie delivering a box of books I ordered from Bendigo. Yippee! Now, where was I? Oh yes, Camille and Malcolm's marriage. But I think I've said enough about that. Let's talk about something else."

Merran says, sipping her coffee, "I think we've talked long enough. You must be exhausted. But before we go, I have an important question. I know that you're fine with my using George's letters in a paper or a book. At least, I assume you are fine with it, though I need to get that in writing. I'll bring you something to sign when I come back for Helen and Owen's wedding. You'll be going, won't you?"

Dorrie's voice is ecstatic.

"Of course! Helen is an old friend. If I were forty years younger, I'd be jumping up and down at the prospect of seeing you again. Instead, I'm going to have a nice piece of apple pie for morning tea. A la mode, of course."

"Don't hang up yet, Dorrie. I need to get Malcolm's permission to use the letters as well. Because he wasn't part of our discussion much at all, it didn't cross my mind. Have you told him anything about me?"

"No. I rarely see him. He shops in Budgerong, so I go to meet him there once in a while. We enjoy each other's company so long as he doesn't get onto the past."

"Then I'll have a challenge on my hands. When I get back to Wirrim, let's put our heads together and work out a strategy."

She imagines the sparkle in Dorrie's eyes.

"All right, I look forward to it. Better you than me, though. He can be contrary. My dear, it's been such a delight hearing from you again. With all of your usual bounce, I imagine that you'll now be in top gear for the rest of the day. Bye."

What a lovely thing to say, Merran thinks as she locks her office door. It sure is energizing to talk to old people once in a while. She breaks into a few bars of "You Make Me Feel So Young," but quickly stops when she sees Blake stepping down the corridor. He's heard her, though, and breaks into a smile.

"Thank you, Merran. I'm glad you feel that way!"

PART IV
LATE MARCH 2018

Chapter 45

A WEDDING

On a clear evening in late summer, Helen and Owen are married. Owen's two children, Bronwyn and Dylan, have made long journeys from Europe, delighted to be reunited with each other and their father after several years apart. Helen's daughter, older son, their spouses, and her youngest, Danny, have joined a large group of local friends and relatives. Merran has brought a toy vintage model cable car from San Francisco for Danny, which makes the young man laugh with joy. Dorrie arrives wearing what looks to be a new floor-length silk dress and flowers in her hair. Merran chuckles to herself when she overhears Dorrie say to James that it was so expensive she'd need several years of wear out of it.

So many have offered food that Helen is able to relax and enjoy the occasion, so unlike the pressure she'd put on herself at the reunion. Her physical transformation has continued as the months pass. Now she is glowing, her long, close-fitting pale cream gown setting off the shine in her hair. Her short veil is topped with a sparkling tiara, which she jokes was her granddaughter Vanessa's wish and command.

Owen's glowing as well, Merran thinks. An old saying of her mother's comes to mind: "Men perspire, but ladies glow." Owen is proving her wrong. It's certainly warm, but all that perspiring and glowing is undoubtedly also due to what Dorrie calls pheromones. If such things exist, do they fly around lovers' heads like tiny butterflies or bats? Watching as Helen paces slowly after Vanessa, who is scattering rose petals along the path to where Owen is waiting in his tuxedo, Merran's amused by the notion that, in nature, it is the male who is all puffed up and often gorgeously coloured to attract the female. In humans, it's the other way around. As she scans the crowd, looking for familiar faces, she notices that Tom and Vera aren't there.

Earlier in the day, she and Helen had a conversation about them. Helen complained,

"I wish we could have had Tom and Vera do the ceremony," Helen confided when she and Merran were decorating the tables, "but they would have had to become official celebrants. None of this 'officiant for a day,' which you have in the States. To my mind, your system is much more sensible and meaningful, because you can invite friends or relatives to do it."

"I agree. But how are Tom and Vera anyway?" Merran asks. "Are they coming to the wedding?"

"I think so, they said they would. But when it comes down to it they might not be able to bring themselves to celebrate anything just yet. The wait for Hiroshi to be found is killing them."

Despite the absence of Tom and Vera, Owen and Helen's friends and relatives seem determined to shrug off the shadow hanging over the town. As

Merran waits anxiously for Brendan to appear, she wonders whether they'll succeed or not.

She'd arrived from San Francisco only the night before. It's way past her bedtime, but adrenaline keeps her going as she looks out for him with a mixture of longing and dread. In the intervening weeks, they've corresponded regularly. Although some of what he writes is news on the investigation, such as the visit of Hiroshi's father a few days after the boy's disappearance, most of the emails express his affection for her. He knows that Merran won't yet accept a declaration of love—for practical reasons, she tells him. In fact, her relationship with Blake has been growing. He's talked of moving in together as a test of the relationship. But something is holding her back.

It doesn't feel fair to either man for her to be two-timing like this. And is she, indeed, two-timing? In her own mind, she is. She does have strong and sincere feelings for Brendan—feelings that frankly scare her—but decides not to tell him for a while longer. She'll have to decide between the two of them soon. She feels stumped, though a new thought is creeping in: if logic tells her that she belongs—for so many reasons—in San Francisco, then why is she holding onto fantasies about Brendan? Is it possible that, all things being equal, he would be her choice? Whatever that means.

Just as the party is at its end, with tipsy guests bidding a noisy good night, she spots Brendan, looking out of place in his uniform and obviously stone cold sober. His eyes sweep the garden and alight on her. With a warm smile he makes his way through the throng, pulls her close with his arm, and whispers into her ear.

"Would you like a walk when I'm off-duty in half an hour? Meet me at the corner? Are you too tired?"

"Sure, I'm tired, but very glad to see you. I've been waiting for hours."

"Sorry, but I had to sort out a domestic dispute, involving knives and broken glass. Worst night for that, don't you think?" He squeezes her arm and walks away. She hears his police car heading towards the station, catches Helen's eye, and tells her she'll be back a little late. Helen doesn't look a bit surprised.

It's after midnight when they meet at the corner. There's no moon, and between the few streetlights, the brilliant stars of the Southern Cross are visible near the river of light, the Milky Way. The town is silent, tucked up and snug. They kiss, then walk hand in hand.

"I hate to put a damper on our meeting," Brendan begins, "but I have some news."

"Hiroshi's been found?"

"No, not that. Remember I told you that Vic Police left a few weeks ago to help deal with that terrorist attack in Melbourne. At least that's the story I was given. But I think they would have stayed if they'd had any good leads. Now the boy's father, Daichi, has come back to put pressure on them for results, and somehow they think that coming back here might be productive. I don't know why. But I don't blame Daichi for pushing. I'd do the same if my kid were missing."

She asks, "What does that mean for you and your schedule? Incidentally, Brendan, I'll be with Mum in Rylands for the next few days."

"A team is due here later this morning, and will pull out the stops yet again, with more searches, though probably scaled back this time. I think they'll also use the station here in Wirrim to send out renewed requests for information, nationwide, on TV and radio. The case went cold for a while, as you know. Now I'd better get some sleep, and so should you. Let's have a cosy evening together after your visit to Rylands." He walks her back to Helen's house and kisses her lightly, starts to leave, then returns with a longing look to kiss her again, this time passionately.

"Remember our night together?"

"How could I forget?"

"I'd love a repeat, but this isn't the right time."

Merran hesitates before allowing her deeper feelings to form into words. She's surprised at how nervous she feels. This is the real thing.

"Do we have a future, Brendan? It would be my fondest wish, if we could work out how to bring it about. You are very special to me. You know that, don't you?" She notices moisture in his eyes. He nods wordlessly, hugs her tightly, and disappears quickly into the dark.

Chapter 46
MALCOLM

Merran and Dorrie talked briefly at the wedding, but the music was too loud for meaningful conversation, so they made plans to meet after Merran had visited her mother. Now Dorrie flings the door open so rapidly that only her walker saves her from falling.

"I saw you from the window. Come in, it's so good to see you again. Are you ready for a cuppa? I have the British one, Tetley's this time."

Again, she has laid out a tempting spread of cakes and biscuits.

"I'm always ready for a cuppa," Merran says, "and Tetley's was the tea I often came across in my travels in Asia. Delicious. But I need your advice as to how I should approach Malcolm. My flight is tomorrow. I can't afford to bungle it."

"Well, if you'd come a month earlier, I would have told you that he seemed depressed when I met him for lunch in Budgerong, but that's nothing new. Now he seems a bit better since one of his daughters, Priscilla, came to visit for the first time in years."

"What's she like? Full of drama like her mother?"

"Well, she's a lawyer like her mother, smart and well educated, but she has Malcolm's temperament, rather quiet, no drama. It was a pleasure to see her. I rang Malcolm after she left, and he told me they'd had a long talk about his marriage to her mother, how it and the divorce had affected her and her sister, and so on. He was more talkative than he'd been for years. He sounded relieved to hear that she's now having quite a good life. Still single but happy with it." She pours more tea. "So, all in all, you might find him less grouchy and difficult than usual."

"Should I just land on him, or ring him first?"

"In the country, remember, people are used to others just dropping in. Besides, if he wants to be difficult, he'll have no time to prepare." She laughs. "Catch him off-guard."

"Sounds fine to me. I'll be off soon, then. But there's something I want to tell you, news about the search for the Japanese student."

"I already know. My friend Val met Brendan O'Neill down the street and heard the news. Vic Police are coming back. Brendan is someone I like very much. I do hope he is the one to find the boy; it would give him such a boost. He's been a bit down lately." She stops and looks hard at Merran, who says nothing. Damn, she knows. After a beat, Dorrie continues.

"You know, I heard some rumours about the boy's father when he was here after Hiroshi disappeared."

Merran pricks up her ears. "What?"

"Well, they say he's an arrogant man. He insisted on talking to the high-ups in Melbourne and gave short shift to the locals. Of course, you'd expect he'd need to deal with Vic Police, and James and Brendan

239

knew that, but they'd expected he'd want to see the school, meet Tom and Vera, et cetera. Everyone thinks that his rudeness to the Wirrim folks was quite unnecessary. He complained that the motel and the food were beneath his standards. I agree that the motel is only average."

Merran nods, remembering the lukewarm water, the threadbare towels, and the absence of soap the previous year. She'd rate it below average.

"But the hotel restaurant down the road is pretty good," Dorrie says.

"Then the father laid it on even thicker and said that if he'd taken more care about where Hiroshi would be located for the programme, he wouldn't have let him come. A dump in the desert, he called it. I ask you! James was mortified. He told someone later that all Daichi wanted to talk about was how disruptive this all was to his work. As though Hiroshi's disappearance was inconvenient rather than a tragedy. That part's hard for me to believe though. He can't be that callous, but he was certainly unpleasant. He really laid into Tom and Vera too. They were terribly upset."

So that's why Brendan gave her only a bare bones account of Daichi's visit: it had cut to the bone for all concerned.

"How important is he, really?" Merran asks. "I heard he's in the Diet, but I haven't come across his name in the newspapers."

"Brendan says he's close to the prime minister and is pushing the re-armament of Japan. Most of what I've seen on the news is that there's a lot of opposition."

"Yes, I'm fairly acquainted with the arguments pro and con," Merran says. She doesn't mention that she routinely reads the *Asahi Shimbun* and the *Yomiuri Shimbun*, two of the leading Japanese newspapers with differing political views.

She stands slowly and stretches. "Now I'd better set off for the farm. How do I get there?

She locates the farm about two-thirds of the way to Budgerong, on a dirt road a couple of k's from the highway. A barbed-wire fence surrounds the property; two large she-oaks flank Malcolm's wide gate. In the distance she can make out a long stand of eucalyptus, which she imagines marks the far boundary. A small creek flows fitfully along one side, where a mob of kangaroos is hanging out. They watch Merran, their big ears alert for danger, but do not hop away. Whirling above her is bird paradise. In the few moments before she gets out of the car, she identifies several species of birds who are gliding, skirmishing, and conversing. It's apparent that Malcolm poses no threat to wildlife. This is a good sign.

She climbs out of the car and notices his face at the window. He comes out and meets her at the gate, an energetic Blue Heeler at his side, his expression neutral. He's dressed in Yakka overalls, a sweater whose sleeves are unravelling at the wrists, and a pair of boots that have seen better days. His face is tan and lined from years of sun and wind.

"Malcolm Richardson?" He nods. She introduces herself. "Your mother Dorrie told me where to find you. I have something important to discuss with you."

"Well, then, you'd better come in," he replies noncommittally, his voice a deep, melodious bass. He leads the way to the back door and signals her to enter first. Immediately, the aroma of fresh bread hits her nostrils. And something else, possibly wild. She glances around the room and spots a young magpie hopping towards her, obviously expecting handouts. Malcolm's expression changes. He smiles at the bird and holds out his hand. He's quite a handsome man when he smiles, Merran thinks. But I imagine he doesn't do it too often.

"Here, Mate. Here, Mate." The bird changes direction and hops onto the table.

"I hope you don't mind," he says. "He's clean, just has a broken wing which I'm nursing back to health. I only took the bandage off this morning. He'll be ready to fly with his friends in a day or two." He breaks off a piece of bread and Mate grabs it.

"Cup of coffee?" he asks. "I was about to make one. And this loaf is just out of the oven. Vegemite? Jam? Peanut butter?"

"Coffee would be wonderful. And Vegemite. I don't get it too often," Merran replies, still watching the magpie, and hoping he'll sing his glorious song, but Mate hops off the table and flies low to his little bed in the corner. He settles down, but his beady eyes remain fixed on them.

While Malcolm rinses the teapot, assembles cups, milk, and sugar, and slices the bread, Merran glances around the room. It's a large country kitchen with an old Rayburn range, a clothes drying rack overhead, and a table and chairs for four, which looks dwarfed by the space. Along one wall there's a built-in oak bookshelf crammed with volumes old and new: Australian authors including Kate Grenville, Patrick White, Tom Keneally, and Henry Handel Richardson; as well as Tolstoy, Dickens, Hemingway, Phillip Roth, and more. Malcolm's open laptop sits on a desk on the opposite wall. The space is spotlessly clean.

When they've settled with their bread and coffee, Malcolm gives her a questioning look. She decides to come right to the point, and explains where she lives and works, how she met his mother, her wish to write a paper or a book including his father's letters from World War II, and her need to have his permission to do so.

What Malcolm says next stuns her. "What letters?" he asks. "There were no letters from the Burma-Thailand Railway."

"Yes, she told me that. But she has a bunch of letters from the Middle East, which he wrote before he was sent back to Australia and captured in Java on the way. Haven't you seen those?"

"Oh, those love letters. She showed them to me once, but they didn't do much for me. Too sentimental, and little information about the war itself due to censorship. I don't care about those; do what you like with them. It's his experience on the Railway that I care about, where he really suffered. Did she tell you about that?"

"Not at first. She explained later that she thought I was only interested in letters, and that there were none from his captivity."

"Yes, I would have expected that from her." He almost spits out the words. "She prefers to live in a fairyland of optimism. She's still flattered by his

'Sincere Lover' letters." He uses air quotes. "But I'll bet she doesn't know squat about his prison camp experiences. When my father died she just went on as though nothing had happened, all in the name of looking to the future."

"I got the impression that this was the attitude she learned from him, that he viewed his death as just a passing over."

"But what I was left with, at the age of twelve, was a dirty great gap in my life which Mum was not interested in filling. God, I missed him, and still do. There's not a day that I don't sit outside looking at his handiwork around the farm. I know it was impossible to get letters out of that hellhole, but I sure wish something remained."

"Why didn't he write a memoir after the war? His writing skills were pretty good."

"I suggested it to him a few times before he died, but he wasn't interested. It wasn't fair to me. Now I have to rely on books written by others to piece the story together." He turns to his shelves and grabs an armful of volumes.

"These books show what actually happened in the camps," he says, and sets them before her in a pile. Out of politeness she spends several minutes paging through them, though she's seen most of them before, and has even taught classes on the Burma-Thailand Railway. She looks up at the bookshelf and spots two volumes with titles written in Japanese. "What are these?" she asks.

"I picked them up in a used bookstore in Melbourne not long ago. The owner told me they contain propaganda from World War II. I never cared to have them translated, as they would have made my blood boil. Don't know why I bought them really. I imagine they contain infuriating stuff, for example that Allied prisoners were cowards because they surrendered."

Merran nods and says, "They probably do," then asks, "May I look at them? I read and speak Japanese." Malcolm, surprised, hands them over. He pours more coffee while Merran peruses the books. After twenty minutes, she turns to him.

"The bookseller was wrong. They're present-day revisionist theories about the way the prisoners were treated and attempts to equate the whole prisoner of war experience with the bombings of Hiroshima and Nagasaki. You know about the recent push by the Japanese government to rearm the country, don't you?"

"Yes, I've heard about that, and it makes me furious." He slurps his coffee so energetically that it spills on the table. After mopping it up, he continues, "Don't get me wrong, I don't hate the Japanese people, and feel sorry that so many lost their lives in the two bombings. I just hate the militaristic ones." He hesitates, his face reddening, then adds slowly, "That goes for militarism everywhere. As a matter of fact, I discussed rearmament with a young Japanese boy out at Coopers Lake a few months ago. I think he was on a cultural exchange with Wirrim School. The boy who went missing. I didn't think I needed to tell the police, because it was just a conversation."

Merran opens her mouth, but nothing comes out. She feels her heart beating wildly. This is the man at the lake who the bully boys talked about. Keep calm, she tells herself.

"So, what did you talk about?" Malcolm picks up the bread knife and cuts off two more slices. His hands are shaking a little as he spreads butter and Vegemite on Merran's slice, and jam on his. But his voice is strong.

"He was an interesting fellow. His English wasn't too good, and my Japanese is nonexistent, but we discovered that we both speak French—my ex-wife is French—so we were able to talk for a few minutes. I was on my way to the other side of the lake to do some sketching. Quite quickly we got onto the subject of the war, and he mentioned that his great-grandfather had been a prison guard on the Railway. Of course, I took note and asked if we could talk another time about that. I told him I had some books he might want to look at. See if he could identify his great-grandfather in any of the photographs."

"What was your goal, Malcolm? To shame him?"

He looks surprised.

"Not really, though I was wondering what his reaction would be if I showed him pictures of prisoners who looked like they'd come out of Auschwitz. We arranged for him to come here a couple of days later, when he thought he'd be able to slip out. I picked him up just outside Wirrim and brought him here."

"Then what happened?" Merran could hardly breathe.

"We had a look through all the books. He said he was shocked at the pictures, and it confirmed his attitude to war in general. He told me he'd lived with his mother in Toulouse, France, for the past few years, but was now back in Japan with his father, Daichi I think he said his name was, who he said was strict and unloving. Not violent, nothing like that, but he didn't intervene when Hiroshi told him he was being bullied at school. In the father's opinion, this was an excellent opportunity for the boy to toughen up, because one day he would be a soldier."

"My goodness, I had no idea," Merran exclaims.

"You know him?" Malcolm asks sharply.

"I've heard bits and pieces about all of the students, actually." A lie.

Malcolm seems satisfied with this.

"Hiroshi told me that he'd recently visited the Peace Park in Hiroshima with his school group, and they'd delivered a long garland of origami peace cranes to the memorial. They'd also sang songs about peace. Some of the boys thought it was corny, but Hiroshi said he decided then and there to be a peacemaker all his life."

"I've been there too, and it does make an impression," Merran said.

Malcolm ignores her, intent on his memories of Hiroshi.

"He said that one of the assignments that day was to interview foreign visitors to the park, using his few words of English. He said that the experience meant a lot to him. How could he fight people who seemed so like him in many ways? He was getting quite worked up. He said he never wanted to go back to his father and would die first." He stops, lost in thought.

"Then what happened?" she asks, after a moment.

"It rattled me that he was hinting at suicide, so I thought I'd better take him back to Wirrim. It would have been too much for me to handle. He protested all the way, until I dropped him off at the railway line.

It must have been another day that he went missing, even the next day. By then I'd left for Alice Springs to visit an old friend. My caravan was already loaded up when I took Hiroshi back to Wirrim." He takes a gulp of coffee and grimaces. "Your coffee must be cold too. Here, let me heat them in the microwave." They sit for a few minutes, sipping and eating. It's all Merran can do to stop herself pushing Malcolm too fast; he might stop talking altogether. After finishing his coffee, he takes his cup to the sink and sits down again in his chair.

"It took me over a week to get to the Alice. I stayed with an old university mate, Ross Campbell, who's lived for the past thirty-odd years out there. He works as a doctor in some of the more remote clinics. I could have flown there, but I drove so I could see the country on the way. It's stunningly beautiful, you know, even the deserts, which it is mostly." He looks at Merran as though expecting her to agree. Instead, she says, "Go on."

"Then when I got there, Ross's work in the clinics was so interesting that I stayed longer than I'd planned. He's quite the humanitarian. He inspired me actually. Made me think about what more I could do with my life instead of rotting away here feeling sorry for myself. I only got back a couple of weeks ago, just in time to see my daughter Priscilla. I'm glad I didn't miss that. But I was amazed to hear that Hiroshi was missing."

"Well, Hiroshi's disappearance was a big deal around here. His father came over from Japan, and from what I've heard, was as much of a bastard as Hiroshi described. No wonder he didn't want to go back. Now as you're talking, I'm wondering if he committed suicide. But we don't have a body to be able to tell either way."

Malcolm looks startled at the word 'suicide.' He puts his head in his hands, muttering, "Poor kid."

They sit for a while without speaking, then Merran gets up to leave.

"The police need to know about Hiroshi's visit here, and especially his mental state. Will you call the police in Wirrim, or will I?" Finally, he mumbles, "I'll call." He looks drained. Merran drives back to Wirrim, wondering why.

She's at the airport the next day, ready to fly home, when a text arrives from Brendan. A constable from Vic Police has questioned Malcolm. The latter's story is identical to what he told Merran.

Chapter 47
A Shift

Blake is waiting for her at the airport in San Francisco, and affectionate in a way he's never been before, kissing her in public. Despite his skill at *Kama Sutra* lovemaking, he isn't a particularly warm person. She's sometimes wondered, as they work through the book of positions, whether he regards each as merely a goal to be achieved, rather than as an expression of love. Will he discard her when they reach the end? Has he worked through the book with other women? He's revealed very little about his past. Now he pulls her close and tells her he's missed her presence, her intelligence, and—with a grin and a wink—her body.

"Let's go straight to your house," he whispers into her ear. At that moment, though, sex is near the bottom of her to-do list, after she's sat up in cattle class for fourteen hours. Surely he can wait until she's slept. But as she glances at him on the drive home, she realizes from his private smile and his caresses of her leg with his free hand, that he will do nothing of the sort.

Blake parks the car outside Merran's house, then leads her up the path and lets her in with his key. He puts her bag down, lays his hand on the small of her back, and gently pushes her towards the bathroom.

"I expect you'd like a shower and some coffee first. I'll go make the coffee."

Not many days afterwards, Merran is struck by the realization that in the course of a little more than a week away, her attitude towards Blake has changed. It still isn't hard to respond to him sexually, but their conversations are becoming dull. Rumors from their departments, who's in and who's out, the burden of students' demands, the competition for grant money. There's also the sticky issue of Blake's new friendship with her boss, J.L. Both men look surprised one evening at dinner when she leaves the room during a discussion about graveyards. Although she also enjoys searching in graveyards, it's the tone of the conversation that annoys her. Each is attempting to outdo the other with accounts of amazing findings. As she clatters dishes in the kitchen, she muses that J.L. and Blake have more in common with each other than with her. She's spent her entire career in one place, while the two men have already distinguished themselves at Duke and Harvard (Blake), and Northwestern and the University of Iowa (J.L.). It's clear to her, even shocking, that as part of Catherine's therapeutic makeover, she's become weary of one-upmanship. The alternative is not necessarily the huge and quite impractical step of moving to Wirrim, but she believes she does need a change and, as she loads the dishwasher, vows to spend time job-hunting in the near future.

The one-upping stops. J.L. pokes his head in the door to say good-bye. He looks puzzled. She hasn't jumped into the fray to boast about her research conquests. This is most unusual.

"Are you OK, Merran? You've been quiet this evening." She pleads a non-existent headache, and he goes away. How could he know that by pushing her to teach Australian studies the previous year, he'd set in motion a series of events neither of them could have imagined? Although she plans to continue to teach Asian studies, and regards Australia as a side interest, when honest with herself she has to admit that she now feels homesick for a place she hasn't lived in for decades.

As the days wear on, she notices that her attitude to other aspects of her life are shifting too. San Francisco's weather, frequently cool and foggy during the summer and winter, and sunny during the spring and fall, seems out of whack for the first time. She longs for Wirrim's hot, dry summers and cold, wetter winters. It's the way weather should be.

When she examines her home with a dispassionate eye, she imagines flushing thousands of repair dollars down the toilet. Richard, though a talented writer, hadn't brought in much money, but he'd been a dab hand at repairs, something she'd never been interested in learning. She feels restless and unsatisfied.

Chapter 48
Coober Pedy

A few days later, Merran's sipping a glass of white wine in a nearby restaurant and waiting for a colleague to join her, when an email from Brendan pops up. She's been trying not to communicate with him often in case their relationship becomes more complicated. But this isn't about the two of them.

Vic Police are going on with the search in this area. Guess what their divers found when they dragged Coopers Lake? A handgun; someone wasn't very thorough the first time. Both Malcolm and Hiroshi's fingerprints are on it. Lucky the police finger-printed Malcolm the other day, as he has a clean record and wouldn't have been in the system. And Hiroshi was fingerprinted, like everyone else, on his entry into Melbourne. It's all very fishy, if you'll excuse the pun. The surprise is that the gun is still fully loaded.

To add to the confusion, Vic Police also told me about an incident a few days after Hiroshi disappeared, when someone at a petrol station near Coober Pedy, way outback, was looking at the "Missing" photo in the newspaper, when she realized she'd seen a boy of that description getting into a truck pulling a caravan at their last stop. We didn't hear about it because, after the local police questioned her, she became doubtful when they showed more photos, so the investigation was dropped. But the question in the back of everyone's mind is, why was the sighting on the exact route that Malcolm would have taken on his trip to Alice Springs?

So now we have a gun in Coopers Lake, still loaded, a sighting of the boy in South Australia, Malcolm telling you he dropped Hiroshi at the railway line. To make it more complicated, there's Malcolm's reputation as a steady person who wouldn't hurt a fly.

And think of this: why would Malcolm even mention Hiroshi to you, if he's guilty of anything?

Merran takes another sip of wine and notices her friend Sabina opening the door. Darn, she's early. Brendan continues:

Also, a new piece of information's turned up. Malcolm's doctor friend Ross Campbell in the MacDonnell Ranges was questioned, and vouches that the visit took place, but that Malcolm was anxious all the time and glued to newspapers and television accounts of the missing boy. He told Ross that he'd met Hiroshi a couple of times, and worried that he might have met with foul play. He told Ross that, in fact, he had left his farm several days before the boy went missing. But the date he gave Ross is two days before the students arrived in Wirrim in the first place. So that's a lie, because it completely contradicts what he told you. The police have decided to question him again.

Sabina is looking for Merran now, and smiles as she notices her. When she arrives at the table, Merran asks, "Would you mind if I just email a friend in Australia? I'll be quick."

Sabina picks up the menu.

"Of course not. I always have trouble deciding what to order. Take your time."

Merran replies to Brendan.

That's strange. Why would Malcolm need to lie?

Very suspicious, Merran. Stay tuned.

Brendan writes again the following day:

Vic Police have taken a statement from Malcolm. He says pretty much what he told you—at the beginning. I talked with the lawyer appointed for Malcolm, and he agreed that I could send you this attachment, since you've been part of the action, so to speak. Get ready for a surprise!

Merran opens the attachment.

I heard that the gun has been found in Coopers Lake, so need to add some new information. It's true that I brought Hiroshi to my house and showed him the books. As he looked through them, I could see that he was becoming more and more agitated. The photos are very graphic.

I asked him what was wrong, expecting him to say he was upset seeing the prisoners' treatment. Of course he said he was, but then followed up by saying that his great-grandfather despised the prisoners' weakness in allowing themselves to be captured. This wasn't the first time I'd heard this opinion. I asked him if he believed it too. He said that he struggled with it himself. The Peace Park in Hiroshima made a big impression on him, as I said before. In the pile on the table there were the two books in Japanese which I'd bought recently, the ones Merran Scofield looked through later on. Hiroshi sat with them quietly for a long while. When I asked what they contained, his expression changed. He stood up, paced around the room, and told me that his great-grandfather was right: the accounts of cruelty in the prison camps were exaggerated. The prisoners had invented their stories. These books confirmed it. But he looked upset as he said it. Frankly, he looked confused.

I asked him how he accounted for the photos. He said the theory was that they'd been staged as propaganda by the Allies to justify the Occupation after the war. I'd heard this theory before, but it was unsettling to hear it come out of the mouth of a fifteen-year-old boy.

'Now I understand why my father is so hard on me,' he said. 'He wants to make me into a soldier in a new Japanese army, strong and able to stand up to the Chinese, the North Koreans, and any other aggressors.' 'But do you want this?' I asked. He put his head in his hands and cried.

I suggested that we take a walk around the farm to calm him down, but it did no good. He talked about his father's role in the Diet, which was to assist the prime minister to get the rearmament legislation through. He began to sob, and said, 'I've hated my father for so long because I don't want what he wants for me.' My mind was whirling.

Just then we were interrupted by a neighbour, who dropped by in his truck. He's very talkative, so it took a while to get rid of him. Hiroshi had gone back to the house when Ken arrived. When I came back inside I was surprised to find him quite calm. He said he was ready to go back to Wirrim. His face had changed, though. He seemed to be focused on something internal, but I was so glad he wasn't upset anymore that I didn't ask any questions. I was anxious to get him back to Wirrim.

We set off, but when we reached Coopers Lake, Hiroshi asked me to drop him off on the far side, away from the caravans. Said he liked the place and wanted to sit there for a few minutes. Then he would walk on to his host family's house. I was doubtful, even though it was still a few hours until dark. I wanted to be sure he'd be able to walk the whole way, but I did have chores to do and was rather glad of the extra time. He seemed OK, and had only a light bag with him, so I set him off and he walked down to the water. I was heading back to my ute, when I noticed he had a dark, heavy-looking object in his hand, and was pointing it at his head. I realized it was a gun. I yelled and ran towards him. He stopped, looked at me blankly, threw the gun into the water as far as he could, then fell on the bank, crying. I asked where he'd got the gun. He said he'd found it in my house. I was shocked, and afraid that if it were found later, I might be under suspicion for something I did or didn't do, whatever that might be. So I didn't mention it to Merran or the police earlier, because he didn't die, and it would complicate things unnecessarily. Now, of course, it's been found.

Then Hiroshi fell apart. He begged me to help him, take him anywhere but back to Wirrim. I was stuck. I knew that if he wasn't there by nightfall there would be a search, and that his caretakers would be blamed. His parents would be called and want to come. We discussed all of this together. He said that he regretted causing trouble, but was adamant that he wouldn't go back. I'd already told him I was driving to the outback, and he pleaded with me to take him with me.

I wanted to do the right thing, but I didn't know what the right thing was. Finally I took him back to the farm for the night, to think it over. After he'd gone to bed I tried ringing the police station in Wirrim, which was of course closed. I let it ring only once. I didn't want to leave a message. Even calling the station made me feel that I was betraying Hiroshi, so I didn't do it again.

Merran replies,

This gets curiouser and curiouser. There are pieces of the puzzle still missing, that's for sure. Why are the two stories so different? The police will be on the warpath now, to get to the truth. I'll have a think and get back to you.

Chapter 49

CATHERINE

Merran is bursting with information and questions from the moment Catherine ushers her into her therapy office. It isn't until a half-hour has passed that Merran sinks down into the couch, having covered the wedding, her growing friendship with Brendan and the current state of affairs with Blake; meeting Dorrie; and her few days with Ruth. But what has occupied her mind the most is the mystery of Malcolm's relationship with Hiroshi, and the missing pieces yet to be discovered. Catherine takes the opportunity to jump in at last, with a kind smile.

"I can't help remembering how difficult it was for me to get you to talk when we were first getting to know each other. Now you're like a river in full flood."

Merran laughs. "I felt ashamed asking for help and was angry with you for being the person I asked for help. How crazy is that? But don't you agree that my few days away have been chockablock?"

"That's for sure." Catherine glances at the clock, whose face is visible to both of them, then back at

Merran. "Half of our time has now gone. What seems most urgent to you to discuss right now?"

Merran stares at the ceiling, then says,

"The inconsistencies in Malcolm's story. Something I didn't mention is that when I went out to his farm I was struck by the paradise of bird and animal life he had there, and by the magpie whose broken wing he was nursing back to health. And yet he is often depressed, sad, and of course angry about how his father suffered during the war, and how he lost him far too early. There are two sides to him. I was shocked that he would tell lies. Does that mean he could hurt someone as well?"

"I really don't know," replies Catherine, "but you said that you were struck by Malcolm's love of wildlife. He sounds to have a kind heart that has been broken more than once."

"That's an understatement. His father's death, his own divorce, his separation from his daughters, taking on all of his father's tragedy. So many losses."

"Have you noticed, Merran, that when people suffer losses, they can go in either direction? One way is to hurt others as a kind of reenactment, an unconscious repetition. The other is to care for others, so they won't have to suffer the same way."

"Funny thing, Catherine, Dorrie read me a letter from George that poses that very question." She describes the account of the monkey, Jerry Lindberg, and how some of the soldiers cared for it, while others teased and kicked it.

"That's a good example. Which direction do you think Malcolm has taken?"

"Well, from his account of conversations he had with Hiroshi, I would say that he takes a humanitarian direction." She glances at Catherine, who is staring out the window, and adds, "When he's not too depressed."

After a moment of silence, Catherine turns and says, "Let me tell you something that can be a problem for therapists, teachers, anyone who works with children. You're not a big lover of children, so you may not have experienced it." She smiles mischievously, and Merran laughs.

"When children are harmed physically by their caregivers, those abuses are reportable because they are so obvious. On the other hand, the day-to-day slow drip of coldness, criticism, and emotional neglect can be just as traumatic, but is not usually reportable. That's when the urge by those in the helping professions to take children home and protect them can sometimes be overwhelming. I've felt it myself, many times. It's not a good idea for several reasons, but I'm wondering if Malcolm felt that urge, even though he knew it would be unmanageable."

Merran can only wonder.

She's finishing dinner and is logging onto her computer to let Brendan know about her conversation with Catherine, when her phone rings. It's Brendan himself. What a surprise; this is his first phone call. Could be awkward if he keeps doing it.

"Sit down before you hear this. Hiroshi's body has been found a hundred metres off a hiking trail outside of Alice Springs. A hiker went to do a pee and found him. At least, the police think it's Hiroshi. There wasn't much left of him, but he was wearing a Wirrim High T-shirt, and there was a note in his pocket in Japanese, which has yet to be translated. The body is to be flown to Melbourne for the postmortem. Shocking, isn't it? But it does fit with that question we had all along about the possible sighting. Oh, and Malcolm has been taken in for more questioning."

Merran collapses into a chair. "So the worst has happened. It doesn't look good for Malcolm now, does it? But I was just about to email you to let you know what my therapist said. I was feeling hopeful after my session with her, but now it's looking more complicated."

She recounts her conversation with Catherine.

"It's very sad," he says. "I'll get back to you as soon as I have more info."

"Can you send an email instead of calling next time, please Brendan?" Blake is coming to dinner and a phone call might be risky.

The day drags slowly. Merran is glad that her students are giving oral presentations about their chosen research topics. She can tune in often enough to get the gist of what they're saying, while her mind is otherwise occupied. Her eyes are red, she knows, and she's not surprised at the somber mood in the classroom, and the glances of her students. During the mid-afternoon, Brendan emails again, with a PDF attached.

The lawyer says it's OK for you to see this one too. Merran opens the attached document and reads the newest statement from Malcolm.

Chapter 50
THE TRUTH

Malcolm writes: *I've just found out that Hiroshi is dead, so it's time to tell you the whole story. You've probably realized that I've been holding back in my statements, and that's because I didn't think it necessary to tell you everything. I very much regret what I did but was hoping that Hiroshi would turn up unharmed. I did tell some lies, but the part about how the gun got into the lake, that was true. And it led to what I did next. The fact that he was suicidal really shocked me. It made me realize how intent he was on not going back to his father. I knew that keeping him away longer would cause all kinds of trouble, and I knew it was impractical, but I believed I should protect him. He was like a bird with a broken wing, and I might be able to help, though as yet I didn't know how. I suppose that, in the back of my mind, it was a way to reach out to someone whose nation I'd despised for so long and now felt differently about.*

Hiroshi seemed to be having a nervous breakdown, so I did what seemed best at the time. The caravan was packed and ready to go, and the next morning I took him with me. I thought I might be able to come up with a solution as we went. I was glad I'd alerted my neighbours that I would be

*leaving a few days earlier than when we did leave, so that's
what they would have told the police. Hiroshi had delayed
me, but the police wouldn't think to pursue me.*

*About the fourth day, at Coober Pedy, I was filling
the fuel tank when I noticed a newspaper with Hiroshi's
photograph on it as a missing teen. It seriously rattled me,
and I had to tell him to stay in the caravan unless we were
away from the towns. He was upset to hear it—he hated to
think he was causing trouble—but he was still hell-bent on
not going back. By then I didn't know what to do, so I just
kept driving.*

*We reached Ross's place, and I made Hiroshi stay in the
caravan. The news was on, and Ross had already seen the
missing teen report. He asked me if I'd heard of it, because
it took place in Wirrim, but I said only that I'd met him
once at the lake. I pretended to be surprised, although I was
shaking from head to toe...*

*I thought that Ross might help me to hide him, but when
we watched the news accounts he was so condemning of
anyone who would kidnap an innocent teenager, or even
harbor a teenager without their parents' permission, that
I felt I couldn't rely on him. It became harder and harder
to keep Hiroshi hidden. He could only come out after Ross
had gone to work. We discussed what we would do next,
but we couldn't come up with any ideas. Then I woke up
one morning, and Hiroshi was gone. Of course I looked for
him, but he'd had a few hours' start and I didn't have any
idea which direction he'd taken. I didn't feel I could call the
police. That's the last I saw of him.*

*I was frantic, even though I expected that he would
come back, so I stayed with Ross for a couple more weeks,
until the publicity stopped, and I'd adjusted to the shock of
what had happened. I hoped he was still alive. Perhaps he'd*

hitchhiked and come across someone else who would hide him, some other kind person. Of course the language barrier would make this very unlikely. And after a while I realized that if he'd been rescued, we would have heard about it by now. So he was probably dead. I lied in my earlier statements because I was still hoping he was alive, and I didn't see the sense in implicating myself more than necessary. But now there's the body, and it's time for me to tell the truth. I would like to emphasize that all along I was doing what I thought was best for him. I knew I could have simply told the police about Hiroshi's fears of his father but could not have been sure of the outcome.

Malcolm Richardson, McKenzie Farm, Near Budgerong, Victoria.

Brendan comments: "Astonishing, isn't it?"

Merran types back.

It sounds as though Malcolm did it with the best of intentions, but he certainly wasn't thinking straight when he thought he could save Hiroshi forever. But what I'd like to know now: why did he tell me about his meeting with Hiroshi in the first place? It's such a coincidence that I needed his permission to publish his father's letters. If I hadn't, the case might have stayed cold.

The renewed search by Vic Police did result in the gun's being found. But I don't think Malcolm knew that when he talked to me. If the gun had been found without Malcolm's statement about the trip with Hiroshi to the Alice, I would expect that the nationwide search would have been called off and limited to the Wirrim area. So there wouldn't have been any report from the woman near Coober Pedy; Ross wouldn't have been questioned. Remember, Ross' comments did show up the lie.

Is there any more, she thinks. There are so many threads here. Another thought comes to mind.

And yet, when I look back on my conversation with him at the farm, you'd think he would have shown nervousness at having spilled the beans. Mysterious, isn't it? It's as though he wanted to be caught.

Brendan calls her the next day.

"I wanted to hear your voice again, and I have more news. The piece of paper in Hiroshi's pocket was a suicide note, all right. He planned to walk into the desert and never come back. He wrote that Malcolm was the only person apart from his mother who really cared about him, that Malcolm had acted out of kindness, and should not be punished. It fits with what you and Catherine talked about, the urge in some people to take youngsters under their wing, despite the hazards."

Merran says, "This brings me to another thought. Therapists, teachers, and so on, are trained not to let their impulses lead them to mistakes like Malcolm made, but he'd had no such training. I remember something I didn't mention earlier, that when I talked to him at the farm he told me he'd applied several times to obtain custody of his daughters to protect them from their mother's rage and nonstop criticism, but the courts had refused. He thought it was partly due to the fact that he lived so far out in the country, and partly that he was depressed much of the time. Rage and criticism aren't reportable offences, but they can have long-lasting effects. So when Hiroshi pleaded with Malcolm not to send him back, Malcolm saw it as a way to make things right somehow."

266

"Great analysis, Merran. You could come over here and testify at his trial, help to mitigate what he did. I'll check with his lawyer. The date won't be set until we get the results of the postmortem."

Chapter 51

RESOLUTION

Brendan emails again two days later.

It looks as though Hiroshi died from dehydration. There were no blows or gunshot wounds. Malcolm's been charged with kidnapping and making false statements, but has been released until the trial, which has been set for May 23rd. Can you come?

Merran consults her calendar quickly and emails back.

Perfect! The semester will have just finished, and I can hurry my grades through. Do you think I'll be able to testify? I'm not exactly an expert witness in psychological matters, but my therapist would help me put something together and vouch for the information.

Brendan's reply comes quickly.

Don't know. I'll speak to the lawyer. You know by now that he's a decent bloke. Unfortunately, the prosecutor is an attack dog. From what I've heard, though, the judge is level-headed. Hard to tell which way it could go. Cross our fingers that the judge and jury will consider Malcolm's clean record. And his remorse. We're a bit worried about him, actually. Oh, and here's some good news: Daichi can't come. Apparently, there's an important vote coming up, and he'll be tied up until early June.

When the trial is over, and all is done and dusted, Brendan is given the task of driving Malcolm to a minimum-security prison farm to serve his sentence of five years, with the possibility of parole for good behaviour after eighteen months. In addition, he will have to complete one hundred hours of community service. As soon as they leave town, Brendan stops and removes the handcuffs, then invites Malcolm to sit in front with him so they can chat. The first thing the latter says is how grateful he is to Merran for her statement in his defense at the trial. By putting Malcolm's actions into a psychological context, she seemed to have put her finger on the scale of justice, pushing it towards mitigation and away from harsh punishment.

As they drive, Malcolm shares with Brendan the tough decisions he's already made about the farm, having expected a longer sentence. His neighbour has bought the sheep. The land will have to lie fallow for a while, but Brendan now offers to check on the property regularly. He's already taken home "the Woof," as he calls boisterous Bluey, saying, "It's high time I had a dog around here."

Chapter 52

FAMILY ROLES

With her departure near at hand, Merran calls on Dorrie. They'd had a few words here and there at the courthouse, but there'd been little privacy. At the end of the trial, Dorrie slipped away while everyone else was gathered around to debrief. Merran knows only that the old woman has received a body blow and imagines that she's had trouble deciding whether to be proud of Malcolm or to condemn him.

After knocking at Dorrie's door several times with no answer, Merran finds it unlocked and eases herself in, calling as cheerfully as she can, "Mrs. Richardson, Where are you?" The television is on; canned laughter comes in waves. Then a croaky voice says, "here."

It's late in the afternoon, and the house is in shadow. She walks through to the room where she and Dorrie had talked at such length, and finds her slumped in her favourite armchair., watching a mindless quiz show. Dust has collected on the table's surface, and a vase of once colourful zinnias has withered. An empty cup and a plate of dry-looking cake sit beside her.

Dorrie's voice is no longer cheerful. Her head droops; her skin sags. Merran goes to her, but Dorrie holds up her hand to signal a stop.

"I'm not good company any more. This has finished me off. Now I'm really an old lady." She grins wearily. "I remember telling you once that it was Malcolm who gave up on life, and that I was the one who looked to the future. We seem to have reversed our roles. He's the one who did something . . . something . . . " She's groping for words. "Let me say, misguided, but heroic in its own way."

"Dorrie, I remember that we once had a discussion about the roles people take on in families."

Dorrie nods. "That's what I was referring to."

"Well, we observed that the roles were taken on unconsciously. That, in my book, means that we have no control. But you are aware. You know how this happens. There's no reason you should reverse roles with Malcolm."

The old woman sits up, a hesitant smile breaking out on her worn face. "I'm so sorry for Hiroshi, but hopefully the experience will help Malcolm take on life in a way he hasn't done for decades."

Chapter 53
Second Thoughts

As Merran walks back to Helen and Owen's house for the night, she reflects on what Dorrie said. "Malcolm did something misguided, but heroic in its own way."

The word 'heroic' reminds her of combat. She reaches the bench in the main street and sits, assailed by new thoughts. Then, as if she were on Freud's couch, she begins to free-associate. Heroic. Combat. Fighter. Father. Burma Railroad. Prison guard. Defence of country. North Korea. China. That's a strong part of Daichi's vocabulary. And all of it also fits with the events of George's life.

But Hiroshi's vocabulary emphasized peace, love and tolerance. It was a short list. Then she thinks of the trial, and Malcolm's insistence that, with good intentions, he more or less bumbled his way through the ordeal with Hiroshi. She wonders what would be on Malcolm's list. Peace, love, and tolerance? Probably not. When she'd visited him to get his signature he fitted the profile of an angry man whose life was a classic case of complicated grief. He'd been eager to show both her and Hiroshi the books on the

Burma-Thailand Railway, and told Merran that he thought of his father every day. He was scornful of his mother's attitude that death was just a passing over. The realization that Malcolm's list could easily match Daichi's is a shock.

She tries calling Brendan, but he doesn't answer. He's probably walking Bluey. He's so fond of the blue heeler that he told Merran he'll take him on his visit to Marisol the next day. Perhaps Bluey might turn out to be a good therapy dog, he said. When Merran heard this she laughed and suggested that if Marisol needed rounding up, Bluey would be just the dog to do it.

She stands up and starts walking again. Helen and Owen will be waiting for her to arrive for dinner. But disturbing thoughts keep coming. Her mind goes back to her conversation with Catherine. Yes, they'd agreed that Malcolm was not a threat to wildlife, but they'd each assumed that his care for animals would extend to Hiroshi. Then it hits her: what if the opposite were true? Malcolm knew that the boy was suicidal. What was he thinking when he drove him several thousand miles with no plan of how to care for him? How long did he expect to hide him? Food, clothing, education.... And after the stint in Alice Springs, Malcolm would be driving home again, with or without Hiroshi. The reality was that it would have to be without.

She's now at the gate and sees Helen and Owen through the kitchen window. Thank goodness; they can help her sort this out.

"What's up, Merran?" Owen asks as she arrives at the back door. "You look awful. We were just about to start eating dinner, because we didn't know where you were."

Her hands are shaking, her legs are wobbly; she sinks into a chair.

She can hardly get the words out. "I may have made a terrible mistake." Helen comes around the table and hugs her. "Tell us, what's happening?" Merran knows that they've been talking to Brendan and are up to date with the trial and sentence. Now she repeats what has been going on in her mind, then the devastating conclusion: "Malcolm is no idiot. Of course he'd thought through the implications of taking the boy so far north. Now I realize that if I switch his diagnosis from innocent, naïve protector to murderer, it all fits, and it seems laughable now that I could have missed the evil intent in his stated desire to 'put things right.' When he said that, I assumed he meant that he intended to save Hiroshi. Now I'm wondering if the boy's role in all of this was to be the payback for Malcolm's loss of his father. The story remains the same; it's only the intent that changes." She puts her head in her hands, then sits up and looks at them, desperation in her eyes. Helen and Owen look shocked.

She breaks the silence again. "The lies should have alerted me. He held back important information until it was impossible to do so. Several times. He really thought he would get away with it."

"But how could he have planned this from the beginning?" Owen asks. "He couldn't have known that Hiroshi would ask for help to avoid his father."

"I thought about this on the way home from Dorrie's place, and now I conclude that none of the early part was planned. At first he might well have had good intentions, and thought to help him. This was the case until he brought Hiroshi back from the lake. But I can imagine him lying awake that night and forming a plan. How convenient that the boy, whose great-grandfather was a guard on the very Railway where his father suffered so much, was right here in his home. The opportunity for revenge was impossible to resist. He knew he wouldn't be able to protect the boy forever, and that death would be the only outcome. I think that Hiroshi was the sacrificial lamb."

Helen and Owen are speechless. Merran looks at them without seeing, and goes on in spurts, as new connections come to her mind.

"I've wondered why he told me about his meeting with Hiroshi in the first place. Now I suspect that he wanted his cover story—a rescue—to be in place proactively in case the body was found. But remember, he only eked it out bit by bit, as further clues were discovered. At every turn he filled in a new fragment of the story, as though it were a puzzle. He only tripped up once, when he got his departure date wrong when talking to Ross in Alice Springs."

"But why go to all this trouble?" Helen asks. "Didn't he know he would be charged with kidnapping when the boy was found?"

"That's true, but there's a world of difference between being a confused do-gooder, and a straight-out kidnapper. He knew that the sentence for kidnapping would be harsh. The eighteen months he will serve for good behavior is nothing." She slumps in her chair, and says with a small voice, "And I helped him get the lighter sentence." She turns away.

Helen glances at Owen and reads his face. This is tough. Let's back off, it says. "Didn't you just see Dorrie? What does she think?" she asks.

"Well, it wasn't until I'd left Dorrie that I realized something was missing. She said nothing about Hiroshi's parents, the loss they experienced. My conversation with her was all about Malcolm: was he a hero or just misguided? All Dorrie talked about was Malcolm's future as though Hiroshi's death had freed him to improve his life. That was weird, don't you think? Though she had no idea what the implications were, when she said that."

Owen stands and stretches. "This is stunning, Merran. How about we heat our dinner and have a few minutes' break? I have to let this settle a bit."

As Merran puts down her knife and fork, she looks at her plate and wonders what she just ate.

"That suicide note," she says quietly. "Hiroshi had blind faith in Malcolm. It's so touching but makes me madder than ever."

Merran decides to try Brendan again. As they talk, she hears Bluey in the background, panting. After she's poured out her new, disturbing thoughts, she waits for his response. What he says astonishes her.

"As a matter of fact, I was surprised and a bit unsettled when I drove Malcolm to the prison farm. He seemed happy with the sentence. He never once expressed sadness or remorse about Hiroshi's death, which was a contrast with his attitude during the trial. Do you remember he cried a couple of times? I wonder now if they were crocodile tears. And something else he said stuck in my mind. He used the words 'now I can let it go,' which puzzled me, but make sense now."

They can hear each other breathing.

"Now what?" Merran asks, her voice breaking. "Can I retract what I said, and can he be retried?"

"No, a person can't be retried for the same crime. It's called double jeopardy. But are you absolutely sure of your new interpretation of events?"

"That's the thing, Brendan. I can't. Malcolm's intent could have been what was said at the trial: the misguided saviour. Or he could be a cold-blooded murderer. Do you think we'll ever know?"

Brendan's response is subdued.

"I hate to say this, but we probably never will."

"Then I hope he's miserable for the next eighteen months!"

Chapter 54
MURDER OR SUICIDE?

Merran's time in Wirrim is at an end, and she's tossing and turning in bed at Brendan's house, and is so disturbed that he wakes up.

"Sorry my darling," she says, "but I'm thinking about how little we have to show when we consider all the turmoil of the past months: Colleen and Hiroshi. We couldn't find out definitively whether what happened was murder or suicide."

"True," says Brendan with a yawn. "It's disappointing, but what's left to investigate? We've reached the end of the road." There's nothing to do but return to bed.

There's little work at the police station today, fairly usual for a Monday. Brendan has decided to emulate the London Bobbies, and go for a walk down the main street. Community relations are very important, he thinks. His mobile rings just as he's paying for a newspaper. More suicide bombings, so depressing. He's often thought that suicide bombings could be called murder, in that those who offer their lives are brainwashed into it. It's not too different from Hiroshi's death, really, if indeed Malcolm used him as revenge. Hiroshi thought he was killing himself by running into the desert, but Malcolm had misinformed him about what would take place up north. The innocent boy, with his naïve belief in the old man, and no knowledge of the desert whatsoever, was a willing victim, even to the extent of writing a note. So was it murder or suicide?

Back at the office, he checks his email and is surprised to find one from Jack Fellows, a long-time friend from the Academy and now posted at the Rylands station. They haven't been in contact for months. Jack sounds excited.

"Sorry I've been off the radar for a while. Our daughter had a baby recently and we're just getting used to grandparenthood. But I just had to get in touch. You'll never guess what I found." Brendan reads the email with growing eagerness, then calls Merran.

"There's been a development in the Enright murder/suicide."

Merran stops munching her toast and sits up straight, astonished.

"Fire away." Brendan's voice is excited, even trembling. "It's an email. I'll read it to you in a minute. It fits in with how we became aware of Hiroshi's supposed suicidality.

"You know how suicide has been very much on people's minds during this investigation right from the start. Suspicions that Hiroshi might wander off on purpose and die in the bush. Then we read Malcolm's account of the gun at the lake. This confirmed that

Hiroshi was suicidal. As you know, I'd sent out an all-points bulletin to the stations in this area but got nowhere. Now we know why: Hiroshi was far away.

"Then this morning, quite out of the blue, I got an email from my mate Jack Fellows, the cop from Rylands." He pauses for dramatic effect. "I was blown away."

Merran is fidgeting. "Go on, get to the point."

"He was cleaning out one of the old filing cabinets—time to spare on a Monday—and came across a file labelled *Enright murder/suicide, near Wirrim, August 1933*. Naturally he was curious, as he'd read the newspaper last year when you were doing your search, and of course he wondered why there was a file in Rylands in the first place. Sure enough, the file was almost empty, but what fell out was an envelope containing a report by the constable at the time, Joseph Blackstone, after he'd met with a swaggie named Robert Kendrick. This took place in Rylands, which was why the report was filed there.

Merran broke in. "Never heard of either of them."

"Just sit on your hands and let me tell you what was in the report. It'll blow your socks off. Here it is: Dated 7 December 1933, several months after the tragedy.

Here's what Blackstone wrote."

I met with Kendrick, who said he had come to provide information on what he saw at a farm outside Wirrim a few months ago. He'd seen newspaper accounts and recognized Colleen and Dave Enright from the photographs. He realized that Colleen had been accused, and that this was now called a murder/suicide. But it was not the way he saw it at all. When I asked him why he'd waited so long to come in, he said that he'd been travelling, and when he came back he found out about the accusation. His conscience said that he had to put it right.

He was dirty and smelly, and I was inclined to send him on his way, but as soon as he began to talk I realized that he had something important to say. Here's what he told me, and I had him write it down later.

I arrived at the farm before lunch, very hungry. But as I approached the door, I noticed that there were two small suitcases outside, and more packing being done inside. A young woman, Colleen, came out holding a baby, looking very nervous, and I noticed a couple of small children holding onto her skirts.

Well, my plans were shot to pieces. Ordinarily I would begin by asking for food nicely, but then move on to other methods of persuasion, if you know what I mean. But this was a very different scene. Colleen told me that she was planning to leave the farm with her children and go back to her parents. She was crying; she said she needed some time away from her husband. When I asked if he beat her, she said no, but that the farm had been a disaster and he wanted to go back to Melbourne. She doesn't like big cities, so decided to go in the other direction, further into the bush, where her parents have a sheep farm.

She said she was almost ready to go but had to wait until Dave came home so she could take the buggy. She thought it would have been better if she'd left before he came home, but they only had one buggy. Now I was getting nervous, wanting to help her however I could, but wondering what kind of a man he would turn out to be. Would he take the news quietly, or would he try to stop her?

A few minutes later, we heard the sound of a horse and buggy bumping along the road. As soon as Dave saw us, he stood up and shouted, "What the hell is going on here?"

Colleen was shaking but started towards the gate. I thought she was very brave, given his aggressiveness. She tried to tell him that she would only be going away for a little while, but Dave wasn't listening. He started insulting me, and when he'd finished doing that, he set upon her. 'Whore, so you have your little sessions while I'm away, do you?' He lunged towards her, but I stood between them. I told him I just came by to ask for food and found her getting ready to leave. I wanted to help. Unfortunately, on hearing this, Colleen turned to me and said thank you, you're a true helper.

Then Dave's face turned red. There was no reasoning with him. He ran back to the buggy, pulled out a rifle, and pointed it at me. I'm pretty fast, and I managed to get out of the way, just as he shot, twice. Colleen and the baby fell to the ground and didn't move. I got out of there as fast as I could and never looked back, even when I heard two more shots. Now I realize that Dave blamed Colleen for the four deaths, but it couldn't have been her because she was shot first.

Merran is speechless.

"Are you still there?" Brendan asks.

"Yes, but this is such a shock. So it could only have been Dave. But why didn't the police take him in for questioning?"

"They probably did, and Dave would have denied it. Dave's account of Colleen's use of the gun may have been more persuasive. Or perhaps they couldn't find him once he'd moved to Melbourne. Or they got busy and decided to let it lie. It was over. The swaggie's report came later and it might have been too much trouble to dig it all up again."

"Can I tell Owen? He'll be thrilled," Merran says, her shock now being replaced by excitement.

"Of course. But wait a minute: I'm surprised you haven't recognized that this story must be true, Merran."

"What?"

"If Dave is telling the truth, then why did the swaggie make up such a story, if he wasn't there?"

"I doubt that Dave would have shot anyone if the swaggie hadn't been there. You know I've always thought that," Merran says. "It was one thing to see Colleen packed and ready to go, but surely he would have tried to reason with her rather than shoot her. It would have been his pride that tipped the balance. Coming home to find someone else—and a smelly, rough swaggie at that— helping his wife leave him, especially if he suspected that they were having sex." Brendan stands and paces the room, frowning.

"Scot free seems to apply to our two cases, hey Merran?"

"I have to say yes, but reluctantly. It makes my blood boil though. Two murderers getting off, but it happens all the time."

Chapter 55

Night Sky

It's Merran's last night in Wirrim. She wants to see the Milky Way and the Southern Cross one more time, and she needs darkness for the full effect. It astonishes her how many trips she's made over the Pacific in recent months. She could move to Melbourne. There might be university positions in Asian studies; she's definitely qualified. Her friendship with Brendan might become something more. He might even move back to Melbourne to be with her. She feels a surge of excitement.

She and Brendan said goodbye after lunch, but now he's on the road to visit Marisol, being forced yet again to adhere to Lilibeth's unyielding schedule. Merran invites Helen and Owen to walk out of town with her, but Helen's exhausted. After checking that she's OK, Owen agrees to go. There's no moon, and after they've passed the last house they are wrapped in a cloak of black velvet. Not even the Milky Way is visible through the fast-moving cloud cover.

They sit in the middle of the road to wait. At last Merran says,

"I've been focusing on Malcolm and Hiroshi so much that I completely forgot to ask about Tom and Vera's programme. Will it be continued?"

"We don't know yet. The only obstacle would be Daichi's objections, but I've heard that he's feeling rather ashamed that Hiroshi would plead with Malcolm to shelter him, even though, of course, Malcolm may have had murderous intent. The decision could go either way, but so far it sounds hopeful."

Just then the clouds part, and the Southern Cross comes into view one star at a time, until the entire constellation, including the two pointer stars, is visible. The Milky Way, a river of light, glows right overhead. A few minutes later, all of it has disappeared. Neither of them speaks, too moved for words. Finally, they get to their feet, and set off arm in arm, back to town. As they arrive at the gate, Owen stops and says, "One more thing before you go back to San Francisco. I happen to know they're hiring at Bendigo Uni. Not to be pushy, but I need to say this: will you and Brendan hurry up and make a future together? I've talked to him and he's raring to go down that path. It's obvious to everyone but you that it's a match made in heaven."

Merran laughs at the cliché and responds with another. "We'll see," she says.

Author's Note

When my Australian mother-in-law died in 1981, a part of what she left behind was a sizeable bundle of letters written by her lover, later her husband, who was stationed in the Middle East during World War II. We brought the letters back to California, stuffed them unread into a file, and forgot about them for over three decades. Finally, on reading them, I hoped to be inspired to write about the times and their lives. The book was to be titled *Your Most Sincere Lover,* the words used by the soldier as his signoff to every letter.

It didn't take long before I realized that these letters had no other purpose than to serve as expressions of love to a young woman who he'd met a few short months before sailing. I decided that I needed more characters to frame the story.

Fictitious creations began to populate the pages. Merran, the historian from San Francisco, who returns to her small Australian country town, 'Wirrim,' only reluctantly, and attends a life-changing class reunion. Owen, also a historian and onetime rival of Merran, who becomes aware of a Depression-era murder/suicide involving his grandfather and grandpa's young wife, Colleen. The elderly Dorrie, who shows Merran the letters from her lover, later to be her husband. Hiroshi, a Japanese exchange student visiting Wirrim, who goes missing. Brendan, the local policeman who falls in love with Merran. Mystery abounds: are we dealing with murder, or suicide? Or both?

Some of the events in the novel are autobiographical. Wirrim resembles the town where I grew up. I did attend a school reunion, where I encountered the mystery of an unsolved murder/suicide from the Depression era. A chance meeting with an old woman in Wirrim's main street was the inspiration for Dorrie. Although the woman in Wirrim quotes our family's letters verbatim, the other details of her life are fictitious.

There are several complex relationships: Merran with her father; Owen with his wife; Dorrie with her son Malcolm, who brings about a turning-point in the novel. It's interesting to think of Malcolm as my husband, but other than the fact that his father did die on the family farm when Roy was twelve years old, there is no other correspondence. In fact, their farm was in another state. Owen, Helen, and Brendan are fictitious, as are Vera and Tom, though I wish they were real. I'd like to spend time with them. And as for Merran? She's a bit nicer at the end than at the beginning. She might be an interesting dinner guest.

Finally, I have used American and Australian spelling according to the location of the action.

Acknowledgments

I owe a debt of gratitude to loyal friends and other readers who have stuck with me over the years I was writing this book. Some, who read earlier drafts, may be surprised that this final one diverges quite a bit from what they saw. Many of the changes took place during two quarters of fiction classes at UCLA Extension. Thanks to Robert Eversz, the instructor, who managed to be kind but firm when insisting that beloved and hard-gotten passages—my "babies"—needed to be removed. The novel, of course, is all the better for it. Thanks also to my cohort during this intense time, who were close and supportive readers.

My two daughters insisted that I create an experienced therapist to help transform my protagonist, rather than the newbie I dreamed up first, thus showing my profession to its best advantage. My son developed my beautiful website. My scientist husband performed numerous reality checks. Not only that, but he consistently went above and beyond in discussing plot lines, helping me untangle knotty problems, and demonstrating enormous patience as the novel came together.

Finally, I would like to thank EditPros LLC partner Marti Childs, who designed the book's cover and interior. She was a pleasure to work with.

About the Author

Susan Curry grew up in Victoria, Australia, and now lives in Davis, California. She imported and sold Australian books throughout the United States for many years. She later trained as a psychotherapist and treats survivors of traumatic events.

CPSIA information can be obtained
at www.ICGtesting.com
Printed in the USA
FSHW020422250119
55150FS